Medium Roast

Shannon Ryan

Medium Roast

Shannon Ryan

Broken Typewriter Press • Cedar Rapids

Cover Design by Blair Guantt
https://bygauntt.com/

Broken Typewriter Press
https://broken.typewriter.press/

ISBN 978-1-940509-37-2

Version 1.0.1

Chapter 1

Cars, Conflict, and Coffee

Sara knew it was going to be a shitty day the moment she saw the look on Fred's face. The mechanic had always been sure of himself in the past, a big man swaggering in to tell the little lady what was wrong with her car. Now he looked hesitant, apologetic, and even a little bewildered.

"I've got some bad news," he said. "I'm guessing you're going to need a new engine. I haven't located the exact problem yet, but from the way it's acting, there's a crack in the block." Fred looked ashamed of his failure. "Again, I apologize for not knowing exactly what's going on. Usually, we'd be able to isolate the issue from the codes on the computer, and there'd be some physical sign of the problem. With the amount of fluid you're losing, I should be able to see where it's leaking."

Sara's stomach churned. What did you do when the expert had no idea what was wrong? And worse, how was she supposed to afford major car repairs when she'd been laid off from her lab tech job at Verdegrowth six weeks ago? The severance package had helped cushion the blow initially, but that money was quickly dwindling. "So, are we talking heart surgery or funeral?"

Fred hesitated before answering. "If we're talking engine replacement, the usual cost is around five thousand. That's with a brand-new engine with all new parts. We can knock a bit off if we go with a rebuilt, but a lot of that is the labor. Of course, if there's a secondary problem, it could be quite a bit more."

Sara's jaw dropped. "Well, that's... astronomical. I don't even know what to do. I guess I'll check with my husband and get back to you." She did a quick mental tally. Between what was left of her severance and their savings, they should have just enough to cover the repairs. But spending their entire cushion on fixing a car that had always been temperamental seemed foolish, especially when she was still job hunting.

The little BMW had constantly nickel-and-dimed them with repairs. Brad had insisted on buying it, claiming it was a status symbol that would help his career. "It's all about projecting success," he'd said, puffing out his chest. "You never know who you might run into in the parking garage." Sara had thought it was ridiculous at the time, but she'd gone along with it to keep the peace.

If they had to spend so much money, she'd rather buy a more modest car—something reliable and sensible. But she could already imagine Brad's protests about "downgrading." Maybe he'd see reason given their current situation. Six weeks ago, she'd had a steady job, and they were planning for a tropical getaway. Now they had to decide whether to sink thousands into a temperamental German status symbol or admit defeat and start car shopping.

"I'm sorry," Fred said sympathetically. "I know it's a lot to take in. I topped off all your fluids. Just make sure you check your coolant and oil occasionally, and that will buy you a few days, but the more the engine heats up and cools down, the worse it's gonna get. Give me a call if you decide to go ahead with the repair, or if you have any questions."

Dazed, Sara nodded her thanks and walked away, her mind racing with the implications of the expense. She dialed Brad's cell, but he didn't pick up, so she tried his business phone—still no answer.

Sara considered her options. She could drive home, but the apartment was across town. Brad's office, however, was only a few blocks away. If he thought she should bring the car back to Fred's European Customs, the trip to his office would put less strain on the failing engine.

Sara pushed through the glass doors of Brad's building into a lobby filled with snug leather chairs and tasteful local artwork, including one Grant Wood original. Nancy, the receptionist, stood up from behind the wrap-around receptionist desk, flashing a too-bright smile. "Mrs. Sterling! I was hoping you'd stop by. Someone locked that filing cabinet again—"

"Ms. Jenkins," Sara snapped, her tone cutting enough to make Nancy flinch. Did this woman forget on purpose, or was she just that dense? Sara didn't care. Not today.

"Oh, of course," Nancy said, fumbling. "Sit down, and I'll buzz your husband—"

"No need," Sara interrupted, quickening her pace past the curved desk. "I know where his office is."

Nancy lunged forward, her hand darting out over the high counter, but the desk's design trapped her behind its wrap-around barrier. "Mrs... Ms. Sterling, I really should announce you. Your husband—"

If Nancy said anything more, it was cut off as the inner door closed. Sara strode down the hallway toward Brad's office. Normally, she would have knocked on the door in case he was in a meeting, but today she threw the door open and walked in.

Brad and his supervisor, Kim, were on the couch in an embrace. Her shirt was unbuttoned. His hand was up her skirt. For some reason, he was wearing a sombrero—a big, black one, decorated like the ones in mariachi bands.

Sara's breath caught in her throat, and her hands clenched into fists. With a rattling sound, Brad and Kim jumped apart, their faces a mixture of guilt and shock. Brad had something in his hand... Oh god, was it... No, surely not a sex toy. The rattling came again, and Sara's brain finally processed what she was seeing. A maraca. Her husband was holding a maraca.

"I... I came to talk to you about the car," Sara stammered, her voice shaking. She was numb from shock and confused about the sombrero. "But it looks like you're a bit... busy."

She took a step back, and her foot brushed against something. It rattled. She looked down to see another maraca on the floor.

Brad's voice filled with desperation. "It's not what it looks like!"

The words escaped before she could stop them. "Cultural appropriation?"

She turned and left without looking back.

Sara drove home, her car coughing and lurching with a stubborn determination to stay on the road. Each jolt sent a ripple of unease through her, although she couldn't tell if it was the car or the general state of her life twisting her stomach. When the car backfired, she flinched, her hands tightening on the wheel. She thought cars only did that on TV shows.

Her phone buzzed again, the sound echoing through the Bluetooth. She put it in airplane mode. If she heard Brad's voice right now, she might be sick.

She spent an hour weighing her options, her thoughts circling: How long had this been going on? Who else knew? That bitch receptionist obviously knew. What signs had she missed? Was their whole marriage a lie? Finally, she decided she needed distance—a couple of weeks away to clear her head and figure out her next move. Somewhere quiet, somewhere that felt safe.

Her thoughts drifted to Grandma's house, the one place that had always felt like home. It had been a little over a month since her grandmother passed, leaving the century-old Victorian in probate. But as the sole beneficiary, the family lawyer assured her she could stay there while sorting through Grandma's things. The idea of being surrounded by her grandmother's presence, even in memory, felt like exactly what she needed.

She packed two suitcases, one full of clothes and essentials, the other full of coffee beans, a grinder, and her new roasting machine. She'd gotten into home roasting after watching some YouTube videos about it and had become very particular about her coffee. She'd be damned if Brad was going to wake up tomorrow and enjoy a cup of her single-estate, small-batch, custom-roasted coffee. He could go stand in line at Starbucks and choke on a bitter, over-roasted Arabica blend in a paper cup.

She stopped at the bank to take out some cash. Her bank didn't have a branch in Downcastle—the sole provider there being Farmers Savings Bank. She gave her name and account number to the teller and asked for two hundred dollars.

The teller shook her head. "I'm sorry, ma'am. There's not enough money in that account."

"There was six thousand in there yesterday," Sara said a little testily. She'd logged in to pay the phone bill, so she knew they had money.

The teller tapped on her keyboard a little more. "There's only seventeen dollars in that account. According to this, a large amount was transferred to another account about an hour ago. Perhaps your husband forgot to mention he was moving the money."

Oh, Sara was sure he'd *forgotten* to tell her, just like he'd forgotten to mention he was screwing his boss.

Up until this moment, Sara had been telling herself that her marriage might still have a chance. Maybe she had overreacted. Maybe it hadn't been what it looked like. Deep down, though, she'd known better, and the speed at which Brad emptied their accounts suggested he'd been planning something for a while. It hit her like a punch in the gut.

In a bit of a haze, she thanked the teller and went to the ATM to try her credit cards. Every single one was canceled, except for the Amazon Prime card. Brad must not have known it was a full Visa card and not just a store account. She took out a cash advance of a couple of hundred dollars, probably at a criminally high interest rate, and prayed her car could make it the hundred miles to Grandma's house.

In one day, her life had turned into a bad country song. Sara hated country songs.

She was exhausted by the time she parked in front of her grandma's house. Her car had managed to make it from Des Moines, but in her current mental state, she'd gotten turned around twice and taken the wrong exit, adding about half an hour to her drive. Now, many of the little lights were lit up on her dashboard.

Deciding she'd done enough ruminating on her day, she turned off the car, and the engine continued to chug along for a minute, no doubt indicating more damage. Eventually, it stuttered to a halt.

She turned her phone back to normal mode and noticed three missed calls. There were also a couple of texts. Not ready to re-open communications, she activated the phone's flashlight and walked up the front stairs. She'd been to her grandma's house a month ago for the funeral, but the old Victorian seemed different in the dark. Last time, the house had been full of Grandma's friends and funeral casseroles. Now it was just her, alone with the echoes of her sweet, old grandma who wasn't waiting inside.

She tried the front door. It was locked, of course, so she started digging in her purse for Grandma's keys. She didn't find them. She looked around the front porch for a place where Grandma might have hidden a key. There were some potted geraniums, but she didn't want to dig in the dirt.

She reached into her purse and pulled out her little lock-picking kit. With Brad "working late" all the time and her recent layoff, she'd fallen down quite a few YouTube rabbit holes. Like her coffee roasting obsession, this particular hobby had started with a few innocent tutorial videos.

She inserted a tension wrench and rake into the lock and pulled the rake across the pins. She could feel the pins popping into place, but she wasn't getting all of them. Using a pick on a padlock at the kitchen table was quite a bit different from kneeling in front of a door in the middle of the night.

She tried to change her grip on the tension wrench, but it slipped out of her fingers. The tool hit the wooden porch with a sharp ping, then *tink-tink-tinked* its way into the darkness like a tiny alarm bell. She shined her phone's light on the porch, looking for a flash of metal, but she eventually gave up. She'd have to look for it in the morning.

Sighing, Sara gave up and decided to look for an unlocked window. As she made her way around the house, she saw the trellis under the dining room window. When she was a teenager, she'd gotten in that way a couple of times. She climbed the trellis, and with a lot of persuasion, managed to get the window open.

She'd gotten her shoulders and torso through the window, legs still outside, when she heard footsteps crunch on the gravel driveway.

"Police! Who's there?" called out a deep, male voice.

Startled, Sara lost her balance. Her foot slipped off the trellis and something—it felt like a huge, jagged splinter—caught her thigh. She froze, half in and half out of the window. If she tried to back out, she'd tear a nasty gash in her leg. If she went forward... well, that would require upper body strength she didn't currently possess.

A flash of light came through the window. Someone was shining a flashlight at her—well, at least at the half of her still stuck outside.

"Uh, hi, I'm Sara Jenkins," she called out, trying to be heard through the window while facing the wrong way. "This is my house. Well, it was my grandma's, but I inherited it. I couldn't find the keys."

The policeman yelled back, "I got a call. One of the neighbors said someone was trying to force the lock."

Sara couldn't help the sarcastic retort that bubbled up. "Well, it wasn't my first choice, but I can't find my keys. I didn't want to sleep on the porch."

"I don't suppose you would mind coming down from there, so I can establish your identity?"

Sara sighed. She would have to set her embarrassment aside and admit her predicament. "I seem to be a bit stuck. Could you either pull me out or give me a boost?"

"Of course, ma'am. Let me lend a hand." A hand clamped around her ankle and pulled. She didn't move, but she heard the sound of tearing from her pants.

"Stop!" When he let go of her ankle, Sara said, "I seem to be caught on something. Could you give me a boost the other way? I promise not to steal the house while you're not looking."

"I suppose I'll have to take your word for it."

Sara waited and nothing happened. "Um, were you going to help sometime soon?"

"I'm strategizing. There are some places you don't want to grab a woman."

Sara sighed. "Please just get me out of this window. I promise not to scream 'bad touch' if you have to get a little handsy."

This time, he took hold of her left ankle and placed his hand on her right buttock to stabilize her, pushing her upward. She launched forward through the window, where she promptly gripped on the edge of a table and chair to prevent a tumble to the dining room floor. It had been a little humiliating, but at least she was free.

As she was getting her bearings, the policeman called from outside, "If you could come around to the front door and let me in, I need to ask a few questions and take a look at your ID."

Sara sighed but nodded, even though he couldn't see her. "Sure, just give me a moment to get myself together."

After disentangling herself from the table and chairs, she made her way through the dark rooms until she reached the front door. She felt around, located the entryway light switch, and flipped it on.

When her eyes adjusted to the light, she unlocked the door and swung it open, revealing the policeman, now illuminated by the porch light. He had rugged good looks and the tan of someone who spent a lot of time outdoors. His handsome face, however, supported a less-than-flattering mustache, and she thought he looked slightly familiar. She was sure she remembered his mustache from her grandmother's funeral. A hint of a smile played on his lips as if he was trying to suppress a chuckle.

"Thank you, Ms. Jenkins," he said, stepping inside. "I'm Adam Mitchell. I live next door." He pointed to a beige ranch with a porch swing out front.

"I know. I remember you from the funeral. I thought you said you were a cop."

"I am, ma'am. I'm a detective for the Cedar Rapids Police Department."

"So, when you say a concerned neighbor saw someone breaking in..." Feeling a draft, Sara reached down and realized the ripping sound she'd heard was the entire left seam of her pants, which were probably gaping open. showing her thigh. She tried to nonchalantly hold the seam together.

"That was me. I am the neighbor."

"Aren't you a little out of your jurisdiction, Detective?" She didn't think Cedar Rapids and Downcastle were in the same county.

"Yes, technically I should have contacted the county sheriff, given that Downcastle no longer has a town policeman. However, I'm glad I didn't bother them with a long drive for a false alarm. Perhaps in the future, you can plan ahead so you don't have to crawl into a window around midnight."

Sara didn't like his tone at all. He had no idea about the shitty day she'd had or why she was here. "Look, Detective Mitchell, I didn't plan on getting here this late, but when I was packing everything I own into the back of my car, I kind of lost track of time. Also, I am sure I packed the keys to the house. I'm just not sure where they are. Haven't you ever misplaced your keys? Or are you always perfect?" As she'd spoken, she'd gotten a bit louder than she'd intended, and as she let the question hang and her voice echoed down the street, she realized Downcastle could get pretty quiet this late at night.

He held up his hands as if to surrender. "Hey, there's no need to get emotional. I withdraw the statement."

"What do you mean by emotional?" she demanded. She knew her raised voice made his assessment reasonable. That didn't mean she currently had the mental energy needed to calm herself down.

The detective looked like he wanted to say something more. Then his face went blank, and he blandly said, "Sorry if I offended you, ma'am. I'll be going now. I live right next door if you have any other problems." He pointed to the little beige house again. Then he took two steps back like she was an animal he'd enraged.

Sara crossed her arms, suddenly feeling defensive. "Well, thanks for your help, Detective Mitchell. I'll be sure to remember I have a police officer living next door, in case any other 'problems' arise. Good night, Detective."

"Good night, Ms. Jenkins," he replied, his tone matching hers. With that, he turned and walked back to his own house, leaving Sara standing in the doorway, wondering how she'd managed to alienate her neighbor and an officer of the law within the first few minutes of meeting him.

She shut the door and leaned against it, trying to process the bizarre encounter. One thing was for sure, her new life in Downcastle was off to a rocky start. Her purse banged against the door, and she heard a jingle. She reached in and pulled out Grandma's keys without even digging for them. She let out an exasperated sigh.

Sara slept in the guest bedroom that night. The bed was already made up, and it had been her room when she was in high school. It felt comfortable and familiar. Eventually, she knew she'd want to move into the master bedroom, but for the moment, it still felt like Grandma's room.

Despite her exhaustion, sleep came fitfully. She kept waking up, and each time she did, she could swear she saw Grandma standing in the doorway. Once or twice, she thought she caught a faint trace of Shalimar perfume. Grandma had checked on her like this quite often during that first year after the car accident claimed Sara's parents—standing in the doorway, watching over her, the scent of her perfume a gentle comfort in the dark.

When she woke up the next morning and walked downstairs, the house felt cold and empty without Grandma drinking coffee in her robe and making something wonderful for breakfast. Sara put some medium-roast Sumatra beans in the grinder and considered what to do next.

With no food in the refrigerator, Sara decided to walk downtown and see if there was anywhere she could get some decent food. She was by no means a stranger to Downcastle. She'd spent her summers here as a child, and she'd lived here during her last two years of high school. However, since college, she'd only come here to visit Grandma.

Sara wasn't the only person walking downtown. It looked like it was going to be a warm spring day. There was still a chill in the air, but the bright morning sun was already taking the edge off it. Many of the people greeted her, and she returned their waves and hellos, wondering if they remembered her from high school or Grandma's funeral—or whether they were being "Iowa nice."

As Sara strolled through the familiar streets, she noticed Mel's Diner had been replaced by Marge's Diner. It looked like the only change to the building was a sign with the new name, promising the "Best Breakfast in Town." Intrigued, she decided to give it a try.

The moment she stepped inside, the delicious aroma of frying bacon and pancakes enveloped her. Untouched for seventy years, the decor had accidentally stumbled into looking deliberately retro chic. Sara took a seat at the counter and was greeted by a waitress, a tall, blonde woman with ice-blue eyes. When Sara saw the name tag, "Marge," she realized she was talking to the owner.

"Morning, hon," Marge said with a smile. "Coffee?"

Glancing at the large coffee maker in the front of the cafe, Sara saw a large ReliaRoast box. ReliaRoast was a lower-tier coffee marketed to convenience stores and cafeterias. Sara thought it tasted like sadness. "How about an orange juice and a glass of ice water?"

Marge jotted it on her pad. "What else can I get you?"

Sara quickly scanned the menu. "I'll have a stack of pancakes with a side of eggs and bacon." Her stomach growled loudly enough that Marge smirked. Between Brad's Mariachi performance and her hasty exodus, she'd managed to skip an entire day of meals. At least her appetite was making a comeback.

"We'll get that right out." Marge smiled at her, then something caught her eye, and she scowled at something behind Sara.

As Sara waited for her food, she couldn't help but turn around and see what Marge had scowled at. A lady was talking quite loudly about the Downcastle Harvest Festival. Sara recognized the loud woman by her bright pile of red hair. Her name was Iris Pilkington. At Grandma Laura's funeral, the woman had given every single person the same speech. "Whenever we lose such an esteemed elder, it hurts us all. Laura Jenkins's death leaves a hole in our community." Sara was sure she'd heard the woman recite those words at least five times. By the end of the funeral, she'd been about ready to punch her in the face.

Marge returned with Sara's food. Sara didn't know if this was the best breakfast in town, as the sign outside had promised, but the puddle forming under the bacon and eggs proved it was the greasiest. Sara decided to set health concerns aside for the day and poured a generous amount of syrup onto her pancakes.

She had just shoveled a large forkful of eggs into her mouth when Iris hurried over to her. "You're Sara, right? Laura Jenkins's granddaughter?"

Her mouth still full, Sara nodded, surprised at how quickly the news of her arrival had already spread. When she finally managed to finish her bite, she replied, "Yes, that's me."

The woman stuck out her hand. "I'm Iris Pilking-ton. We met at your grandmother's funeral."

It was a small town, and Sara didn't want to get off on the wrong foot. She smiled and took the prof-fered hand, only slightly worried about how sticky her fingers might be from handling the syrup. "Of course. Nice to meet you again, Iris."

"Your grandma was the neatest lady. Whenever we lose such an esteemed elder, it hurts us all. Laura Jenkins's death leaves a hole in our community."

Sara's mind wandered as Iris recited the mantra, and she realized she'd missed a question. "Sorry, what was that?"

"I was wondering if you were going to be moving into your grandmother's house."

"Well, I was—"

"I'm the organizer of the Harvest Festival, and I was hoping you might take over Laura's role in the event."

Before she asked about her grandma's role in the event, Sara had to ask, "As the organizer, maybe you can answer a question for me. Why is the Harvest Festival in June?"

The smile momentarily slipped from Iris's face, then it returned. "You see, the Harvest Festival was in September, but the local farmers were too busy with the harvest to participate, so we moved it to the end of October, but then it kept getting in the way of Hal-loween events. We pushed it back to mid–November, but it was sometimes too cold, and we had to schedule around the Hawkeye football. Then we decided to move it to summer, but August is too hot. Swisher Fun Days are at the end of July, and the Cedar Rapids Freedom Festival is at the beginning of July. So now we have it in June."

"But you still call it the Harvest Festival?"

Iris shrugged. "Well, it's tradition. Speaking of traditions, your grandma used to run a mediumship booth at the Harvest Festival every year. It was a real hit. I was hoping you might be interested in taking it over this year."

"Medium ship? Like boat rides?" Sara wasn't aware of any nearby body of water other than the creek and the town's sewage lagoon. Neither was suitable for a small boat, let alone a medium one.

"No, honey. Your grandmother was a psychic medium."

"You mean, like, talking to dead people?" That was a side of her grandmother she knew nothing about. Then again, Grandma did have a weird sense of humor. She might have done it just to screw with people. "You've got to be joking."

"Oh, I'm sure she didn't really talk to dead people. It was all in good fun. I guess she didn't teach you any of her techniques. That's too bad. She was quite gifted. I'm sure it was all carnival tricks, but many people thought she was the real deal."

Sara shook her head. Her grandma always had a little bit of a wild streak. However, Sara was a little surprised her grandma was spending her spare time communicating with spirits, even just for fun. Why had she never mentioned it? "No, she never said a word about it to me. I'm not sure I'd be any good at that kind of thing."

Iris's smile dimmed slightly. "Maybe you have a hidden talent that you don't know about. You know, your grandmother's booth brought real comfort to people. Mrs. Henderson still talks about how Laura helped her find peace after her Harold passed." She touched Sara's arm. "Having the best town festival is a point of pride for our community, and your grandmother's booth was always one of our biggest draws. But I understand if you're not up for carrying on her legacy."

Sara nodded. "I'll think about it, Iris. Thanks for letting me know."

There was absolutely no way in hell she was doing it. If she had a hidden talent, it was better hidden than the character development in a Michael Bay movie. But it wasn't just about embarrassing herself—pretending to connect people with their lost loved ones? That was playing with dynamite. Her grandmother had brought comfort to people like Mrs. Henderson, but what if Sara got it wrong?

But as Iris walked away, Sara felt that special kind of small-town guilt settling in her stomach. The kind that came with knowing everyone would hear about how she'd refused to help with the festival.

Coming home from breakfast, Sara saw Ruby Mae Walker on the front porch, about to ring the bell. Normally, Ruby Mae dressed like she had somewhere important to be—smart slacks, a bold blouse, jewelry that made a statement. Today, she was in sweatpants and a t-shirt, a scarf wrapped tightly around her head.

When Ruby Mae moved to Downcastle in the eighties, she had been the only black person in town, and being married to a white man hadn't exactly made her the town darling. Sara's grandma took this as a good reason to get to know her, and the two had been best friends ever since.

"Hi, Aunt Ruby," Sara called.

The old woman turned around and waved. "Hey, girl. Have you been out already? I heard you got in late last night."

News did travel fast in a small town. "I went to the diner and got some breakfast." She walked up the front steps and gave Ruby Mae a hug. "Come in, and I'll make some coffee."

Sara was always happy to see Ruby Mae. Not only was she practically family, but the woman had an infectious aura of happiness and positivity. Today, though, Sara was extra eager to see her, fueled by her own burning questions about Grandma's mysterious hobby as a medium.

Sara wanted to make a splendid cup of coffee for Ruby Mae, so she brought out the last of her custom blend, a medium–light roast Casa del Sol Bourbon Arabica with a hint of Kona. As they settled down in the cozy living room with steaming mugs of coffee, Sara couldn't contain her curiosity any longer. "Can I ask you something? Did Grandma really run a booth at the Harvest Festival?"

Ruby Mae chuckled. "Oh, yes, she did. She was a psychic medium. She started it the year after you left for college. That was back when the harvest festival was in November, and with you going off to school, I think she needed something more to keep her busy. Your grandmother turned out to be quite the entertainer. People loved her booth, and it was all in good fun. She put up all the 'for entertainment only' disclaimers, but she had a way of making people feel comforted and connected to their loved ones."

Sara furrowed her brow. "Iris Pilkington approached me earlier today and asked if I would take over the booth this year. She made me feel like I was letting the whole town down. But I could never do it. I don't know the first thing about how to entertain people like that."

Ruby Mae's eyes narrowed a little. "Iris, huh? Be careful around her, Sara. She's quite the puppet master in this community. She's got her nose up in every-body's business. If you don't want to, don't listen to Iris. If you want to take over your grandma's booth, you do it for you and for her memory."

Sara smiled. "I suppose you're right. Maybe I should go look at her psychic stuff at least."

"I know exactly where she stored her crystal ball." Ruby Mae's tone brooked no argument. "That's why I'm here—to help you sort through your grandma's things. And don't even think about arguing with me, young lady. Your grandmother would never forgive me if I let you tackle this alone."

"That's so sweet of you." The simple directness of her offer touched Sara more than she expected. After years in the city where everyone was too busy and self-involved to lend a hand without being asked, she had forgotten what it felt like to have people quietly show up for you. Aunt Ruby's presence was a poignant re-minder of the way people looked out for each other in tight-knit towns like this. Sara suddenly realized how much she had missed that sense of unspoken under-standing.

"Of course, dear," Ruby Mae said, her warm smile returning. "Why do you think I'm here, just to have coffee? I'm here to work."

Even though the generosity came as no surprise, Sara was momentarily overcome with emotion, and she felt her eyes water a tiny bit. "Oh, that would be so wonderful. My cousin Jennifer offered to help, but I felt bad, she's like a senior software engineer, and she works crazy hours sometimes."

The doorbell rang, and Sara said, "I'll be right back." She set down her coffee and walked to the en-tryway. When she opened the door, a young man was standing outside wearing business casual and saturat-ed with the overpowering scent of musky body spray.

"Hi there, ma'am. I'm Dwain Hart. This might seem like an odd question, but did your grandmother leave anything behind for me?"

Sara shrugged. She had no idea what he might be talking about. "I haven't seen anything. But I haven't really started going through the house."

"You see, I'm a realtor at Kelley and Hart, and I had been talking to your grandmother about selling the house. I'd like to provide you with this assessment of homes in your area." He handed her a glossy pamphlet. "I understand you've recently inherited the house, and if you're interested in selling, I'm sure we could make you an exceptional offer. The housing market in Downcastle is—"

Sara took the pamphlet. "Thanks. I'll think about it." Her eyes were starting to water from the body spray, and she closed the door before the young man could say another word.

Returning to the living room, she set the pamphlet on the coffee table. "Some young realtor trying to buy the house. He had on so much body spray, it smelled like he'd run over a skunk."

"Oh, that would be Mayor Hart's boy. He's been going all over town trying to buy houses. I don't know why anyone would want to own so much property here. Then again, they say land is the only thing they can't make more of."

"Funny, a week ago, I might have considered it. Even after Verdegrowth shut down, I had no intentions of leaving Des Moines. Until yesterday..."

Ruby Mae gave her a scrutinizing look. "Is there something wrong, girl?"

Sara sighed. "I found out Brad was cheating on me with one of his coworkers. I had to get away. I just packed a suitcase and came straight here." She found herself spilling her guts; she'd been holding in so much. "He'd cleaned out the bank accounts, and my car needs a new engine, and all I have left is the clothes I could carry and my coffee roaster. This house is still technically in probate."

"Honey, men like that aren't worth the leather on their spinny office chairs. My Harold, bless his soul, couldn't balance a checkbook to save his life, but at least he was honest. He was no good in bed, but your grandma would occasionally help me out in that department."

After a moment of silence, Sara realized her mouth was hanging open and closed it.

Ruby Mae started to shake with laughter, before letting out a laugh at her own joke. "Oh, I'm just kidding, sugar. Your grandma and I were strictly platonic. Well, there was that one time in Cancun..."

Despite the events of the previous day, Sara found herself laughing and smiling. She rolled her eyes for effect, "Ruby Mae, inappropriate."

She shook her head. "Don't you worry, though. You're part of my family, and I'm going to help you restart your life and get you back on your feet. Speaking of which, do you know what you're going to do once you are settled in? This is a pretty good area for jobs, between Cedar Rapids and Iowa City."

Sara did have an idea, but she was wondering if it was silly. "Well, this may sound crazy, but I'd like to roast my own coffee and run a little coffee shop. I was thinking maybe I could convert the downstairs of the house."

Ruby Mae pondered it for a minute and said, "Well, I think that would be a great idea. It would give people somewhere to go other than Marge's Diner. Her coffee's so bad even the spoons try to escape."

Sara hesitated for a moment, "But I don't have any money, and I'm afraid Grandma wouldn't like me turning her house into a business."

Chuckling, Ruby Mae said. "Girl, your grandma left you this house to make your own life in. I think she'd just be glad you're going to stay here instead of selling it."

"But what about the money?"

"Well, you'll own this house, so you can always borrow against it. And you should at least try to take that cheating husband for all he's worth."

Sara smiled at that, and perhaps because of Ruby Mae's belief in her, she made up her mind to at least try. "You're right. I'm going to do it. I'm going to open a coffee shop right here in Grandma's house." It still seemed an impossible pronouncement with less than two hundred dollars in her purse, but at least she had nothing to lose.

"And I'll be your first customer," Ruby Mae promised, raising her coffee mug in a toast. "To new beginnings and honoring the ones we love."

Chapter 2

Festival Fiascos and Financial Woes

After she finished her coffee, Ruby Mae set down her cup. "Sara, do you think you're ready to look through some of your grandma's things today? I do have some boxes and garbage bags out in the car in case you are up to it. We could start with her clothes and things you know you're not going to need."

Sara nodded. "Yeah. I think I can handle doing a little today."

"That's good, sweetie. Best to tear off the bandage and get started. I told my boy, Joe, he should stop by this afternoon with his big pickup truck. By then, we should either have a good pile to take to Goodwill or the dump. You remember Joe, don't you?"

"Oh, yeah. I remember Joe." Joe had been away at college most of the time Sara had lived in Downcastle, on a Division Three football scholarship. But whenever he was home from school, Grandma would invite Ruby Mae over for dinner, and he would come along. He was built like you'd expect a college football player to be, broad-shouldered and solid, but that's where the stereotype ended. He was a quiet guy, always having his nose stuck in a book or watching football on Grandma's old TV, the sound turned all the way down. "I guess we should get started."

After they retrieved the supplies from Ruby Mae's car, the old lady led the way up the stairs to Grandma's bedroom, garbage bags in her hands. Sara followed her with a stack of broken-down boxes and a roll of packing tape. When Ruby Mae pushed the door to Grandma's room open, a faint smell of Shalimar hit Sara, making her expect to see her grandma just around the corner. Not seeing her made the room feel even more empty.

Throwing the boxes on the bed, Sara said, "You want to start in the dresser? I don't think I'll want to keep any socks or undergarments, but I do want to look through the clothing. Grandma had some nice outfits, especially the dresses."

"Oh honey, your grandmother's dresses!" Ruby Mae's eyes lit up as she moved to the dresser. "That woman knew how to make an entrance. Half of Downcastle clutched their pearls when she wore that sparkly number to the Fourth of July picnic. Mind if I look through them after you? Some of those outfits deserve a second act, though we don't share quite the same color profile."

Sara heard a clink of glass from the depths of the drawer Ruby Mae had opened. Curious, Sara peered over Ruby Mae's shoulder just as the older woman triumphantly pulled out a set of garishly colored shot glasses.

"Well, would you look at that!" Ruby Mae exclaimed, holding the glasses up to the light with a mischievous grin. "I haven't seen these in ages."

Sara leaned in for a closer look. Each glass was emblazoned with the word "Chicago!" in swirly, cursive letters. But it was the designs on the opposite sides that really caught her eye:

A deep-dish pizza, steam rising from its center, with the slogan "Cover me in your sauce!"

A loaded hot dog proclaiming "Get your buns ready!"

The iconic Wrigley Field sign, arched over the cheeky phrase "Check out our balls!"

And finally, a commuter train on the famous elevated track above the words "You can ride me all night long!"

Sara couldn't help but laugh out loud at the audacious slogans. She could totally picture Grandma Laura shooting tequila from these tacky, exclamation-point-laden glasses.

Ruby Mae must have been thinking along the same lines because she turned to Sara with a conspiratorial wink. "We got those when we went to Chicago with the Baptist Women's Circle. Did your grandma ever tell you about that?"

Sara knew her Grandma's opinion of church had been, "The Lord gave us Sunday to rest. Why would I want to get out of bed early and dress up?" With Grandma not being one to regularly visit a church, Sara realized she didn't know much about the religious preferences of those close to her grandmother. Turning to Ruby Mae, she asked, "Are you a Baptist, Ruby Mae?"

"No. I'm not all that religious myself."

"Then, how did you end up on this trip?"

"What were a couple wild women like me and your grandma doing with the uptight Baptist Women's Circle of Downcastle? Well, they all wanted to go to Chicago to hear Pastor Jimmy Mundy speak about his visit to the Holy Land and tour the First Baptist Church of Chicago. They let us come along because they needed twelve women to split the cost of the charter bus.

Ruby Mae grinned. "Of course, we didn't give a fig about Pastor Jimmy Mundy. As soon as the bus let us out at our hotel, we took the El train downtown and went from jazz club to jazz club. At one point, we ended up at this tiny, smoky club where the air was thick with the scent of stale beer. A man sat down next to us in this sparkly outfit. I thought he was going to offer to buy us drinks, but instead, he started talking about life and death, freedom and slavery, the nature of the Universe vs the Omniverse, and how he was originally from Saturn. We'd had a few drinks at that point, so we just smiled and nodded along with him. Then they invited him up on stage to play piano. I found out later that we'd been talking to Sun Ra!"

Sara laughed, delighted by the unexpected twist in the story. "Wait, so you had a whole philosophical conversation with a jazz legend without realizing it? That's wild!"

"There were plenty of other men hitting on us that night. Your grandma was just a little older than you are now, and she wore the tiniest little blue dress. She was a knockout. However, when the sun went down, it started to get cold."

"You know," Sara said, "she never let me out of the house without at least a light sweater if it was under seventy degrees."

Ruby Mae nodded. "Well, it was the voice of experience from what she learned that night. We got turned around trying to find an after-hours party. There was a rumor Von Freeman was going to be there and maybe Miles Davis. We ended up drinking coffee and trying to sober up at four in the morning in an all-night donut shop waiting for a cab to pick us up. We got back to the hotel three hours before we had to get up and go to the sermon."

"Ouch."

"Let me tell you something. Pastor Jimmy Mundy is not an engaging speaker when you're hungover and going on three hours of sleep. We took turns prodding each other awake. After the sermon, we went back to the bus to sleep while the women's circle toured the church. They did not invite us on their next trip."

Sara laughed. "It sounds like the kind of thing you guys would get up to. Sometimes, Ruby Mae, I think you moved to Downcastle just to stir things up."

"Honestly, our decision to move to Downcastle had more to do with the price of housing than making things uncomfortable for people. Back in those days, you could buy a nice house here for less than a 'fixer-upper' in Cedar Rapids."

Sara nodded, absorbing the information as she continued exploring her grandmother's closet. Behind the dresses, Sara found a small shelf with a number of jewelry boxes. She picked up the first one, a tiny wooden box that looked older than the rest, and opened it. Inside was a heavy, silver pendant with an intricate design. "This is nice." She turned and held it up by its thick, silver chain.

Ruby Mae squinted at and nodded. "Your grandma used to wear it during her mediumship act. She called it her magic amulet. She said it was some kind of family heirloom, but I never got the full story behind it."

"It's beautiful." There was a micro-fiber polishing cloth in the box, and Sara gave it a few wipes to bring out the shine. She walked over to the mirror and slipped it on. The piece settled heavily against her chest, and with that weight came a calm she hadn't felt since before she'd caught Brad cheating on her. She took a deep breath and let it out.

Leaving the amulet on, Sara went back to sorting her grandma's dresses. Her "try on" pile kept growing larger than the others. She couldn't help herself—each piece she touched was pure Laura. The designer labels weren't what made them special—it was how her grandmother had worn them, turning heads at seventy the same way she had at twenty. That sparkly purple dress that she often wore to her card games. The clingy, red silk number she liked to wear to board game night at the library just to annoy the librarian. Even now, Sara could hear her grandmother's laugh: "Age is just a number, honey, and mine's unlisted."

They had been working for a solid couple of hours when Ruby Mae stopped and said, "I'm sorry, honey. I'm not as energetic as I used to be. Do you mind if I go downstairs and have another cup of your fine coffee?"

"Of course. I could brew a fresh pot. It has been sitting out for a while."

"Don't you bother. I'll warm it up in the microwave."

While Sara would never have reheated coffee herself, if Ruby Mae was comfortable with it, she wasn't going to complain. The woman had been a whirlwind all morning, sorting and organizing with the energy of someone half her age. Sara needed a break herself.

Tired of looking through dresses, Sara decided to pull the rest of the jewelry out of the closet and start going through it. She set down a stack of boxes on the dresser and looked up to see someone standing behind her in the mirror.

Sara screamed. She turned around to see a woman standing in the middle of the bedroom. The woman was attractive, reminding Sara a little of Elizabeth Montgomery in "Bewitched", one of Grandma's favorite shows. She was wearing a white mini-dress cinched with a gold belt, casual but a tad dressier than an oversized t-shirt, like something from the cover of one of Grandma's disco albums. She was also slightly transparent.

"I thought she would never leave," the woman said.

From downstairs, Ruby Mae called out, "Are you okay up there?"

Sara opened her mouth to answer, but she wasn't exactly sure if she was doing all right. Had a crazy woman sneaked up on her? That didn't explain the transparency. Was she hallucinating? Did Grandma have some LSD hidden somewhere, and she'd accidentally ingested it? You never knew with Grandma.

"Can you stop gathering wool and tell her you're fine? You're going to make Ruby Mae nervous."

Sara had only known one person who regularly used the phrase "Stop gathering wool." Between that and the smell of Shalimar, she knew who she was facing.

The woman waved her partially transparent hand in front of Sara's face. "Hello? Tell her you saw a spider before she tries to run up the steps and breaks a hip."

"I'm okay, Aunt Ruby," Sara yelled out the door. "I saw a big spider under the bed."

Ruby Mae yelled back. "Leave it alone, honey. They kill the other bugs."

"As long as it keeps its distance, I'm prepared to live and let live." Sara turned back to the transparent woman. "Grandma Laura? Is that really you, or am I losing my mind?"

Sara had to admit, there was a more than even chance she was losing her mind. She was under huge amounts of stress. She'd lost her closest relative. Her marriage had imploded just when she'd burned through most of her emergency savings from being laid off six weeks ago. Her asshole husband had stolen what was left, and to top it all off, her car was mostly dead. When she compared the possibility of a break-down with the possibility of seeing ghosts, a complete mental collapse made a lot of sense.

Then again, the woman had accused her of wool gathering and she looked a lot like her grandma in old pictures. Still, if Sara was hallucinating, she obviously would make it a believable one.

The transparent being that looked a bit like her grandmother chuckled, a sound so familiar it sent shivers down Sara's spine. "You're not losing your mind, sweetie. It's me."

"But you're…" Sara tried to think of something to say other than dead. "You're so young."

"The perks of no longer having a physical body. I can appear to people however I want, so I decided to go for young and hot. I never did take well to being an old lady. I always felt like a young person trapped in an aging vessel."

"Fair enough," Sara said. "But that brings me to my next question. If you don't have a physical body, how can I see you?"

"The ability to see ghosts does run in our family. However, that amulet you're wearing can boost that gift. Before, you might have gotten the vague impression that I was in the house somewhere, but when you put that amulet on you can see me as I am now and speak to me directly."

Sara's eyes widened. "So, you're really here? You're talking to me from the afterlife?" Her voice cracked on the last word, all the grief she thought she'd processed rushing back.

Grandma nodded. "I thought we'd established that. I crossed over to the other side, and now I'm back checking up on you."

"I know. I know." Sara sank onto the edge of the bed, her legs suddenly unsteady. "It's just... God, Grandma, why didn't you tell me before you died? All those years, you were doing carnival reading for the whole fucking town, and you never thought to mention it to me?"

"I was trying to protect you, honey." Grandma's form flickered slightly, like a candle in a draft. "This gift... it's not always the blessing people think it is. Sometimes what you see..." She paused, something dark crossing her transparent features. "Let's just say not everything that comes through is pleasant. Some are trapped on Earth and miserable, and some who've crossed over can still be a-holes. And living people... well, once they know what you can do, some of them never leave you alone."

"So why not make it into a carnival act for the whole town?" Sara couldn't keep the biting sarcasm out of her voice.

Grandma shrugged, a gesture so familiar it made Sara's heart ache. "I figured, what the hell? I thought it would piss off a couple of people with sticks up their butt. Look, is every decision you make one hundred percent logical?"

Sara lifted the amulet and gazed at the pattern. It seemed to move as she tilted it to catch the light. "Where did this thing come from anyway?"

"My grandmother brought it with her from Turkey. Not even the ghosts of our ancestors remember the full history."

31

Sara looked around nervously. "The ghosts of our ancestors? They're not hanging out with us, are they?"

Grandma chuckled again. "Don't worry. Mostly the dead don't hang around with the living." She gestured at the boxes around them. "Speaking of which, do whatever you want with all this stuff. I certainly don't need it anymore." Her eyes twinkled. "Though, before you ask, there's no box of gold doubloons hidden around here."

"I wasn't going to–" Sara started to protest.

"Honey, if I had them, they'd be all yours." She shrugged. "Now, what else can I tell you? There are a few souls stuck on this side, but most people cross over sooner or later. It gives you a lot of perspective, and from what I hear, it's kind of a pain in the butt sitting around and watching your descendants make the same mistakes generation after generation."

Sara made a face. It made a lot of sense. "So, you're here because you want to check in on me?"

"Of course. I wanted to see how you were doing, and after listening to you and Ruby Mae earlier, I feel that I was right to do so. You got laid off. You're having trouble with Brad. You have the amulet now, and the responsibility that comes with it. That's a lot—"

"Responsibility?"

"Well, now that you can see ghosts, they might start coming to you for help. Remember how I said some people are stuck? Some of them can use a hand crossing over."

"Like that kid in the movie, *The Sixth Sense*? Will dead people just be everywhere?" Sara's voice rose with barely contained hysteria.

"Not exactly, but a lot like that, yes. They kind of nailed it on that one."

"Hold up. How the hell am I going to help? Help with what? I am barely keeping my shit together!" Sara ran her hands through her hair. "Jesus, Grandma, I have my own problems. I have a house full of your things to sort through. I am not equipped to be some kind of... ghost social worker!"

Grandma's laugh sparkled like wind chimes. "Ghost social worker? Oh honey, that's a new one." Her smile turned gentle. "But you're more equipped than you think. And I doubt even social workers have it all that together."

"But why me, Grandma?"

Her grandma shrugged. "Why you? Why me? Why anybody? You've been given a chance to do something, but whether you take that chance is up to you. I can teach you to shut down your gifts as easily as I can show you how to use them. You never have to put the amulet on again if you don't want to. But you know what I'd do?"

"Help other people?" Sara asked.

"Before I did anything, I'd hook up with that cute detective next door. Both as a way to get back at Brad and as friends with benefits."

"Grandma!"

Her grandma shrugged. "Well, there are worse ways to spend an evening. I grew up in the free love era, but I met your granddad and got married young, so I never got to experience it. I have to admit I was a little bit jealous of women who waited to get married and dated a bunch of guys. Of course, I saw a few gentlemen after your granddad died, but I would have liked a few more notches in my headboard when I was younger, or they were younger for that matter."

Sara's brain stuttered to a halt. Wait. What? She thought back to all those nights in high school, her grandmother heading out with her purse and a spring in her step. "So when you told me you were going to play cards with the girls..."

Her grandma nodded. "I don't even like card games."

"O–M–G!" Sara pressed her hands to her temples. "You were... while I was still living here?" She started laughing. "I was sitting at the kitchen table, all innocent and virginal while you were out... Grandma! I thought you were playing bridge."

Again, Grandma gave her that unconcerned shrug. "Too many rules. I like to keep things loose."

Before she felt compelled to comment on "keeping things loose," Sara decided to change the subject. "I still don't know if I'm ready to deal with this whole amulet thing."

"Don't worry, Sara. We'll figure it out together." Grandma reassured her.

The stairs creaked with slow footsteps, and Ruby Mae appeared in the door with a mug in her hands. "I got tired of resting. Now that I have my second wind, we can get back to work."

Sara's cheeks still felt warm from the conversation with her grandma. "Sure, Ruby Mae, let's do that."

Grandma waved. "I'm going to go so you can work without distraction." As she faded away, she added, "And think about bumping uglies with the detective." She added a lewd hand gesture as she vanished.

They returned to going through Grandma's belongings, but Sara found herself repeatedly looking at the spot where her grandma's ghost had stood a few moments before. She felt simultaneously frightened and excited about the possibility of talking to ghosts, but it was also making it damn hard to concentrate on which Christmas sweaters she wanted to keep or sort through twenty years of shoes.

After another couple of hours, the doorbell rang. Sara hurried down the stairs and opened the door to find a beautiful man standing outside. Joe had dark skin, like his mother, and he was very muscular under his thin shirt. His serious expression melted into a warm smile. "Hi, Sara. I'm Joe Walker. Remember me? Your grandmother used to have me over for dinner occasionally."

Sara could have sworn he had grown three more inches since high school. She felt a flutter in her stomach as she took in Joe's broad shoulders and chiseled jawline. The scent of pencil shavings and cinnamon enveloped her, and she found herself leaning in unconsciously. She shook her head, trying to dispel the unexpected reaction. She hadn't even started her divorce paperwork yet. This was not the time to get a schoolgirl crush no matter how good Joe looked in a t-shirt.

"Yes, your mom said you'd be stopping by to help. I appreciate everything. Your mom's upstairs. We've been going through Grandma's clothing all day.

"Yeah, I remember your grandma always liked to dress fancy. She was one classy lady."

Sara had a flashback to her grandma's ghost making suggestive hand gestures a couple of hours ago. "That's so sweet of you to say."

She made a conscious effort to look away from his huge pectoral muscles. Outside, a big white contractor truck with "Walker Building and Design" written on the side caught her eye. Joe followed her gaze. "I brought my truck, so we can get quite a bit in there. If you lead the way upstairs, I can start carrying things. Are we doing garbage or charity first?"

"Follow me." She turned and started leading him up to Grandma's bedroom. "I think we should start at garbage. There's a bit more of it, and it will be nice to get it out of the way."

Ruby Mae was still working hard when they got to the bedroom. She looked up at Joe and said, "There you are, boy. It's about time you showed up."

"Hey, Mama," Joe said, giving Ruby Mae a big hug. "You know I had to supervise the painters today. If the Fincher brothers start smoking weed before noon, I never get any work out of them."

"I don't know why you hire those boys all the time."

"They work hard when you can keep them on task. They can splash primer on a wall just fine as long as you keep them sober and make sure they've taped everything off properly."

"Well, I wouldn't tell you how to do your business."

"No, mama, I know you wouldn't do that." He turned his head and rolled his eyes so Sara could see, just in case she hadn't heard the subtle sarcasm in his voice. "Now, point me at what you want to go, and I'll start hauling."

As she worked, Sara found herself stealing glances at Joe. She tried to stay focused, but she couldn't deny Joe had really filled out since she last saw him. When he lifted a heavy box, his biceps strained against his sleeves, making it even harder for her to concentrate.

Joe ended up having an entire load of donations and a trip to the dump. Sara felt kind of sad throwing out her grandma's things, but she didn't have any use for them, and there was a lot of stuff a charity wouldn't take—opened makeup and lotions, well-used undergarments, and shoes that were mostly worn out. A lot of it was stuff Grandma probably would have thrown away if she'd taken a closer look at it.

After returning from his final trip, Joe came upstairs and said, "I put supper out on the table. Everything's set up."

"Supper?" Sara asked. "I was going to take you both out to eat for all the help you've given me today." While this was true, she was glad she wouldn't have to, as a sit-down dinner for three people would have wiped out her supply of cash.

Ruby Mae stood and stretched. "I'm sure you would, honey, but I made a few sandwiches and some iced tea in case we worked through the whole day. I'm glad I did. I'm feeling pretty worn out. If you still want to treat us, we can go out to eat some other time."

They went downstairs and gathered around the dining room table. After she'd gotten a ham and cheese sandwich, Sara said. "I appreciate everything you did today."

"I'm glad Mom asked me to come help," Joe said. "Your grandma was a big part of my life, growing up. She used to babysit me when I was little."

"Yeah. The same for me. Of course, when I moved in, you were a little old to be hanging out with a high school girl."

"You know," Ruby Mae interrupted, "Sara's going to turn this house into a coffee shop. She sure could use a contractor to do some work for her." Ruby was not so subtly poking Joe under the table.

Ignoring the literal prodding, Joe thought for a moment before shaking his head like it was the worst idea he'd ever heard. "Turning a residence into a commercial eatery? Not a trivial task. You've got zoning to deal with, accessibility issues, health codes—and don't even get me started on installing commercial appliances or upgrading the plumbing."

"Joe," Ruby Mae pursed her lips and gave her son a murderous look, "stop making excuses and tell the woman that you'll help. She's family."

"Of course, Sara. I'll help in any way I can. Mom! Stop poking me."

37

The busy work with Ruby Mae and dinner had kept Sara's mind off ghosts for a while, but that night, she found herself jumping at every sound the old house made, thinking that either Grandma or someone else might be watching her sleep.

Even if she had been able to ignore the possibility of voyeuristic spirits, she kept turning the scenario over and over in her head. She was down to only three rational explanations. One: As she had considered earlier, she was going insane from the stress of her situation. Two: There actually were ghosts hovering around us all the time, but most people couldn't see them. Three: Hallucinations brought on by some kind of toxic mold in her grandma's closet.

Needing to clear her head, Sara decided to go for a walk. She put on the clothes she'd been wearing earlier and grabbed a coat from her grandma's closet, knowing that even after a warm spring day, the temperature could dip below freezing at night. As she stepped outside, she was pleased to find a full moon made it easy to see. Sara walked a block over to Ely Road, an older street that wound through town and continued out into the country. About a mile down the road, where the small town began to turn into cornfields, cattle pastures, and the occasional farmhouse, she heard a strange sound—someone was moaning.

She moved in the direction of the moaning, hoping she wouldn't run into some kind of injured farm animal or something else she was completely unprepared to deal with. She squeezed between a gate and a chain-link fence with some warnings from the town on it and found a transparent young man. She tapped her chest under the light jacket and felt the amulet there. She must have slipped it on when she got dressed, although she couldn't actually remember doing it. That was odd—she usually deliberated more carefully about jewelry.

The ghost moaned again, and Sara felt like she needed to say something. "Hey, are you okay?"

He looked up at her, a confused look on his face. "You can see me?"

She nodded. "Yes, I can. My name is Sara. What's your name?"

"I'm Ethan."

"So, what are you up to tonight, Ethan?"

"I'm doing what I do every night. I come out here to gaze across this beautiful lake."

"Um... I hate to tell you this, but you're gazing out over the town's sewage lagoon. There are signs posted outside the fence."

"I gaze out over this beautiful lake—"

"So, we're going to ignore that fact and keep going then."

"I gaze out over this beautiful lake, and I think about losing my one true love and how I'm going to be alone forever."

If she had been talking to a living person, Sara might try to convince them that they had plenty to live for, but she didn't think that was going to help Ethan. Instead, she changed the subject. "You seem pretty young and healthy, Ethan. How did you die?"

"I..." He paused for dramatic effect. "...was a poet. I wrote the greatest love poem ever written, and when the girl I sent it to failed to reciprocate my feelings, there was nothing I could do but take my own life."

For Sara, who had recently found the man she considered her true love *in flagrante delicto* on a leather office sofa, harming oneself over another person, who didn't even like you, sounded like a pretty bad idea.

Still, he was dead, and she wasn't going to give him a lecture over something that couldn't be changed.

She felt like she should do something to cheer Ethan up, so despite her better judgment, she asked, "Could you recite your poem to me?"

He nodded enthusiastically. "Yes!" Taking several pages of transparent paper out of his hoodie, he began to read.

Sara didn't consider herself to be any great judge of poetry. She'd taken a couple English classes in college, but just basic literature classes she needed for language requirements. However, even she knew that Ethan's poem was not something to be remembered for posterity.

Ethan waxed lyrical for a while about the attributes of his imagined love. Her eyes, he claimed, sparkled like stars, only to reveal their full splendor beneath the moon's glow—an impressive feat, unless one happened to be a werewolf.

The poem didn't stop at celestial comparisons; it ventured into mythology, invoking Aphrodite and Cupid. Sara, though not exactly a scholar of ancient tales, had a hunch that mixing Greek and Roman deities was sort of frowned upon.

With mythology put to rest, Ethan's verses took a gastronomic turn. He praised her cherry-like lips and dubbed her 'sugar-dipped.' And then came the comparison to fondue, which, frankly, was laying on the cheese a bit thick.

At the completion of his recitation, Sara wasn't sure whether she should applaud or critique him. So instead of doing either, she just nodded and said, "I see."

"She didn't even respond to my poem," Ethan complained. "It's like she never even read it."

This made Sara stop and think. Even the worst poetry should get some kind of response—even if it was just a restraining order. Being called a "sugar-dipped visage with eyes like stars" who needed to be "covered with cheese" wasn't the kind of thing most people could ignore. "Are you sure she got your poem? I mean, did you hand it to her directly or read it to her?"

"Well, no. I slipped it through the vent in her locker."

Sara raised an eyebrow. "Don't you think it was possible she never even saw your poem? Maybe she never knew how you felt. Maybe your note got caught somewhere or fell down to the bottom. Are you even one hundred percent sure you got the right locker?"

"Well, not exactly. I mean, I never thought of all that. I guess I just assumed she'd rejected me."

Sara bit her lip. She wanted to scream at this kid and call him a moron, but Sara felt a pang of recognition in her chest. His misunderstandings and jumping to conclusions hit uncomfortably close to home, reminding her of her own recent inability to gauge Brad's character.

"Ethan," she said softly, "I know it hurts to feel like you've been rejected by someone you love. But holding onto that pain, letting it consume you... it's no way to live. Or to die, for that matter."

Ethan's ghostly form flickered, and for a moment, Sara thought she saw a flash of anger in his eyes. "But how can I let it go?" Ethan asked, his voice raw with emotion. "She was my everything."

The temperature around them seemed to drop, and she shivered involuntarily.

Sara took a deep breath, choosing her words carefully. "Sometimes, people get so caught up in their own pain that they can't see the bigger picture. They make assumptions and close themselves off to the truth. But if you can find it in your heart to forgive, to release that anger and hurt... it's the only way to truly be free." As she spoke, Sara felt a weight lifting from her own shoulders. The irony wasn't lost on her—here she was giving advice about letting go when her own wounds were still raw.

Ethan was silent for a long moment, his form shimmering in the moonlight. Then, slowly, he nodded. "You're right," he said, his voice barely a whisper. "I've been holding onto this for too long. It's time to let it go and move on."

Smiling, Sara said, "I think that would be the best thing for you, Ethan. And I want you to know, that if I was a teenage girl and you wrote that poem to me, I would have been impressed." There was no reason to point out that you could be impressed with how disproportionate a gesture could be.

"Do you think, if you were a little younger, you might have dated me?"

"Sure," Sara said. She couldn't see where this line of questioning was going, but she might as well humor him. What was the worst thing that could happen?

"So, yeah. There's just one thing before I can move on. I died a virgin. Do you think I could see you naked?"

Sara shook her head. "No. Absolutely not." She hadn't been sure what he was trying to get at, but this hadn't been on her list of possibilities.

"Well, look at it this way, if we had been in high school together, and I had given you that poem, which you said was an impressive gesture, maybe you would have gone out with me."

"That's a big maybe."

"But there would have been a possibility. And then if we had gone out a few times, there would have been a possibility we would have gotten to third base."

"Okay, yeah." Based on her own personal history, Sara had to give him that one. She'd spent her fair share of time being groped in an old car parked in a secluded area. "Still, that doesn't change that you're like fifteen."

"I appear to be fifteen. However, we're actually quite close in age. You see, we went to Downcastle High together, and the girl I was trying to give that poem to was you."

"Bullshit. I think I would have remembered if a kid I went to high school with had committed suicide. There were only forty-five people in my graduating class."

At least he had the decency to look embarrassed. "Okay, fine. I might have graduated in 1988. Or would have, if I hadn't... you know. But you're smoking hot, and I did die a virgin."

"Can't you just walk into any house and watch people undress?"

"Yeah, but I'm horny, not a Peeping Tom. Besides, what's it going to hurt? It's not like I can do anything other than look. This isn't *Ghostbusters.*"

Sara hadn't seen that movie for a long time, but she did remember a very disturbing ghost sex scene. "Look, even if I wanted to help you out, it's too cold out here. You might not feel the cold." Did he? "But if you haven't noticed, I'm wearing four layers."

"What about a flash of your boobs? You never know, it could help me cross over."

Sara had pretty serious doubts about that. She shook her head. "Sorry, not going to happen."

He looked at her with pleading eyes. "What if I wrote you a poem? It's the only thing I have to offer. I've been working on my metaphors since 1986."

Sara felt a chill of genuine horror. Over thirty years of pent-up teenage poetry? Given his last poem, she was afraid his next creative attempt might be the poetic equivalent of a war crime. With a defeated sigh, she started to unzip her coat. "I can't believe I'm going along with this. And it better fucking work or I'll..." How did one punish a ghost? "I'll figure out some way to make your afterlife terrible."

Pausing for just a second, she looked left and right, making sure no one could see her from the road, then she worked her sweater up around her neck. Quickly lifting her shirt and bra, she pulled them back down after about four seconds.

Ethan let out a sigh of contentment. "Beautiful." Then a little light appeared above his head, like a little spotlight, and he disappeared.

Honestly, Sara found the whole thing a little anti-climactic. She'd expected to see the gates of heaven open and angels singing with Liberace on piano and things like that. Instead, there was a tiny light. It didn't even look like it had come from outer space, just a point about two feet over Ethan's head. Like the afterlife had a strict budget.

Sara walked home, shivering from her brief exposure. Her teeth chattered like she'd never get warm. Even with all that, she felt like she'd done something good.

She walked through the front door, and Grandma appeared before her. She was so excited, she blurted out the whole story, flashing and all.

When they got to that part, Grandma started laughing uncontrollably. "You have magic boobs. My tits never sent anyone to heaven."

Sara's cheeks burned. "Um, yeah. I guess so."

"Be proud of yourself. I wish I had magic boobs." Grandma grabbed her chest and shook her cleavage as if she was using them like a magic wand. There were also sound effects.

Sara shook her head, torn between laughter and mortification at her grandma's antics. Only Grandma

Laura could make ghostly voyeurism and supernatural strip teases seem like just another Tuesday night.

As she climbed the stairs to her childhood bedroom, the weight of the amulet cool against her skin, Sara couldn't help but marvel at the strange new world she'd stumbled into. Talking to dead people, guiding restless spirits, getting love advice from her deceased grandmother... It was a lot to take in.

Sara shook her head in disbelief as she replayed the night's events in her mind. Just yesterday, she'd been a woman scorned, drowning her sorrows in coffee and contemplating a future of crippling loneliness. Now, she couldn't stop thinking about her encounter with Ethan. Sure, the kid had been a bit of a horndog, but helping him move on had given her a strange sense of satisfaction. It was like she'd finally found her calling in life: Sara Jenkins, Topless Ghost Whisperer. She could almost picture the business cards now.

Chapter 3

Breakfast, Bureaucracy, and a Blacksmith

Having finally gotten to sleep, Sara woke up late the next morning in the comfortable bed she had slept in all through high school. Her cat Patches purred loudly, kneading on her pillow, and she smiled for a moment and reached over to find nothing there. Through the haze of waking up, she remembered Patches had died while she was away at college. She put her hand on her chest and felt the amulet still resting there.

She walked downstairs and found Grandma standing in front of the stove in a vibrant, low-cut, polka-dot dress. Cinched at the waist and flared at the hips, it clung to her curvy, young body. She'd added a playful red scarf and matching lipstick for a pop of color.

The outfit seemed a little flashy for so early in the morning, but Sara held her tongue. She was going to have to get used to Grandma's new look. It wasn't like the neighbors were going to see. If anything, Sara was a bit jealous that Grandma could look so good first thing in the morning. Sara would need a half pot of coffee before she could even think of making herself presentable.

Grandma smiled at her. "I wish I could cook you breakfast like back in the old days, but I don't have the ability to move things around."

"Don't be silly, Grandma." Sara chuckled. "I think you get out of breakfast duty when you die. I'm just glad you're still here with me. Not everyone gets this. Yesterday, the house felt so empty, I went to Marge's diner instead of making breakfast. I found her greasy spoon a little too greasy."

"Marge is a menace. You're lucky you got out of there without food poisoning. You wouldn't be the first person she put in the hospital."

Sara raised her eyebrows. "Is she really that bad, Grandma? The place was full of people."

"It's a small town, honey. Where else are they going to go? Drive over to Swisher, or all the way to Cedar Rapids or Coralville? I'm surprised the place hasn't been shut down by the health department. Then again, I don't know if the health department knows Downcastle exists."

"Well, it's a good thing I'm planning my coffee shop." At the mention of coffee, Sara turned on the electric grinder. "Maybe you could help me with baked goods," she said hopefully.

Grandma smiled. "Now that's the spirit, dear. With my recipes and guidance, you'll be able to cook rings around Marge. We'll have people lined up around the block. I can't wait to see the look on the woman's face when she finds out she has competition."

Sara laughed. "Well, let's not get too excited. I have the recipes, and you can give me advice, but I'm not the best cook in the world. I'll need a lot of guidance. At the very least, I know I can outdo Marge's coffee. She's using second-tier cafeteria stuff. She could literally switch to a grocery-store brand and the quality would improve considerably." She poured herself a cup of lightly roasted Nicaraguan single estate. "If I'm going to sell coffee, it's going to be the absolute best."

Sara had just cracked an egg when there was a knock at the door. She looked down at the outfit she slept in, an oversized Lake Okoboji t-shirt that had seen better days. It was not a suitable outfit for answering the door.

She ran to the door and peeked through the curtain. Joe Walker stood outside with a clipboard and a laptop. "Sorry," she called through the window. "Wait out there a minute while I get dressed."

She resisted the urge to call to Grandma and tell her Joe was outside. He might hear her through the door, and it wasn't like Grandma could invite him inside and offer him a coffee while he waited.

Running upstairs, she located some clean clothes that did not have large holes in them. She washed her face and ran a brush through her hair so it looked slightly less awful. It still looked like a bird lived in it, but a much tidier bird than had lived there before. She badly wanted to put on some makeup, but she also didn't want to keep Joe waiting.

After bounding down the stairs, Sara paused for a moment to catch her breath. Composing herself, she strolled over to the door and opened it with a smile. "Joe, hi. What brings you here so early?" The scent of wood shavings wafted off him, and his t-shirt and jeans hugged his frame in all the right places. Sara felt a sudden urge to touch him, to explore the contours of his body. She shook her head, trying to dispel the inappropriate thought. "Sorry, I'm still waking up."

He raised an eyebrow. "It's ten thirty, Sara. You know, if you're going to serve people breakfast, you're going to have to get up very early in the morning." His tone was playful, but she blushed, embarrassed because she knew he was right.

They shared an awkward moment of silence. He cleared his throat and held up the clipboard and laptop. "I brought some forms and some design software over. I thought we should start talking about what it would take to renovate the house." He glanced left and right and lowered his voice. "If I drag my feet on this, Mom's not going to be too happy, and there's *a lot* of work to do."

Sara wasn't crazy about the way he emphasized *a lot*. After all, didn't Grandma say the health inspectors didn't know where Downcastle was? Sara had imagined baking and making coffee in the kitchen just as it had always been. "Is it going to be that bad?"

Joe shook his head. "No, I don't think 'bad' is the right word. But..." He pulled up a page on his clipboard. "With a business open to the public, especially a restaurant, there will be a lot of hoops to jump through. There's zoning, permits, and insurance. Then there's the structural stuff—kitchen equipment that will meet a health inspection, building codes, ADA accessibility, fire suppression, bathrooms, parking, and signage. Now, I can cut you a break and even float you some credit on the framing and finish work, but when we get into plumbing and electrical, I have to subcontract it out, especially anything that goes inside the wall or connects to city services, like a commercial grease trap." He looked up from his clipboard, and his expression turned to panic. "Are you crying?"

"Sorry," Sara said, wiping her face, "I can't help but get emotional when I think about commercial grease traps." She sighed. "Seriously though, I'm feeling a little overwhelmed. I wanted to sell coffee and maybe a little breakfast."

Joe leaned in closer, his dark eyes intense. "I know it seems daunting, but I promise I'll be with you every step of the way. I've been through this before, and none of this is impossible." His reassuring smile made Sara's heart skip a beat, but her bank account balance made it plummet right back down. Two hundred dollars wouldn't even cover the permit applications, let alone the actual work.

As Sara saw her dream washing down the drain, the old, unimproved drains, she gave him a brave smile, desperately needing an excuse to leave before he realized she was one bounced check away from complete disaster. "Speaking of coffee, can I get you some?"

"That would be great. While you're doing it, I'm going to take some measurements. I pulled the plans from the county assessor's website, but sometimes their numbers aren't as exact as I need them to be."

Sara retreated to the kitchen and took several deep breaths. She blinked, trying to dispel any tears that might be trying to form. When she'd regained her composure, she saw her half-started meal. She called back to Joe, "You want some scrambled eggs and toast? I was in the middle of making my breakfast."

"I'd appreciate it," he called from the living room. "I had to get up early to check the Fincher brothers' work. They sometimes forget that you can't put the bathroom closet door behind the sink."

She counted eggs—two for her, two for Joe, at five dollars a dozen. Everything was math now, whether she wanted it to be or not. But she was good at math. Being generous now was a luxury. As she was scrambling the eggs, Grandma appeared. "You have the hots for Joe," she said.

"No, I don't," Sara answered automatically.

"Honey, I know that look," Grandma said with a knowing smile.

Sara nearly dropped the whisk. "What? No! I mean, he's nice and all, but it's not like that. Ruby Mae keeps saying we're family."

Grandma chuckled. "Just because I changed his diapers a time or two doesn't mean you can't appreciate the fine young man he's grown into. I've seen the way your eyes linger on those big, strong hands of his."

Sara fiddled with the hem of her shirt. "I'm grateful for his help with the house. It's a big project, and I don't know what I'd do without him," she admitted, her fingers worrying the fabric.

"Mmm–hmm. And I'm sure his charming smile and rugged good looks have nothing to do with it." Grandma's eyes twinkled mischievously.

"Grandma, stop! Joe is just a friend, okay? A kind, thoughtful, incredibly handsome friend..."

Grandma laughed. "Oh, honey, you're about as subtle as a disco ball at a poetry reading. But don't worry – your secret's safe with me. Well, as safe as it can be with a meddlesome old ghost."

Sara sighed, turning back to the pan to add salt and pepper. "There's no secret, Grandma. I'm not interested in Joe that way. End of story." Even if nothing else turned out good today, it looked like breakfast was going to make it.

"Isn't it the classic romance, though, children of best friends, almost raised as siblings realizing what they were missing all along."

Sara shook her head. "Grandma, romances lie. There is no such thing as romance, only chemistry."

"In that case, honey, I wish you an explosive reaction." Grandma winked and faded away.

When Sara returned with a steaming plate of eggs and a fresh brewed cup of Nicaraguan, Joe was already sitting at the table putting measurements into his computer. "Breakfast is served," she said to get his attention.

Serving Joe breakfast felt strangely domestic and intimate, more like a post-hookup ritual than a business meeting. Sara's heart raced at the thought, and she nearly dropped his plate. As much as she tried to deny it, part of her wished their cozy meal was the aftermath of a passionate night together. The unbidden fantasy caught her off guard, and her own thoughts startled her. When had she started thinking like a single woman again?

With Ruby Mae calling her family, her inappropriate fantasy also felt strangely incestuous. The thought was disturbing enough to cool her ardor, at least for the moment. Sara took a deep breath, mentally scolding herself for her wayward musings. Their meeting was strictly professional, she reminded herself sternly, no matter what her newly awakened heart might conjure up.

Joe set aside his laptop and pulled the food and coffee in front of him. He took a sip of the coffee and made a satisfied "Mmmm" noise. "That's good."

Sara nodded. "It's a single-estate Nicaraguan Arabica. Taken out of the roaster immediately after first crack. It keeps the nutty, earthy aspects of the beans without introducing the slightly burnt flavor of the darker roasts, and it maximizes the caffeine level."

"I thought dark roast had more caffeine."

"A common misconception," Sara said. "While you need heat to activate the caffeine, if you roast too long, you start to cook it off."

Joe nodded, but the eggs had captured his interest. As he ate, he started discussing possible layouts for the coffee house. While he seemed to understand the warm, casual atmosphere Sara saw in her head, Joe could see beyond her vision of people sitting in comfort and drinking coffee. He saw the need for upgraded wiring and widening doorways for wheelchair accessibility.

When he finished breakfast, he pulled back the laptop and showed her a model of what the house looked like now. Then he started moving walls and upgrading the kitchen. With every minor change, Sara saw the price tag getting bigger and bigger. Even when there was a bright side, it came with a caveat. Maybe they could get a parking exemption and possibly could get away without a sprinkler system. Sara concentrated on not crying again. She didn't consider herself a crier, but apparently the loss of massive amounts of money made her emotional.

"We could take out this wall entirely," he said, gesturing at the laptop screen. "Run a couple of steel posts up to a support beam, then finish them to look like reclaimed wood. It'd give you that open look while keeping the structure sound..." He trailed off, noticing her expression. "Hey, you okay? I know this is a lot to take in."

"This is my grandmother's house." Up until now, Sara could manage, but this was too much. "We can't take out walls. We can't rearrange everything. I mean, widening doors is bad enough, but—"

Joe sighed, his shoulders slumping slightly as he studied her. "I get it, Sara. I do. This place has a lot of sentimental value. But look..." He turned back to the screen and pointed at the diagram. "By the time we widen these two doors, the little bit of wall that's left is just going to be in your way. I promise, I'm not suggesting anything that doesn't make sense."

Sara cleared her throat. "Honestly, I'm a little in shock right now. I wanted to serve coffee and muffins, maybe offer a breakfast special. I thought the hardest part would be learning my grandma's recipes. I guess I forgot the real world demands things like ADA compliance, parking plans, and commercial dishwashers reaching an internal temperature of one hundred and eighty degrees. Maybe I was being naive, but I imagined a bunch of people sitting around Grandma's living room having coffee. I thought we might have to add a few chairs. I didn't know we would have to move walls around."

Joe pursed his lips. "Let me think about this a bit and get back to you." He stood up and started to gather his things. "I see more what you're envisioning, but it may end up being more difficult than what I was laying out."

Sara wanted to scream a little when he said, "more difficult." However, he walked over to her and hugged her. "Don't worry. We'll figure something out." He felt solid and smelled good, and Sara struggled to keep thinking of him as a brother.

She took a reluctant step back and put her hand on his chest, marveling at the unyielding firmness of his muscles, as if he were carved from oak. "Thanks for all your help, Joe." She resisted the urge to go in for another hug or even more. "I guess I have a lot of things to think about."

Joe grinned. "It's my pleasure, Sara. If you decide you want to pull the trigger, I'm sure we can make something special here." He made a face. "The hard part is going to be convincing my mama that I didn't talk you out of it, especially since I do feel partially responsible."

She shook her head. "Don't feel responsible. You gave me a realistic understanding of what I was in for."

"Thanks for that. And I can always keep my eyes open for any opportunities."

Opportunities sounded interesting. "What kind of opportunities?"

"Well, you know there are grants and small business loans. Also, the city sometimes has a little extra development money, and if they think they have a need, they can give you a bit of a boost. It might not be much, but with a project like this, everything helps. In fact, if I was you, I'd go over to City Hall and have a conversation with Mayor Hart. It won't hurt anything, and once in a while, Mayor Hart seems to take a liking to people. I've seen him bend over backward to make projects work if he decides the person behind it is worth the effort."

"Shouldn't I have a business plan or something?" Approaching the mayor out of the blue seemed like an aggressive first stop.

Joe shrugged. "It's Downcastle. Your grandma lived here. If the mayor liked her, that's your business plan right there."

Sara nodded. "Thanks, Joe. I think I'll do that. After all, it can't hurt, right?"

"And if you do ever decide to move forward, getting building permission and zoning changes are going to be the first thing to take care of, so even if you don't get any money, it might still help to establish a relationship with City Hall."

Sara spent much too long trying to find an outfit to impress the Downcastle mayor. She kept telling herself there were towns bigger than Downcastle that had cats and dogs as mayors. There was no reason to be intimidated.

While she was digging through her suitcases, Grandma appeared beside her. "What are you up to, young lady?"

"I'm trying to find an outfit. Joe suggested I check in with the mayor to see if he has any economic development money. I'm a little lost however, I didn't really pack carefully when I left Des Moines."

"Hmm..." Grandma looked over Sara's options.

Sara turned to her. "Do you think I'm doing something wrong?"

Grandma shook her head. "No, you're not doing anything wrong. My worry is about our mayor."

"Don't tell me you two had a blood feud or something."

Grandma made a face. "No, we were polite enough, but the best way to get something out of him is with a little quid pro quo, if you know what I mean. As badly as I think you need to get laid, I wouldn't wish him on my worst enemy.

Sara made a face. "So, I guess I shouldn't dress in a way he might find provocative?"

"I would strongly recommend against it."

"So, I guess I'll be skipping any of your clothes." Despite the jab, Sara ended up in one of Grandma's button-down plaid shirts from the grunge era along with a pair of dark jeans she'd brought with her. She rolled up the sleeves of the plaid and tucked it in, so she didn't look too casual.

She completed the outfit with a pair of Grandma's ankle boots. They were a half-size too small, but her other choices were heels, tennis shoes, or hiking boots. Also, the nearest shoe store was in Cedar Rapids, and her car would never make it.

Grandma took a look at Sara and nodded. "Perfect. He's not going to hit on you in that outfit. You look like a Midwest lesbian."

"Grandma! Inappropriate!"

"I'm just calling it like I see it. You may not win any fashion awards, but at least you won't have to worry about the mayor undressing you with his eyes."

Sara closed the front door and walked down the front steps. Her toes were already feeling pinched in Grandma's boots. She thought about going back inside and getting her hiking boots, but then she thought about Grandma's Midwest lesbian comment and decided to tough it out.

She also gave a longing look at her car, which had done nothing but leak fluids since she arrived. She hadn't even tried to start it up since she'd parked in front of the house. She guessed trying to get it running would probably do more harm than good. At least the weather was nice for her walk.

She shook her head and turned around. She thought she heard something behind her, like someone yelling in the distance, but when she turned, she didn't see anyone there.

She had never been to the Downcastle City Hall, but she had seen it from the outside as it was right across the street from the library. It was a charming little brick building with white trim. It absolutely screamed, "I am a small-town government building."

There was even a little bell tower with a rooster weathervane on top.

The lobby was a small waiting room. In one corner, a woman in her forties with dark, curly hair sat behind a desk. She smiled at Sara and said, "Hi. How can I help you?"

Sara returned the smile and said, "Hi, I'm Sara Jenkins. I was hoping to speak to the mayor about opening a business in Downcastle."

"You are in luck. The mayor is in today. Let me try to locate him." She hit a button and said, "Mayor Hart, please call the front desk." Her words reverberated up and down the hallways.

The receptionist's phone rang, and she answered it. Sara couldn't hear the other side of the conversation, but from the poor woman's expression, she was being chewed out. Finally, she said, "I'm sorry sir, but there's a young woman named Sara Jenkins here who asked to see the mayor. I... No, I don't know how young. Yes sir."

Convinced she was about to be dismissed, Sara had already started to turn toward the door when the receptionist said, "The Mayor will see you now. He's in the Reubens Conference Room. It's down the hall, the third door on the left."

She bit her lip and then continued. "Oh, and Sara?" The receptionist's expression was carefully neutral, but her eyes held concern. "The conference room can get a bit... uncomfortable. You might want to leave the door open during your meeting. And my name's Deb. If you need anything—anything at all—don't be afraid to yell for me."

"Thank you." Sara walked down the hall until she found a door with a little placard reading "Paul Reubens Conference Room." She knocked.

A tall man with silver hair and a friendly face opened the door. "Ms. Jenkins?" he asked.

Sara nodded. "Yes, Mr. Mayor. Call me Sara."

"In that case, you can call me Mike." He gave her a warm smile that made him look like a mischievous old man.

When he stood back and let her enter, she saw a nicely furnished conference room, but the thing that caught her eye was a large portrait of a stern-looking man in a wingback chair. "Ah, I see you noticed the portrait of my ancestor, Paul Reubens, Downcastle's first mayor," he said as he pushed the door closed.

Sara stepped closer to examine the painting. The man's stern expression and tightly pursed lips gave him a slightly constipated look, as if he were perpetually displeased with the state of his digestive system. "I'm sure he had quite an impact on shaping Downcastle in its early days. He looks like a formidable man." A formidable man who badly needed a number two.

The mayor nodded. "Oh, yes. He was a real go-getter. Started out in the livestock business before settling down and becoming a pillar of the community. He even donated the land for the town square."

With his sweet-old-man demeanor, Sara had trouble imagining Mike Hart as the manipulative womanizer her grandma warned her of. Then again, he was forty years older than Sara, a lot closer to Grandma's age.

There was a momentary lapse in the conversation, and Sara searched for a piece of innocuous small talk to fill the silence. However, a voice behind her took care of it for her. "It's good to see you again, Sara. I'm so glad you're taking an interest in local affairs."

Sara turned to see Iris Pilkington sitting at the other end of the room. Her bright red hair was extra poofy today, and she was wearing an equally poofy, white spring jacket, reminding Sara of a marshmallow catching fire. "Hi, Iris. What brings you to City Hall today?"

Iris smiled. "Honey, if a town this size didn't have volunteers, it would cease to exist," Iris said, her eyes twinkling. "Harvest Festival doesn't organize itself, and someone's got to sit on the town council, the school board, and any number of other things that keep this little slice of heaven ticking along. I just can't help but stay involved."

Hart nodded. "I think this town would fall apart without Iris. She spends more time in City Hall than I do." He gestured to the table. "Why don't you take a seat, young lady, and tell us why you're visiting us today."

Sara didn't like when men called her "young lady" but given their age difference and the power imbalance, she decided to allow it. She took a seat at the table. "Well, I was thinking about opening a coffee shop in Downcastle, and I was wondering if the city had any sort of economic development fund or anything like that."

Hart's smile faltered. "A coffee shop, you say? That's an interesting idea, but I worry about the impact on our existing businesses. We have to be careful not to oversaturate the market. "

Iris's head bobbed in an enthusiastic nod. "But I think a coffee shop would be a lovely addition to Downcastle, don't you, Mike?"

He glanced at Iris, his smile tight. "There are a lot of factors to take into account. For instance, we need to consider what businesses Downcastle really needs right now. Take our car wash situation—when Eddy Van Husen died, it left our only car wash closed. Now that's a real opportunity, young lady. I bet you could buy it up for a song. Have you ever looked at the profitability analysis of a restaurant compared to a car wash?"

Sara felt her stomach tighten as the mayor's words sank in. She had known starting a business wouldn't be easy, but she hadn't expected some sort of Spanish Inquisition. "I um... I think a coffee shop would be good for the community. And I was hoping to offset some of the costs by starting the restaurant in my grandmother's home."

Hart nodded thoughtfully. "So, you come here asking me for money, but you haven't even considered proper zoning or building permits. Do you know what it takes to convert a residential property into a restaurant?"

"I was talking to Joe Walker about renovating the house—"

Hart glanced at his watch and rose from his seat. "I'm afraid I have another meeting to get to. Iris, I trust you can continue this discussion with Sara and fill me in later?" As he was leaving, he said, "Think about that car wash, young lady. It could be a real money maker."

Iris yelled after the departing mayor, "Of course, Mike. Leave it to me."

"Um..." Sara looked to Iris. "I guess that could have gone better. Does he own part of that car wash or something?"

Iris smiled. "Don't worry, dear. The mayor can sometimes be... difficult. I'm glad I happened to be here to join the meeting" Iris's slight smile held a sharp edge. "Especially with young ladies. It helps to avoid... misunderstandings."

Changing her tone, Iris got down to business. "Now, there is a bit of economic development money in our budget, and Mayor Hart does not have the ultimate say. The town council makes a lot of those decisions. Yes, he chairs the meetings, but he only gets to vote in the event of a tie, and I can make sure there's not a tie. I think that with my support, we can take care of all those piddling little details... zoning, parking exemptions, building permits. My cousin is the building inspector. And I'm always happy to step up and help someone who takes the interests of the community seriously."

"Interests of the community?" Sara had a sinking feeling she knew where this conversation was going.

Iris nodded. "You know, Sara, I think running your grandmother's booth at the Harvest Festival would be a wonderful way to honor her memory and connect with the community. People loved her readings, and I'm sure they'd be thrilled to see you carrying on her legacy. Plus, it would give you a chance to promote your new business and drum up some buzz before the grand opening. It's a win–win, really. Besides, what better way to show your commitment to the public good than making sure we have more attractions than Swisher Fun Days."

Sara fought the urge to squirm in her seat as Iris's words washed over her. On the surface, the older woman's suggestion sounded reasonable, even generous. But the thought of being branded as "the town psychic" before she'd even opened her coffee shop made her stomach clench. In Des Moines, she'd worked hard to build a professional reputation as a scientist, and while she might have inherited her grandmother's gift, she wasn't ready to inherit her role as Downcastle's resident medium. Still, she was going to have to play along with Iris's game if she wanted to have any hope of getting her coffee shop off the ground. "I suppose I could try running Grandma's booth. I'll try my best, but I have never done anything like it before."

Iris absolutely beamed. "Oh, I think you'll do just fine. I bet once you get started, you'll feel like your grandmother is right there with her hand on your shoulder telling you what to do. I tell you what, I'll even waive the booth fee."

Sara walked home, so lost in thought she barely noticed the pinch in her shoes. Her first exposure to small-town politics had left a bad taste in her mouth. Although, from talking to Grandma, it could have been much worse. And what was that crack about her grandma being there with a hand on her shoulder? Did Iris know something about the amulet, or was it her creepy version of a pep talk?

When Sara got home, she called out, "Grandma, I'm back."

Her grandma appeared beside her, still looking young and now wearing a little black dress. "Did you enjoy your walk? Isn't it a beautiful spring day?"

"Yes, I did, but I do have to get these boots off." Once she had gotten the boots off and settled into the couch, she told Grandma the whole story.

Grandma's only comment was, "His great-great-grandfather, Paul Reubens, was a cattle rustler. He used his dirty money to found the town."

Sara didn't care about the local gossip in 1850. "So, tell me how I do this booth thing."

Grandma smiled. "There's nothing to worry about. The city gives you a table, and the other things you need are upstairs in the storeroom. There's a credit card machine, some linens, and a canopy for privacy and shade. Oh, and I added a cheap crystal ball I got off Amazon. People like that touch. I also usually pay the extra $25 for an electrical run so I can run a box fan and plug in the credit card machine."

"But how do I do it? How do I contact spirits?"

"Oh, that's easy, trust the power of the amulet. Envision the person you're trying to contact, or at least focus on their name if that's all you've got. If they want to come to you, they'll come to you."

"But what if they don't come to me?"

"Then tell the person their loved one is happy and they are glad they're doing well, but they don't feel like talking. It should be true enough. Once someone is dead, they tend to set aside any petty grievances and only want the best for their loved ones, so there's nothing untrue there. If they don't think that's enough, give them their money back and apologize. Just tell them the spirits are having trouble coming through."

"I guess so. I'd kind of like to practice, though." Sara had a thought. "Do you think I could contact Mom and Dad?"

Grandma held up her hand in warning. "We might want to try that later. Your father knew about my ability, but he never approved of it. For your first try of calling a spirit to you, you might want to try for someone who won't challenge you." She snapped her fingers. "How about Sam Douglas? He was the town blacksmith about a hundred and fifty years ago."

"I'll try." Sara put her hand over the amulet and said, "Sam Douglas. I'm calling Sam—"

"You don't have to do all that," her grandma said.

"All what?"

"Holding the amulet or using that silly voice. You can just call to him in your head."

"Fine." She concentrated. *Sam Douglas, Downcastle blacksmith, would you like to come and speak with me?*

A burly man wearing old-fashioned work clothes, including a worn, leather apron, appeared in front of her. "Hello there, young lass. What do you need from me?" He had a hint of what might be a Scottish accent.

Sara's breath caught. "Holy shit," she blurted. "I conjured a ghost!"

"She's with me, Sam," Grandma said calmly, as if this were the most natural thing in the world.

"Well, if it isn't the beautiful Laura Jenkins. How long have you been on this side of the veil?"

"A couple of months now," Grandma answered.

"And you didn't think to come and see me right away?"

"What do you think I'm doing now?" Grandma answered. "My granddaughter just found the amulet yesterday and I'm showing her how to use it. You're the first person I had her call."

"Well, that makes me as happy as a piper on Hogmanay."

Sara guessed this must be very happy.

Grandma said, "Tell my granddaughter what you've been up to."

"Well," Sam thought for a moment. "Not too much, really, being dead for a century and a bit."

Grandma shrugged. "You see, running around and doing things is for living people. There's not a lot of news to pass back from the other side. Mostly things like, 'I'm doing well,' or 'I'm not mad about the car anymore.' It takes a lot of the pressure off."

"Oh, the other hand," Sam said. "I might consider doing a little bit of running around with you, fair one, for it's no hardship to follow where beauty and wit lead.

Grandma twirled a strand of her hair and let it fall lazily between her breasts. "That sounds like fun," she said with a coy smile.

"Grandma!" Sara said, "You can't date. You're married to Grandpa."

"Oh, honey, your grandpa and I had a good run, but he's been gone for years now. I'm sure he's up there in the great beyond, tinkering with his old car and not giving a hoot about what I get up to. He spent more time with the car than he ever did with me." She took hold of the blacksmith by one of his beefy arms. "Come on Sam. Let's go watch the sunset over the sewage lagoon."

"Speaking of which," he said, "whatever happened to the wee poet that used to hang out there?"

"Oh, have I got a story for you," Grandma said. She turned to Sara and winked as they disappeared together. As they faded away, Sara was sure she heard the sounds effects that Grandma had used when talking about her magic boobs.

Chapter 4

A Shade at the Schoolyard

Over the next few days, Sara found all the stuff from Grandma's mediumship booth. The only difficult part was changing the promotional materials and signs. Apparently, Grandma had done them all on her ancient computer that used a version of Microsoft Word that didn't even run on Windows. Sara had to sit at the computer while Grandma walked her through how to use it. Then she printed everything out on the amazingly slow printer. She wasn't sure about the printer's age, but it needed special paper with little holes up the side.

On Saturday morning, Joe stopped by—this time he called ahead, and she dressed up just a bit. She wasn't trying to seduce him per se, but she wanted to show him a little interest.

Joe wanted to show her some beautiful models he'd done on his laptop. As he pointed out this feature or that feature, she found herself leaning over him and resting her hand on his shoulder. When he got done with the presentation, he asked, "So, how did things go at City Hall?"

She walked around the table and plopped down in the seat across from him. "I didn't know what a horse trade it was going to be. Mayor Hart just gave me a flat-out 'No.' Worse than that, he nearly called me stupid for wanting to open a business. Iris Pilkington, on the other hand, would be more than happy to push everything I asked for through the city council as long as I do Grandma's mediumship booth."

"That's weird," Joe said. "Why would it be so important?"

Sara sighed. "It has something to do with having more attractions than Swisher Fun Days."

Joe nodded, looking more than a little amused. "Yeah. Yeah. That sounds right. So, are you planning to go through with it?"

"I guess." She shrugged. "I might even make a little money, and I could use some right now. Iris is even going to waive the booth fee."

"Wow. She is serious. Do you have everything you need?"

She nodded. "I think so. But do you know how to set up the canopy?" She almost added that Grandma told her to ask Joe to help with the canopy. Well, first she'd told her to ask Detective Mitchell next door, as he'd always helped in the past. She even suggested some creative ways in which Sara could thank Detective Mitchell, to which Sara said, "I'll figure it out." So far, she had failed to figure it out.

"I can sure take a look," Joe said with a grin. "How hard can it be?"

70

As Sara led Joe to the garage, Patches, the ghost cat, darted through the door, startling her. She stumbled over the step, losing her balance.

"Careful!" Joe's strong arm swiftly encircled her waist, pulling her back against his solid frame. "You okay?" His breath tickled her ear.

"Yeah," she managed, acutely aware of his body pressed against hers. "Just tripping over my own feet."

Reluctantly, she stepped out of his embrace and continued into the garage. The space was mostly empty, save for the scattered canopy pieces. Grandma had sold her Buick a few years ago after a close call on the highway, deciding she was too old to drive. Sara deeply regretted not having the car now. A second vehicle would have solved so many problems.

Joe looked over the pieces of the canopy and started to poke and prod at them. He picked up a couple of PVC pipes and slotted them together. Then he tried another, but it didn't fit. He shook his head. "It's like they made this hard on purpose. Let's open the garage door and get some more light in here." He walked over to the inside door and pushed the button.

The door slid open to reveal Adam Mitchell working in his yard. He looked over at what they were doing, put down his pruning shears, and walked over. "Hi, Sara."

"Detective Mitchell," she responded.

"Call me Adam. Hey, Joe, how's it going?"

"Not too bad," Joe said. "Still enjoying the new deck?"

"No complaints." He turned to Sara. "I needed a new deck, and your grandmother suggested I get Joe to do it. He did a great job." He nodded to the canopy parts spread across the garage floor. "I can help you with those. I always used to put this thing together for

Laura. Unfortunately, we lost the instructions, but it's not too bad if you know the trick."

"I'd love the help," Joe said.

Adam picked up two of the PVC pipes and set them up vertically. "All these pipes look the same size, but there are actually three different sizes that are a few inches different from each other. The longest are the vertical poles, the second longest are for the bottom, and the shortest ones go on the top, so there's a slight taper. There used to be lettering on the ends—A, B, and C, but it's worn off over the years."

Sara was actually a bit disappointed Grandma wasn't around to see this. Grandma would have had so much fun making comments about men comparing the length of their poles.

Looking at Sara, Adam said, "Your grandma used this for her medium booth. Are you going to do it this year? I can always pop over in the morning and throw it together for you."

Sara was still a little lukewarm about getting help from Adam. "Well, I did already ask Joe to help me with that."

"I could use the help," Joe said. "I bet it will go a lot smoother with an extra pair of hands."

Adam nodded. "We can get Sara's booth set up in no time."

"That's very kind of you both," Sara said. Wishing she'd never asked. Then again, she didn't think she would have figured out the tent poles being slightly different in length.

The men, having solved Sara's problem, said their goodbyes, and Adam went back to trimming his hedges.

Joe started sorting tent poles. "For now, I can get these separated. It will make things go easier."

"Wait," Sara said, pushing the button to close the garage door. "Leave them. I'll sort them out. It's the least I can do with all the help you two are giving me."

"Okay then." He held up the two he had been comparing. "I'll set the smaller one on the left, and you can take it from there."

After Sara showed Joe out, she realized she'd just witnessed the time-honored ritual of small-town male helpfulness: the thinly veiled attempt to create intimacy through utility. Joe showing he was younger and stronger. Adam exhibiting his experience and... mustache. Or maybe she was reading too much into it.

After Joe left, Sara set about doing some chores around the house. Ruby Mae had promised to come help the next day, and before she came, Sara wanted to get a few more things done, especially in the yard. Because of the long, cool spring, the grass was starting to grow at a good pace, and there were a ton of other little things to do both indoors and outdoors.

Late that afternoon, after finishing the yard work, Sara finally got around to calling Brad. It had been a few days, and she hoped she had calmed down enough to have a conversation with him. He answered his phone on the third ring, but when he picked up, she heard Mariachi music in the background. She resisted the urge to ask about it and pretended he was picking up Mexican food at 2 p.m. on a Thursday.

"Hey, Sara. How are you doing? I worry about you."

Sara was glad they were doing this over the phone. If he were there in person, she would have considered strangling him. "I think I would be doing much better if you'd left a little money in our shared accounts."

"Yeah, I'm sorry about that, but I have to protect myself, you know? If I hadn't acted right away, you could have done the same thing to me."

"No, I wouldn't have done that, Brad, because I would never have thought of it. Besides, you must have already had accounts in place."

"Of course I did. I had to be prepared, knowing how you might overreact to something as harmless as a little sex. It wasn't even serious—it was just... convenience. A work thing."

"So, you're just sleeping your way to the top?"

"Yeah. I did it for us. You were laid off from your job, and I figured if I could get a raise, it would take some of the pressure off. Kim indicated amenability to some quid pro quo, so I decided to put in my application, if you get what I mean."

Sara did get what he meant; it made her want to vomit. "Do you think you could return some of *our* money to the bank account so I can pay for some necessities?"

"No can do, babe. My lawyer advises against it. Now, I know it seems a little harsh, but in his defense, he is exceptionally expensive, and I have to pay him out of that money."

"Well, I wouldn't want to contradict your lawyer, but I think you're going to regret not giving me access to a fair share of *our* money." He would definitely regret getting the bill from his Amazon card, because Sara was going directly to the bank to take out the maximum cash advance she could.

"I still don't see why you have all this hostility. We had a little miscommunication about boundaries in our relationship. I'm sorry. I should have asked before I played El Mariachi with Kim."

"Speaking of which..." Sara's morbid curiosity almost won out, but her white-hot rage at his betrayal reigned it in. "It's not like you booked a holiday without asking or came home late after I cooked supper. You broke our wedding vows."

"*Mea culpa*, babe. In hindsight, I totally see why you're upset. And I promise I'll ask if I ever decide to think about my career before our marriage again."

Sara felt a twist in the part of her gut that used to believe his promises, a part that didn't exist anymore. "Brad, don't you see, it's not going to happen again because I'm not coming back to you? I hope you and Kim and your divorce lawyer are all very happy together."

"Oh, come on. Let's be adults—"

Sara hung up. She felt a little dizzy. She needed to sit down for a minute. Then she put on her most comfortable walking shoes and walked to the bank. She was able to get five hundred dollars more out of her Amazon card.

The bank was across the street from the Downcastle school, so Sara walked over and sat down in one of the swings to watch the sunset. A woman wearing a vintage, navy blue shirtwaist dress approached her. The dress, cinched at the waist with a matching navy belt, fell just below the woman's knees, revealing sensible black Oxford shoes polished to a shine. Her dark hair was styled in a tight poodle perm, with curls framing her face and adding volume at the crown. Horn-rimmed glasses perched on her nose. "Aren't you Laura Jenkins's granddaughter?"

Sara nodded. "I am. I'm afraid I don't remember you, though."

"Oh, I'm Maggie. I used to be a school teacher here about a hundred years ago."

At first, Sara thought Maggie meant she had retired and exaggerated a bit. Then she realized what Maggie really meant. Looking carefully, she noticed a hint of transparency to Maggie. She probably hadn't noticed earlier because the light was fading. "Oh. I'm sorry, I didn't realize..." She tried to think of a delicate way to say—

"That I'm dead?" She found this so funny she actually slapped her thigh. "Yes, I am. In fact, when you went to school here, I used to keep an eye on you for your grandmother. You were a good girl, though." Her face crinkled up a bit. "Compared to some of these other little brats, that is."

Maggie stopped mid–sentence, her mouth dropping open as her face went pale. She pointed past Sara, her hand trembling. "Oh, my God," she whispered. "Behind you."

Sara turned and froze. Mayor Hart was staggering toward her, clutching his bleeding head. His face was twisted with pain and desperation. "Please," he begged, his voice trembling. "You have to help me. Find out who did this. Please."

"Oh, my god!" Sara stumbled backward, fumbling for her phone to call 911. But she'd dropped it after talking to Brad and left it at the house. She looked at Maggie for help but realized that the ghost wasn't going to have a phone either.

"I think you should lay down," she said, stepping toward him. But as she reached to steady him, her hand passed straight through his shoulder. Her entire body jolted as an icy pain stabbed through her, making her gasp.

His face contorted in anger as he moved through her, his voice echoing in her head: "This is all your fault." Then, he growled, "You should have invested in the car wash!"

Sara staggered back, spinning around to see him collapsed behind her. But he wasn't there. No blood, no body, no Mayor Hart. Just an empty street.

Her breath came in short gasps as she clutched her chest. "What the hell was that?" she yelled into the silence, her voice shaking.

"That's what happens when people are on the edge of death. They get pushed out of their bodies, confused and angry." She pointed the way he had come. "He came from that direction. There's a slim chance, but sometimes the soul wanders around a bit when the body is still alive. Come on! We need to find his body. There might be time to save him." Maggie disappeared.

Sara took off at a dead run, grateful for her comfortable tennis shoes. As she sprinted, a whirlwind of thoughts and emotions surged through her mind. Part of her couldn't help but see Hart's death as a potential advantage in securing the economic development grant, but another part recoiled at the thought, guilt gnawing at her insides. She felt freaked out, terrified, and utterly bewildered—freaked out that a man she had just spoken to might be dead.

She knew she should turn around and run to the nearest house with a light on, but her feet kept propelling her forward, driven by a desperate need to do something, anything, to help. Before she knew it, she had reached the front door of the school, and the sight that greeted her made her blood run cold. Mayor Hart's body lay sprawled on the sidewalk, a dark pool of blood spreading beneath his head.

A cold numbness settled over Sara; the world tilted beneath her feet. This couldn't be real. Not here. Not in Downcastle.

Fear and desperation wrestled inside her, but the urge to act propelled her forward. Hands shaking, she reached for a pulse, fingertips grazing the mayor's cold neck. Snatches of a forgotten CPR class surfaced, but her mind was a haze. No heartbeat. The realization hit her like a punch to the gut, and she stumbled back, eyes wide with horror.

She looked up at Maggie, who stood by watching. "Do you think I should still try chest compressions? He was..." She swallowed a frog in her throat. "...cold."

Maggie shook her head. "Not unless you need the exercise. If he's cold, he's about as alive as I am, and I died in 1933."

There were lights on in the school, so Sara yelled. "Help! Help!" Then she remembered the possibility of a nearby murderer and regretted her decision.

She heard the sound of a heavy door open and a rattle of keys. She gasped and looked up to the door of the school.

An old janitor walked through the door. "What the hell's going on out here? Are you all right, lady? Who's that with you?"

"I'm fine," Sara said, "but this is Mayor Hart. I think he's dead."

The janitor shuffled over to the body and poked Hart with the toe of his shoe. "It does look like it." His voice was steady, but his face had gone pale. "Come on with me. I'll get you some coffee, and then we'll call the sheriff. Dealing with a dead mayor requires caffeine."

Rufus, the janitor, led Sara into the classroom and pulled out a chair for her. "Sit here. I'll be right back," he said before disappearing down the hall.

She slumped into the chair, her hands rubbing at her temples. Rufus returned a few minutes later with a cup of coffee. "Here, it's not fancy, but it's hot," he said, setting it in front of her.

Sara took a sip, grimacing at the taste. It was bitter, sour, and faintly reminiscent of an old gym sock, but she kept drinking. Warmth and caffeine were what she needed right now. Was this the same coffee her high school teachers had been given to drink? If so, no wonder they were always so grumpy.

Rufus returned a second time with a blanket and put it over her shoulders. "Isn't this what you're supposed to do when someone has had a shock? I don't know if shock makes you colder or what, but they do it on all the TV shows." He was being sweet, but she also felt he was kind of making sure that she wouldn't run away before the police got there. After his comment about shock and TV shows, Rufus didn't say anything. He sat in the corner, occasionally glancing at her, then glancing out the window, to make sure the dead mayor was still there, and then glancing at the clock on the wall.

The silence was starting to bother Sara, so she decided to say something, but she carefully stayed away from the topic of the dead mayor outside the front door. "How long have you been a custodian here, Rufus?" Sara asked.

"About ten years. Used to work in a data center, but I got bored after retiring. Cleaning up messes, making things nice for the kids—it's satisfying work. What about you, Ms. Jenkins?"

"I've got a chemistry degree. I worked as a lab assistant for an agritech startup, mostly washing test tubes and taking measurements, until they lost their funding. Now I'm thinking about opening a coffee shop here in Downcastle."

Rufus nodded approvingly. "Feeding hungry folks, helping them start their day—that sounds mighty satisfying too. More so than washing test tubes, I'd wager."

"Yeah, maybe."

Rufus's question about Verdegrowth hung in the air, a lifeline away from the body outside. Her dreams of retiring young on stock options, once bright, were now as dead as Downcastle's mayor. She'd imagined turning that tiny equity stake into something real, a coffee shop of her own, but without the constant financial hardship she was now facing. Now, those plans were suddenly, irrevocably gone, just like Mayor Hart.

She was about to tell Rufus about that plan, when a black Suburban pulled up outside, and Officer Adam Mansplain himself jumped out and approached the body. Then he did exactly what Sara had done. He checked for a pulse, and Sara saw Adam make the same determination she had made while Maggie looked over his shoulder.

Maggie looked over at Sara. "I don't think he's doing it right. Not that he's going to find one anyway."

Rufus stood and squinted out the window. "Who's that poking at our body?" He knocked at the windows and motioned to Adam to come over.

Sara wasn't sure she was ready to lay that much claim on the corpse as to call it 'our body,' but she decided not to argue. "That's my neighbor Adam Mitchell. He's a Cedar Rapids cop. The Sheriff probably asked him to come take a look, or maybe he heard it on the police scanner."

Adam stood up, turned to the window, and saw Rufus waving, so he walked over to them.

Rufus cranked the window open. "Hello, officer. I'm Rufus, the custodian here, and I've got the woman who found that body right here."

Sara smiled. "Hi, Adam. So nice to see you again so soon."

"Sara, how did you get messed up in this?"

Sara shrugged. "I was out for a walk, and I stopped here to watch the sunset." She paused wondering what to say next. She couldn't really claim she'd gotten a hot tip from the mayor's ghost, could she? "I guess my intuition just told me to walk this way."

Adam looked momentarily troubled by that answer. Then he nodded. "Okay. I guess you two should wait. I will wait by the body until the sheriff's department gets here."

After another twenty minutes of waiting, two white SUVs with "Sheriff" emblazoned on their sides pulled up behind Adam's black Suburban. Two people emerged from the vehicles: a tall, broad-shouldered man in his mid-fifties wearing a cowboy hat and an athletic-looking blonde woman. Both wore light jackets with "Sheriff" printed on the left chest and in large letters across the back.

Sara watched as they approached Adam. Some kind of argument seemed to be ensuing. Maggie, who had drifted over to eavesdrop (old teacher habits die hard, apparently), shook her head at whatever was being said, but Sara figured if it was really juicy stuff, Maggie would have shouted it over to her.

Just as she thought this, Maggie did turn toward her and yelled, "They're pretty sure it's murder. Something about the angle of the wound and how the body fell."

Finally, Adam nodded and settled back into the stance he had been using while waiting for the sheriff. The tall man walked over to the front door of the school, and the woman followed behind him. Rufus turned to Sara, "I'm going to have to go let them in the front door. Why don't you come with me?"

"Sounds good." Sara stood, discarding her heavy blanket.

They walked into the hallway just in time to open the doors.

The tall man started talking before they were inside. "Good evening, I'm Sheriff Robinson. You're Rufus Harrison, the janitor?" He took off his hat as he stepped across the threshold revealing gray hair, surprisingly thick for a man his age.

"Yes, sir." Rufus confirmed his identity.

Robinson turned to Sara, "And you're Sara Jenkins, the woman who discovered the body?"

Sara nodded. "Yes, that's right."

"Okay, Rufus, you come with me, and Sara, you follow Deputy Johnson."

Sara nodded to the sheriff and followed Johnson, the blonde woman, into an empty classroom. Johnson took a moment to find the switch and then flipped on the lights. When she saw the layout of the room, rows of tables with chairs lined up behind them, she pointed to one of the tables. "Why don't you take a seat, Ms. Jenkins? I have a few questions to ask you, and then we'll get you out of here."

Johnson took a chair and placed it across the table from Sara. She took out a notebook and a pencil. "First, can you state your full name, phone number, and address? If you have any identification on you, that would be good too."

Sara knew how to answer that question. "Sara Louise Jenkins." She added her cellular number and address, then handed over her driver's license. "That's my Des Moines address. I'm not staying there anymore, with my husband." She stumbled over the words, unfamiliar with having to say them.

For a split second, the hard line of the deputy's mouth twitched, as if she were suppressing a sympathetic grimace. But just as quickly, her professional mask slipped back into place. "In your own words, Ms.

Jenkins, can you tell me what you were doing when you found the body?"

Sara repeated the story she'd told Adam, about going for a walk, waiting to see sunset, and her intuition telling her to walk toward the school building. Deputy Johnson seemed just as impressed by Sara's intuition as Adam had been.

"Right... Intuition." The deputy paused to write in her notebook. "Ms. Jenkins, have you ever had any personal disputes or disagreements with Mayor Hart? Any reason he might have been upset with you or vice versa?"

Sara opened her mouth to dismiss the suggestion, but the words caught in her throat. She swallowed hard, her mind racing back to the heated exchange in the mayor's office. "Well... I did have a meeting with him today, asking for some grant money from the town. He got pretty upset with me, and weirdly tried to bully me into buying a car wash..." She trailed off, still a bit confused about that. "But that's all been resolved now. I'm going to do a favor for Councilwoman Pilkington, and she's going to help me out with the grant." Sara mentally kicked herself—why couldn't she just stop talking when she was ahead?

After writing in her notebook for a while, the deputy leaned forward and asked, "What kind of favor?"

Sara shifted in her seat, suddenly feeling like the room had gotten a few degrees warmer. "It's not like it's anything shady. They asked me to help with a project, and in exchange, they're backing my grant request. That's how things get done, right?"

Shit! Shit! Was their deal illegal? This wasn't fair. She was the one being blackmailed. She opened her mouth to explain that part, then snapped it shut. That was not going to make things better. She wiped her forehead on her sleeve.

Deputy Johnson's eyebrows shot up. "Nothing shady? That's an interesting choice of words, Ms. Jenkins. Care to elaborate on the nature of this project?"

"Well, it's kind of a long story," Sara began, fidgeting with her damp sleeve. "But basically, I agreed to run a booth at the upcoming Harvest Festival. A... mediumship booth. You know, talking to the dead."

Deputy Johnson's pen paused mid-stroke. "Talking to the dead?" she repeated, her tone a mix of disbelief and curiosity. "And how exactly does that relate to your grant request, Ms. Jenkins?"

Sara took a deep breath, knowing how strange her next words might sound. "Well, Councilwoman Pilkington says it's about showing my civic-mindedness. And there's something about having more vendors than Swisher Fun Days."

"Right." The Deputy didn't sound very convinced. "Do you have anything to add to your statement?"

Sara, feeling she'd done enough, shook her head. "No."

The deputy handed Sara a business card with a glossy picture on it. "If you think of anything else, anything at all, don't hesitate to call. For that matter, we may have more questions for you as the investigation unfolds." She let those words hang ominously for a moment. Then, as if she could relax now that she had finished her professional business, she said, "Adam said he was your neighbor. Why don't you come with me? And maybe he can give you a ride home."

Sara nodded. "Yeah, that sounds great." She might not need to be covered in blankets, but she was nervous about the idea of walking home by herself with a murderer on the loose.

Johnson walked her outside where Adam's Suburban and the police vehicles had been joined by a van with Coroner written on the side. A man was taking pictures of Mayor Hart, or perhaps she should think of him as the former Mayor Hart.

Adam stood nearby looking bored, and Johnson walked her over to him. "I'm done questioning your neighbor. Do you want to run her home?"

"Sure. No problem. Just glad I could help." He turned to Sara. "Come on. Let's get you home." He turned back to Johnson. "If you guys need me, Emily, you know where to find me."

Sara followed Adam over to the giant, black SUV, her heart still racing from the night's events. After they settled into the seats, Adam navigated through the haphazardly parked vehicles with ease. "How are you doing, Sara?" he asked, his voice filled with concern. "I mean, it's not every night you find a dead body."

Sara let out a shaky breath. "I guess I'm doing okay. I just hope I answered everyone's questions all right."

"I'm sure you did fine." He said it with the same gentle voice he probably used to calm down hysterical witnesses, which was, to be fair, exactly what she was.

He hesitated for a moment, as if debating something, then reached over and gave her hand a reassuring squeeze. "You're handling this incredibly well, you know."

Sara felt a flush of warmth at his touch, and she found herself suddenly very aware of how close they were. She swallowed hard. As Adam pulled the car into her driveway, he left the motor running. "Are you doing okay? Do you need me to walk you in?"

Sara looked at the old house. Usually her safe space, its darkened windows seemed to loom ominously in the night. The thought of going inside alone, with a murderer possibly on the loose, made her queasy. "I would appreciate that," she said softly. "If you want, I can make you some coffee as a thank you."

Adam looked at her, his face calm but serious. "That would be nice." He turned off the Suburban, and the quiet settled in around them, neither of them moving right away.

As they got out of the car and started heading toward the house, Sara felt a rush of gratitude and something else, something warmer and more complicated. "I'm sorry if I'm ruining your evening," she said, her voice barely above a whisper. "I feel a little silly asking a man to defend me in my grandmother's house."

Adam stopped and turned to face her, his expression serious. "Don't feel silly at all. I've stayed to comfort grown men whose houses have been broken into. And don't feel bad about inconveniencing me. I know it might not seem right to say so, but a homicide investigation is a lot more exciting than staying home and watching TV."

His eyes searched hers as if trying to convey some unspoken message. Sara's breath caught in her throat as Adam took a step closer, his body just inches from hers. For a moment, she thought he might reach out and touch her again, but instead, he just gave her a small, reassuring smile. "You know," Adam said, "if you wanted to spend more time with me, you could have just asked. You didn't have to go and stumble upon a murder scene."

Sara raised an eyebrow. "Oh, so you think I orchestrated this whole thing just to get some quality time with the local law enforcement? I'm flattered, but I think you're overestimating my level of interest."

"Hey, I'm just saying," Adam held up his hands in mock surrender, "if you wanted to see me again, there are easier ways."

Sara snorted. "Next time, I'll just invite you over for coffee like a normal neighbor, but don't expect pastry."

As he placed his hand on the doorknob, he took on a more serious tone. "Let me go in first," he said, his voice slipping back into the cool, professional tone of a police officer. "I'm probably being over-cautious, but if someone saw you talking to us about the mayor, I'd rather not take chances. Hold back until I've at least looked through the first floor."

From inside the house, Sara heard something clatter, and then the back door slammed shut. Adam grabbed her by the arm and dragged her into the house. "Forget that. Stay close, and try to keep behind me. Someone is here."

Adam drew a gun and started to walk slowly toward the dining room. As a matter of principle, Sara disliked guns, but in this case, she was willing to make an exception. He turned on the dining room light. Nobody was there. Then he went into the kitchen. At first, Sara thought nothing was wrong in the kitchen, but then Adam tensed. He looked at something on the floor, and Sara peaked around his broad back to see what it was.

Sara's brow wrinkled. Grandma's eight-inch chef's knife lay in the middle of the floor—the same knife Sara had used countless times to help prepare family meals, the same knife Grandma had once jokingly threatened to use on any boy who dared to break Sara's heart. She couldn't understand why it was on the floor, so out of place.

Sara desperately wanted to put it back in the knife block, where it belonged. She took a step forward, her hand outstretched, but Adam caught her wrist.

"Don't touch it," he warned, his voice low and urgent. "It could be evidence."

She nodded, her throat tight, her eyes fixed on the blade. The realization crept over her like cold fog. Someone had been here. Why? Her stomach churned. This wasn't just someone passing through. It didn't feel random.

"Adam," she murmured, leaning against the counter as her knees threatened to give way. "Why would someone...?" She stopped herself, her voice faltering. Her mind raced. The implications felt unbearable.

Adam glanced at her, his jaw tight. "We'll figure it out," he said firmly, but his tone didn't soothe her. It only made the tension feel sharper, the sense of unease heavier. Adam's hands were on her shoulders, steadying her. "Hey," he said softly, ducking his head to meet her eyes. "Look at me, Sara. You're safe now. I'm here, and I'm not going to let anything happen to you." He glanced at the knife. "Don't touch anything in this area. I'm calling this in—we need to process this properly."

He pulled a pair of blue nitrile gloves from his pocket and snapped them on. "Try to keep away from the windows as best you can." He walked over to the kitchen door and locked it. Then he took out his cell phone, again without putting away the gun and dialed. "This is Adam. I need you to come over to the Jenkins house. Someone was here, waiting for her."

Chapter 5

Spectral Mechanics and Legal Maneuvering

Once he had alerted the sheriff's department, Adam devoted himself to securing the house, his movements conveying nervous energy. Sara watched from her crouched position in the kitchen as he paced from window to window, yanking curtains closed and checking locks with sharp, efficient movements.

"Clear," he said, more to himself than to Sara. "All clear."

When he finally seemed satisfied with his impromptu fortifications, Adam's demeanor shifted. His shoulders dropped, and he let out a long breath. He turned to Sara, his expression softening. "Let's get you more comfortable," he said, gently helping her to her feet. "The living room will be safer anyway."

Sara let herself be led to the couch, sinking into its familiar embrace. Almost by instinct, she reached for the throw blanket draped over the back – Grandma's favorite. As she wrapped it around herself, a hint of Grandma's Shalimar perfume enveloped her, a bitter-sweet comfort.

Adam sat beside her, close but not touching, as if unsure of the appropriate distance. After a moment's hesitation, he placed a hand on her back. "It's okay," he said, his voice low and steady. "You're safe. It's all going to be all right."

But of course, Sara thought, her mind reeling, he couldn't possibly know that. Someone had been wait-ing in her house to stab her, for crying out loud. That was pretty fucking far from everything being safe. Just as Sara was about to voice her doubts, a familiar pres-ence shimmered into view.

Grandma's ghost appeared, and things got expo-nentially more confusing. The first thing Grandma did, when she saw Adam sitting by her and touching her, was say, "Go, Sara! Get some of that sweet cop action." Then she realized something was off. "Are you okay, sweetie? You don't seem too excited that a cute guy is sitting next to you."

Sara tried to subtly give her grandma a look that said, "You know I can't answer you, right?" but some-thing was lost in translation, as Grandma stood in front of her and glared.

Needing to be alone to talk to Grandma, Sara said, "Um, thanks for comforting me, Adam. I did really need that, but I have to go to the bathroom now."

"Of course." He stood up. "I don't suppose you'd let me come with you?"

"No."

"I would stand outside, and you could just leave the door open."

"No."

"If you could wait ten more minutes, Deputy Johnson will be here to escort you."

She knew he was trying to help, but she needed to be alone. "No. You're going to sit here on the couch and wait for the sheriff. Thank you for being concerned, but the bathroom has one tiny window eight feet off the ground outside. I think I'll be safe for five minutes. If there was a sniper gunning for me, they wouldn't have waited in the kitchen with my grandma's cooking knives."

Adam looked like he wanted to argue, but he managed to keep his mouth shut and let it go. He sat back down on the couch, looking just a bit grumpy.

As soon as she shut the bathroom door, her grandma was there. "What the hell is going on? I should have never gone on a date. Did someone hurt you?"

Sara held up her hands. "I need you to stop freaking out. Can you do that for me?"

Grandma's ghost took a deep breath, or seemed to be taking a deep breath, or whatever. "Okay, I'm calm now. Go ahead."

"So, I went out for a walk today, and I ran into Maggie at the school."

"Did she do something to you? I'll murder her." She kept pushing at her forearms and after a moment, Sara realized what she was doing.

"Are you seriously trying to roll up your sleeves right now? That dress doesn't even have straps. And no, Maggie didn't do anything. But Mayor Hart walked up with his head smashed in and said it was my fault, whatever that means. He's dead now, and I'm officially the person who found his body because I ran over to see if I could help."

"What did he mean it was your fault?" Grandma asked.

91

Sara shrugged. "I don't know. I'm not the one that killed him."

Grandma relaxed. "Oh well, that's fine then..."

Sara bit her lip. "Well, yeah, but I think someone just tried to stab me."

"What?"

"Adam drove me home from the school. That's where I found Mayor Hart, and I was a little nervous because I knew you were out with Sam, so I asked Adam to come in with me. I was going to make him coffee." She realized she was drifting away from the point. "Anyway, someone was hiding in the kitchen, and they had taken out one of your knives."

"Oh, honey. I'm so sorry. I should have stayed here tonight."

Sara shrugged "You couldn't have known some-one was going to try to murder me. These are sort of extreme circumstances."

"Well, don't worry. I'm going to go get help. You sit still."

Sara sat down on the toilet. She glanced at the time on her phone. It was already ten p.m. She won-dered how long this was going to take.

After about five minutes, there was a soft knock on the door. "Everything okay in there?" Adam asked. Great. Now he was treating her like a toddler having an especially bad bowel movement.

She called back, "I'm fine. I just needed a minute alone."

"The sheriff is on his way."

"Okay. Just let me wash my face." That would buy her another couple of minutes.

Sara leaned over the sink and splashed cold water onto her face. She toweled off and straightened.

There was a strange man in the mirror behind her. She screamed. She turned around, and suddenly the bathroom was very crowded.

Adam pounded on the door. "You all right in there?"

"Sorry!" she called. "Sorry, just saw a spider." Realizing this was her second time using the same excuse, she thought she should invent new justifications for her surprises.

After a second, Adam responded with, "Don't scare me like that. Okay, I'm going back to the living room. Hurry out."

Grandma had returned with Sam, Maggie, and a man she didn't know. "Sara," she said, "this is Tom, a farmer from the nineteenth century. He's going to help watch out for you, along with Maggie and Sam."

"Okay," Sara said. She wasn't crazy about having around-the-clock ghost protection, but she'd had enough of a scare, she wasn't going to argue. "Um, thank you. I have to go talk to the sheriff now, so if you don't mind..."

Tom and Maggie stepped out of her way, which was just a bit disconcerting as the bathroom was small enough that they had to back through the walls. Sara returned to the living room to find Sheriff Robinson and Deputy Johnson waiting for her. The Sheriff held her grandma's knife in a clear evidence bag.

"Um, hi, everybody," Sara said. "Can I get anybody coffee? It's kind of turning into a late night."

As if on cue, Robinson yawned. "If you really don't mind, maybe that would be for the best."

"No problem." Sara turned to make the coffee.

Deputy Johnson followed her. "Just to be safe, I'm going to go along."

With a shrug, Grandma followed her too. "Well, I'm not leaving you alone."

Sara shrugged. "Sure." She wasn't going to argue that.

Sara started grinding beans and got four mugs out of the cabinet to the right of the sink, just where Grandma had always kept them. As she worked, she felt some of the tension leave her shoulders. There was something soothing about the familiar routine of making coffee.

Deputy Johnson leaned against the counter, her posture relaxed but alert. "So," she said, eyeing Sara's coffee setup, "you roast and grind your own beans, but then you use your grandmother's old Mr. Coffee machine?"

Sara found herself smiling for the first time in hours. "Yeah, I'm a bit of a coffee nerd. Want to hear a secret?" At Emily's nod, she continued, "Believe it or not, these old Mr. Coffee machines outperform most of the new, pricey, high-tech coffee makers. Perfect water temperature, just below boiling. Adjusted for inflation, this baby would cost about four hundred bucks today."

Grandma gave her a smug look. "See? I told you that machine would outlive me!" After a moment, she morosely added, "Though, I am a bit worried it might outlive you too."

"Four hundred?" The deputy's eyebrows shot up. "No kidding? And here I thought I was fancy with my French press."

Sara was so busy trying to avoid reacting to Grandma, she almost missed the French press comment. "A French press is a solid choice," Sara said, warming to the topic. "How do you take your coffee, by the way?"

"Just a little milk for me, if you have it. Walter takes his black. Oh, and you might as well start calling me Emily—we're probably going to be spending some time together."

Sara paused, hand on the fridge door. "We are?"

Emily's expression softened, but her tone stayed firm. "Look, I know this is a lot to take in, but someone tried to hurt you tonight. Until we figure out who and why, you need protection."

Sara blinked, still gripping the fridge handle. "And that means...?"

"It means I'd like to stay here for a few days," Emily said gently. "If that's okay with you."

"I'm not sure I need a bodyguard."

"It's not ideal," Emily admitted, "but we have one deputy on medical leave and no night shift. The nearest hotel is all the way out by the airport. This is the best way to keep you safe without either Adam lurking in your bushes all night or me sleeping outside in my car. Trust me, I'd rather be in my own bed, but this seems like the easiest way to handle things."

Sara considered this as she poured milk into Emily's mug. It should have felt invasive, having a virtual stranger move in. But the intruder had shaken Sara to her core. "I guess it makes sense," she said slowly. "And honestly? I'd feel better with you here than Adam checking in constantly. He means well, but..."

"But he's a guy, and there's always that underlying... something?" Emily finished with a knowing smile.

Sara nodded, relieved that Emily understood. "Exactly. Plus, I'm guessing you won't try to follow me into the bathroom."

Emily laughed, a warm, genuine sound that made Sara feel even more at ease. "Scout's honor. Your bathroom breaks will remain sacred and unguarded unless absolutely necessary."

As they gathered the mugs to return to the living room, Emily added softly, "I know this is scary, Sara. But we'll get through this. And hey, maybe between protecting you from mysterious assailants, you can teach me the finer points of coffee snobbery."

Sara found herself grinning despite everything. "Deal. By the time this is over, you'll be a certified coffee expert. It'll really add to your law enforcement skillset."

"Only if it's served with doughnuts."

They shared a chuckle as they headed back to join the others, and Sara felt a small spark of optimism. Maybe, just maybe, she could get through this between her ghostly bodyguards and very much alive protectors.

If she took the dead people into account, it looked like they were having a party, and Sara had to keep reminding herself that there were three people in the room who could not see the other four. She had to side-step to get by Tom and Sam, and she saw Sheriff Robinson raise an eyebrow at her. Despite that, he said nothing as he took the coffee from her.

Fortunately, the dead people in the room had saved her a seat next to the law enforcement officers, so she wasn't forced to sit a questionable distance from them or sit on top of one of the ghosts in the room.

As Sara settled in, Grandma said, "This is the most people who've been in the living room since I died."

It took all of Sara's power not to shoot Grandma a look. "So," Sara said, trying to control her voice, "Emily filled me in on the plan in the kitchen. She's going to be my house guest for a while. I'm cool with that as long as someone is trying to kill me."

Her grandma waved her hands for attention. "And don't forget, honey. You'll have a ghost protecting you twenty-four seven." Sara nodded at her and then made a face as she realized what she did.

Now the sheriff was waving for her attention. "Are you all right, ma'am? I know it's been a difficult night, but I'd like you to try to pay attention for a few more minutes. Do you think you can do that?"

Sara nodded. "Yes, Sheriff. Sorry about that. I think I'm starting to nod off."

"Don't worry," he said. "That's a perfectly normal reaction to something like this. I was just saying that Emily staying here is only part of what I'd like to do. When she's not available, Adam's going to be right across the street."

Maybe Sara wasn't tracking because she was very tired. "But you have to go to work, right?"

Adam shook his head. "I have a ton of vacation saved up and I can finish up paperwork from home. Besides, things are a little slow right now. I'll call in tomorrow, find someone to cover my open cases, and set up a staycation."

Sara wanted to protest and tell him that she already had a group of invisible bodyguards that never had to sleep—or did they?—to keep her safe, but it was a hard conversation to have when she was sure every living person in the room would think she was nuts.

Once they had all finished their coffee, the men went home, and Sara made up Grandma's bed for Emily. Exhausted from the stress of the day, she was out the second her head hit the pillow.

The next morning, Sara woke to the sound of cooking downstairs. For a second, she thought Grandma was cooking breakfast. Then she remembered that the deputy, Emily Johnson, had slept in Grandma's room. Sara looked at her phone and scowled at the time. Emily must be used to getting up early.

She staggered downstairs, mostly led by the smell of coffee. When she dragged herself into the kitchen and collapsed into a stool at the counter, Emily turned and smiled at her. Before Sara was able to respond, a plate dropped in front of her, followed by eggs and sausage.

"I hope you don't mind. I made some coffee and raided your fridge. I'm guessing you're not a morning person."

Sara grunted.

"That's no problem, as long as you're willing to put up with me being an early riser." A cup of coffee joined the meal.

Sara was going to grunt, but Grandma was standing in the corner eying her. "This nice lady is here to protect you, and she even made you breakfast. The least you could do is sit up straight and try to act like a normal human being."

Sara took a sip of the coffee. It wasn't too warm, so she took a bigger drink and cleared her throat. "Emily, thanks for making breakfast. You're right, I'm not so good first thing in the morning."

"I hope I did the coffee right. I watched you do it last night. I'm not used to these older Mr. Coffee machines. It peed out a little water before it got started, was that right?"

"Yeah," Sara said. "That's normal. These old machines drip a bit before they warm up all the way. Nothing to worry about."

Emily took a drink of coffee. "I noticed you're almost out of groceries. Do you want me to pick something up?"

"Um... Well, the truth is, I'm a little short on cash right now. In fact, I have to go talk to a lawyer today about my divorce, and I'm hoping he'll let me put a retainer on my last credit card. Otherwise, I might have to give him what little cash I have."

Emily waved a dismissive hand. "Don't worry about it then. I'm eating here too. Let me pick something up, and I'll charge it to the department."

"Thank you, Emily. I appreciate that." Sara wasn't sure if she could charge it to the sheriff's department or if it was a convenient excuse, but she wasn't going to argue.

"*De nada.* Okay, I'm going to drive into the station." She handed Sara another card. "Here's my number in case you lost the other one. Don't hesitate to call if you see anything strange, okay?"

Sara nodded. "Yes. Thank you."

"If nothing else comes up, I'll see you tonight." She finished her coffee, set the cup in the sink and headed out.

Sara turned to her grandma. "Well, with her out of the way, and the Harvest Festival a few days off, maybe I should do something about my impending divorce."

Her grandma looked at something behind her. Sara glanced around. The ghost farmer, Tom, was standing behind her. Sara jumped, and her coffee mug sloshed dangerously in her hand. "Geez, Tom! Don't you ghosts believe in doorbells?'

Tom looked puzzled. "But... we don't use doors, Mrs. Jenkins. I am deeply sorry for startling you. I meant not to interrupt your talk with your grandmother." The style of his speech and way he stumbled over "grandmother" made her think he might have been born in central Europe.

She didn't like being called "Mrs. Jenkins" either. "Please, call me Sara." Something told her this might be too informal for him, "Or if you have to, call me Ms. Jenkins."

Tom straightened his ghostly overalls. "I shall try to be more plain in my comings and goings, Ms. Jenkins. Your grandmother asked me to look out for you today."

Grandma nodded. "My friends and I are all going to take shifts. Today, Tom is going to watch over you."

Sara nodded. "Sure. Thanks for helping, Tom." Last night, when she was mentally exhausted and thought someone was going to stab her, she was a lot more amenable to having Grandma's ghost buddies follow her around. Now that she'd slept on it, it seemed like it would be a bit of a pain. It's not like they could stop an attacker. She was the only one who could even see or hear them. However, after they'd all offered to help so enthusiastically, she felt bad saying so out loud.

Sara returned her focus to her grandma. "So, do you think your attorney would be a good choice for my divorce?" She hated using that word, but it seemed inevitable now. She might as well be prepared.

"Martin? I suppose so. I think divorce is a good deal of his business."

"Okay. I guess I'll have to go see him. After I finish my coffee."

About an hour later, after convincing Tom that he could patrol the first floor of the house while she showered and got dressed, Sara was headed out the door with Tom following close behind her. When she got to the end of the sidewalk, she again heard, "Far to hurl."

She stopped. "Did you hear that?"

Tom nodded. "It sounded like someone was telling you to go to Hell in German. *Fahr zur Hölle!*"

Sara's car screamed back, "*Fahr zur Hölle!*"

Tom stepped back. "I think there's somebody in there. Can you..." He paused as if looking for the right words. "...pop the hood?"

Sara dug in her purse and located her car keys, which took a moment, as she hadn't used them in a few days. Then she ducked into the car and popped the hood.

As soon as the hood was up, Tom started speaking softly in German. A shrill, agitated voice answered back. This went on for a few minutes, then Tom came around the hood and spoke softly in English. "There is a spirit trapped in your car. Her name is Greta, and she worked at the BMW factory in Munich. She doesn't remember anything after that, but she believes she has been jailed in the motor compartment by a witch. I think she may believe you are that witch."

Sara nodded. "I always thought that car hated me for some reason. I guess I was right." She'd told Brad she just wanted something simple that came with a warranty, but Brad hadn't thought that was fancy enough. Though, to be fair, a warranty wouldn't have covered haunting.

Just then, she saw Adam walking across the street, trying to be helpful, no doubt. "Hi, Sara. I've been meaning to ask you if you were having car trouble. I noticed you hadn't been using it much."

Seeing Adam walking toward them, Tom stepped back. "I'll go talk to her some more. It is common for people to lose their last memory, especially if it's a sudden or traumatic incident. I think she had some kind of accident at the BMW factory. Perhaps I can convince her you are not her jailer."

Sara turned back to Adam. "Yeah. It's been trouble. The mechanic in Des Moines thought it might have a cracked block, but he couldn't locate the crack. He said the computer didn't tell him anything."

"Hmm." He got down on his hands and knees and looked under the car. He said something, but Sara couldn't hear over the loud, German argument going on right next to them.

She walked around the car and squatted down next to him. "Sorry, what was that?"

He winced like she was talking way too loudly. She must have subconsciously upped her volume to be heard over the conversation he had no idea was going on.

Adam pointed to the ground. "You see all these fluids that have leaked out. You're going to want to top off the oil and coolant before you do anything."

"Yeah," Sara tried to look embarrassed. "The mechanic said something about that, but I was so busy with my husband cheating on me, that I never got around to getting any of that stuff."

"Don't worry. I have a jug of pre-mixed coolant and a couple of quarts of oil. I'll be right back."

"Take your time," she said. "I'm in no hurry."

While Adam crossed the street, Sara walked around the front of the car. The German voices had calmed, and Tom smiled when he saw her. "Greta would like to say something."

The woman let out a long string of German, and Tom translated. "She knows now that you were just someone unlucky enough to get the car that killed her. She wants to apologize for any damage she did to your car. 'She says something about... *die Zündkerzen*? I believe that's... spark plugs? My apologies, Ms. Jenkins, I died before these things were commonplace."

"Wait," Sara said, "Grandma and everyone else I met so far haven't been able to touch anything, but Greta could make oil and coolant leak. What's different?"

"I've seen it happen," Tom said, "if a spirit is around long enough and gets angry enough, they can get strong enough to push physical objects. In Germany, we call them *Poltergeist.* I guess if you spend nine years in an engine compartment, you have plenty of time to get annoyed." He turned and explained to Greta what they were talking about.

Sara nodded. "Fair enough."

Greta turned to her and waved. "Auf Wiedersehen," she said, then added something else to Tom. The car engine started and revved a couple of times before a backfire, as loud as a gunshot, sent a plume of smoke from the exhaust. Finally, the car stuttered to a halt. When Sara turned back around, Greta was gone.

"That's it?" Sara asked. "Nine years in an engine bay, and she's gone in ten minutes?"

Tom shrugged. "Sometimes that's how it goes. She just had to know she was dead. She says the car should work fine now. There was nothing wrong with it."

Adam came over and made a big show of topping off her oil and coolant, carefully explaining each step to her. When he was done, he said, "Try to turn over the engine, and we'll see what happens."

Sara sat down in the car and turned the key. It started up with no resistance and purred like a kitten. She got out and shrugged to Adam. "Wow, I guess whatever was causing the problem worked itself out."

Adam stared at the engine in disbelief. "Wow. I could have sworn this car was on its last legs, and now it's purring like a kitten." He shook his head. "I mean, I'm glad it's working, but I've never seen anything like this."

"Thanks for checking everything. I'm going to go over to Martin Settler's office to get an update on the probate and start talking about my divorce." The more she said the word, the easier it was to say. Two or three more years and she might not trip over it at all.

Adam nodded. "Martin's a good guy. I'm sure he can help you."

He looked like he wanted a hug or something, but he also had oil on his hands, so Sara smiled at him again and said, "Thanks for the help." Then she got in her car and drove downtown.

Martin Settler's office did not inspire one to believe they were speaking with the pinnacle of the legal profession. The office looked like it had last been remodeled fifty years ago, when Martin started practicing law. Wood paneling lined walls broken up by the occasional bookshelf. Sara had counted five fish mounted on the wall, along with the occasional net and fishing rod crossed like swords under a medieval crest. A large oak desk dominated one side of the room, along with a little wedge of wood with a brass nameplate reading "Martin Settler, Esq."

There were two old leather chairs sitting across from the desk. Sara had taken one of them, and Tom sat in the other. Occasionally, he would comment on this or that and Sara would respond quite softly, afraid that Martin might come in and find her talking to herself.

When they'd come in the door, Martin himself had met her in the reception area, He'd been sorting several large stacks of paper, and he told her to take a seat in the office and wait for him because things were a little crazy. His assistant, Mimi, was sick. Sara had met Mimi on her one other trip to the office, and she was pretty sure the legal secretary had been working for

Martin's practice since he started it. She estimated Mimi's age to be at least one hundred.

"Sara," Martin said, moving quite quickly for his advanced age while trying not to spill a mug of coffee. "Can I offer you a cup of coffee?"

"No, thank you," she said, having spied the bright red, gigantic Folger's container as she walked in. "I just had a cup at home."

"Good. Good. I always think it's good to keep the caffeine levels up," his tone changed, losing a little bit of its regular joviality, "though my doctor disagrees." The regular tone returned. "Here to check on the status of the will? I'm afraid I'm not quite finished up with it. While your grandmother's estate wasn't the most complicated, I'd be pretty bad at my job if I lost track of an investment account or failed to notify a creditor. Of course, the probate court is always backlogged. And then there's life insurance, they always drag their feet. That's technically outside of probate, but I always like to confirm the beneficiary designations. Missed details can cause family headaches down the line."

"Wait," Sara said, "life insurance? I thought that was for young people."

Martin adjusted his glasses. "Mostly. But your grandmother had what we used to call a whole life policy. That's just how things used to be done. We didn't have Roth accounts and 401ks. You had your savings account, whole life, and stock certificates if you were wealthy." He gave a dry chuckle. "Trust me, I know how boring this sounds, but a lot of people forget the Roth didn't even exist until 1997. Not a lot of people remember that."

Sara definitely didn't remember that. She hadn't been born yet. "That's really interesting, Martin, but before we go off on a tangent about investments, I need to discuss something else. I need to divorce my husband."

"Ah, the D word." His enthusiasm seemed suitably dampened. "Never a fun topic even when my other specialties are death and taxes. Well, you've come to the right place, I've divorced half the people in this town from the other half."

Sara's mind wandered for a moment, picturing a dizzying flowchart pinned to Martin's wall, arrows crisscrossing between names like a deranged game of six degrees of separation. She shook off the absurd image and focused on the task at hand.

Taking a deep breath, she told Martin her story, starting with Brad's affair and ending with her cleared-out account. Martin listened to the whole thing, taking notes with professional detachment which only briefly slipped when she mentioned the sombrero. His eyebrows shot up, and Sara could have sworn she saw him stifle a smirk.

"So," she concluded, "my biggest worry is being able to pay you, at least in the short term."

Martin leaned back in his chair, which complained in a voice of old wood and leather. He steepled his fingers, his eyes narrowed, and suddenly the jovial, old lawyer took on the countenance of a shark at feeding time. Sara marveled at how the quaint, fishing-themed office suddenly felt like the lair of a cunning predator.

"Let me tell you something, Sara. People think I'm a little old-fashioned."

Sara started to protest, but he waved her objections away.

"Part of being old-fashioned is building relationships, and your family has given me a lot of business over the years. Your cousin Jennifer and her husband give me plenty of lucrative work, and your grandmother wasn't just a client, she was my friend. As long as I draw breath, your credit is good with me. Now, down to the business at hand. Let's just say I've cast a few lines in my time, and your husband is a whopper." He gave a nod to the trophy fish hung on the wall. "We'll go after him for temporary spousal support."

Sara raised an eyebrow. "But he's not going to like that. He hired a fancy Des Moines lawyer."

"That's the beauty of it. His fancy lawyer isn't going to want to wade hip-deep into cold water. Brad tried to leave you destitute, unable to afford your own fancy, Des Moines lawyer, and we have the receipts. Now, if you had to hire a divorce lawyer out of the phone book, that would be a serious problem, but you have me to petition on your behalf. The court will take Brad's actions into account. Because he tried to leave you with nothing, they can order him to pay you a portion of his income during the divorce proceedings."

Tom yawned, stood up, and walked out into the lobby, obviously bored with the conversation.

"And the money he took?" Sara asked.

"We'll file a motion for a financial restraining order. Then we'll be squeezing him from both ends, both his savings and his income, and unlike me, his fancy, Des Moines lawyer isn't going to take an IOU. With that kind of pressure on him, he'll be begging to settle as soon as possible. That's when we hit him up for alimony."

"I thought only movie stars from the nineteen fifties got alimony. I don't know if I'd feel right taking money after the divorce."

Martin nodded. "Many people think that way about alimony, but it's actually quite common, especially in cases like yours. Think of it as more of a bargaining chip. We're going to cast our nets as wide as we can and pull in as much as we can get. Also, while I am working on credit, remember my services are quite expensive. Let's stick your adulterous husband with the bill."

"Okay, I guess my only other worry is if Brad can go after Grandma's estate."

"Actually, the timing on that front is quite beneficial, if you'll excuse the pun."

Lost in thought about inheritance and divorce, Sara had missed that there had been a pun.

Martin continued. "Because of the way your grandmother's will was written, by yours truly, Brad has no claim on the estate. I'm sure they'll try to use it as a leverage point, but I don't think we have much to worry about."

Sara felt an uncomfortable mix of relief and guilt. "Part of me knows I should be angrier—he betrayed me, stole our savings, and then tried to make me feel crazy for being upset. But..." She shook her head. "I guess I'm still learning that it's okay to fight back."

Martin's eyes narrowed slightly. "That's why you have me, my dear. I'll do the fighting for you. Unfortunately, it's not the first time I've seen it. A lot of couples still have joint accounts, and there are some shady websites out there giving out bad advice. I never thought I'd have to deal with that when I opened this practice." He put down his notebook and got up from his chair. "Just a moment, I want to pull the folder for your grandmother's estate and find some forms."

He left the office and returned a few minutes later with a large binder and a small stack of paper. Tom followed him back in. "Now, because you are short on cash, I am authorized as executor of your grandmother's estate to make an early disbursement on grounds of financial hardship. Would two thousand be a good amount?"

"Yes. Oh, my god, yes. I was literally worried about buying groceries this morning." She blinked back tears, embarrassed by how emotional she was getting over money, but two thousand dollars meant she could breathe again.

Settling back into the chair, Martin opened the folder and started filling out the form. When he finished, he hand-copied everything onto a second form. "If Mimi were here, I'd have her do this on the computer, and we'd just print two copies, but I don't know how the printer works." He slid the pages in front of her. "Sign and date these by the X. I'm having lunch with Judge Krieger in about an hour, and if Marge's cooking doesn't kill him, I'll have him review these documents and sign them. If you come back at two, I should have a check waiting for you."

"That would be great!" Sara was overwhelmed with happiness. So many of her problems had been solved by this one visit. If only Martin could wave a magic wand and people wouldn't be trying to kill her. "Martin, would it be okay if I hugged you?"

The old lawyer looked momentarily surprised, then he said, "I suppose that would be fine." He stood up, and she went around his desk for an embrace.

On the way home from the law office, Tom couldn't stop talking. "It's unbelievable how much things have changed," he said. "Of course, no one got divorced in my time. We didn't hug our lawyer. For that matter, we didn't murder the mayor, though we probably should have. That Paul Reubens was a real son of a bitch."

Chapter 6

Dirty Deeds and Dirtier Diners

Sara and Tom returned before noon to find Grandma and her friends hanging out in the living room. Grandma and Sam were sitting on the couch and Maggie sat in a chair across from them. Since there was only one other chair in the living room, and Tom couldn't go get a chair for himself, Sara motioned for him to sit down and pulled in a chair from the dining room.

"So," Grandma asked, "how were things with Martin?"

Sara tried to get comfortable in the wooden chair, as she reflected on the fact that she had the least comfortable seat in a room full of otherwise non-corporeal people. "Actually, it's a huge weight off. Martin says that because Brad tried to screw me over, he's in a

worse position, and he's going to get me an early disbursement from the estate, so I won't have to worry
about money as much."

Grandma nodded. "That's good. He should do it. I
told him to write the will so you'd get all the money.
You're the only one who should have it, except for your
cousin Jennifer, and she married a rich man. You
should go visit them, you know, now that you're in
town."

Sara rolled her eyes. "You know Jen and Nick are
in love. She didn't care about his money." Deep down
though, she had to admit she was jealous of her cousin.
Not every person was lucky enough to fall head–over–
heels in love with someone who came from old money.
Some people just ended up with guys like Brad.

"Even so," Maggie said, "a modest income never
undermines a relationship. My husband operated a
shop downtown, and there were times we earned twenty thousand dollars a year. Today, it might seem in-
significant, but back then, it was sufficient for a comfortable life. Now that you are free to court again, bear
it in mind."

Sara decided to switch the subject away from marrying for money. "So, does anyone have any theories
about who killed Mayor Hart?"

"Not really," Sam said. "I say he seduced the
wrong woman, and the husband came to take re-
venge." The assembled ghosts nodded as if this might
be plausible.

Maggie said, "I think he swindled the wrong person. Just like his ancestors, he's as crooked as the Dev-
il's tail."

"Maybe," Tom said, "it's got something to do
with all the land he's buying up all over town."

All heads turned to Tom.

"What was that, Tom?" Sara asked.

"While you were in the lawyer's office," he said, "I got bored and stretched my legs. I could only see the ones on top, but those unsorted papers spread out on the desk in the lobby were land deeds, and they had the names Mark Hart and Dwain Hart all over them." Tom's spectral brow furrowed. "In my time, the affairs of the town were not the concern of us who worked the land. However, it is most irregular for one family to acquire so many properties. When I first arrived, each shop belonged to a different tradesman—the cobbler, the tailor, each to his own craft. This Hart family's actions... they do not adhere to proper order."

Sara took a deep breath and let it out. "So why is the Hart family buying up half of Downcastle? They don't have lots of money, do they?" She looked around the room to the assembled dead. From their faces, she was pretty sure none of them knew if the Hart family had that kind of money.

She picked up her phone and scrolled through the numbers. Then she called her cousin Jennifer. "Hey, Jen, it's Sara. How are you doing?"

"Doing great, cousin. I heard you moved to Downcastle."

"Yeah, that's a really long story."

"Why don't you come out here for lunch? You can tell me what's going on."

"You're offering to cook for me?"

"Not at all. We have a housekeeper who does all the cooking. I know it's a little ostentatious, but neither one of us can boil water."

"Sure, that sounds great."

"Be here in forty-five minutes. I'm sure Gladys can whip something up by then."

This seemed to be Tom's day to tag along with her, as he accompanied her to Jen and Nick's place. They lived in a large house at the edge of town, built when Nick sold the family's ancestral mansion in downtown Iowa City. While Sara had found that previous house intriguing in an Addams Family sort of way, it was creepy as fuck, and she could see why Jen no longer wanted to live there.

Their new residence was about as different as you could get from the Gothic horror show while still being big enough to convert into a small hotel. It screamed ultra-modern. It was the kind of place you'd expect Bill Gates or Tony Stark to live—if they wanted to downsize and live on a hill in a sea of cornfields.

Despite having a housekeeper, Jen met Sara at the door. Sara was struck by how little her cousin had changed since college. Her long blonde hair cascaded over her shoulders in gentle waves, framing a face that was both familiar and subtly matured. Despite living in a mansion that screamed luxury, Jen's outfit whispered cozy comfort, a t-shirt with a faded Radiohead logo paired with jeans that looked like they'd been broken in over years of lazy Sundays. Her bare feet peeked out from under the jeans' hems, toenails painted a cheerful turquoise.

Jen drew her cousin into a comforting and welcoming hug. "It's been so long. Now that we both live in Downcastle, we have to hang out more." The last time they had been together, they'd both been at the U of I, and they were in different departments. They'd mainly run into each other at parties if they hadn't specifically made plans together. "Come in. Come in." She led Sara into a spacious living room, where plush carpets and inviting furniture created a warm, welcoming atmosphere. Floor-to-ceiling windows spanned one wall, flooding the space with natural light and offering a view of cornfields reaching to the horizon.

Tom walked over to the windows and looked out. "Corn's coming in good. Should be knee high by the fourth of July."

A woman in an old-fashioned maid's uniform joined them. She looked to be about the same vintage as Martin Settler's assistant Mimi. "Would you ladies like drinks before lunch? Perhaps some iced tea or some lemonade?"

"I could use a glass of water," Sara said, aware they'd talk themselves hoarse the moment words started flowing.

"I can get that, Gladys," Jen said. "I know where the water is. You can go back to making lunch." To Sara, she said, "I'll be right back."

Jen returned with two bottles of Taiga Water and handed one to Sara. "She still acts like she's working for Nick's mother, who didn't know how to do simple things like find a bottle of water in the refrigerator."

"You've certainly come a long way since college," Sara said.

"As have you. Are you still working in biotech?"

And then Sara had to unload her long story of misfortune, from unemployment to infidelity to divorce. She did leave out the bits about ghosts, though. Through the whole thing, Jen sat in silence, and when Sara was done, her response was simple and to the point.

"Holy fuck, Sara."

"Yeah."

"I had no idea things were going so bad for you. How are you holding up? I have money, you know. I can help."

Sara smiled at her cousin. "I know you have money." She gestured at the huge house around them. "But actually, I think I'm going to be fine. I talked to Martin Settler this morning. He's going to take on my divorce, and he's arranging a small advance on the inheritance from Grandma."

"And if it doesn't work out, you are going to promise you'll come to us, and we're going to make sure you have everything you need."

Sara sighed. "Okay, but you don't have to be that generous." She knew Jen could afford to keep Sara as a pet, but Sara had too much pride to leech off a relative.

Jen shook her head. "No, I don't. But you're my only living relative, and I choose to be."

Now that they had caught up a bit, Sara decided to discuss some touchier subjects. "So, I don't know if you heard about it yet, but Mayor Hart was murdered last night."

"O-M-G. I had not."

"I found the body. Then someone was in my house. It was kind of scary, you know?"

Jen had just taken a drink of water, and she put her hand over her mouth like she had almost done a spit take. "We're going to hire a bodyguard for you. We'll get someone good. I know a guy."

"I'm fine. One of the county deputies is staying with me. Emily Johnson. She seems nice. Anyway," Sara tried to think of a better way to ease into the question, but she couldn't. "I was wondering if maybe you and Nick are financing the Hart family to buy up the whole town." Sure, it was a bit of a leap, but no one else in Downcastle had that kind of money.

"What?" Jen looked at Sara like she had two heads.

Nick picked that moment to walk into the dining room in clothes covered in dirt and mud. "Hi, Sara. I've been gardening, but I thought I'd pop inside and say hello."

"You garden now?" Sara asked. "I thought you were a hardcore gamer."

Nick shrugged. "Well, I probably annoy my landscaper more than anything. But I have a big yard that has to be taken care of, and it's kind of satisfying to grow your own food."

"Sorry," Jen said, "but Sara just asked a question that surprised me. She asked me if we were part of a secret cabal buying up the town with the Hart family."

Nick thought about it for a minute. "I'm pretty sure we're not. I mean, we're diversified. Last week, I found out we own a lumber yard in New Albin. I had to look New Albin up on Google Maps. But I think I would have remembered something like buying up Downcastle."

"I'm sorry I even asked," Sara said, "but when I found out they were buying up property all over town, I figured they had to have backers. And who else around here has that kind of money?"

"I'm pretty sure the Hart family doesn't," Nick said. "If they are secretly rich, they really keep quiet about it."

"Well," Sara said, "they got money from someone, and I think it got Mike Hart killed."

Nick looked a bit skeptical. "Are you sure? He was kind of an ass. There might be lots of reasons someone wanted to kill him."

Sara shrugged. "You've got me there. Sure, he was an ass, but that's not usually enough to get a person killed, unless Downcastle has changed a lot since I lived here in high school."

"Okay then," Nick said. "Do you want me to look into it, see if there are any weird land deals going on? I am pretty good with computers."

Sara nodded. "Sure, that would be great."

After lunch, as they were driving away, Tom said, "I get what the boy's saying about growing your own food. There's a satisfaction to it. So, what are you going to do next?"

"I'm going to go back to Martin Settler's office and get my money."

"No, I mean, what are you going to do next in the investigation?"

"Oh, Tom, I'm not investigating anything." Or was she? Should she be? She did just question her only living relative. That was dramatic enough.

Sara drove back to Martin Settler's office, and the old man had the check as he'd promised. "Now, you go and take some of this to open a bank account. We're going to need a direct deposit address for when we start taking part of Brad's pay."

Sara nodded. "Yes, sir. I will do that right away." Of course, she had to go to the bank to cash the check anyway. She paused, wondering if she should press him about the property deals. He'd been so nice to her, and she already felt like an asshole for questioning her own cousin. "Do you mind if I ask you something?"

"Ask away, my dear."

"Do you know anything about any land deals involving the Hart family?"

Martin made a face. "You know, it puts me in a tough situation, but I've been doing this for a long time. So let me tell you why I won't answer that kind of question. If they were, Sara, I'd likely be representing either them or the other party, and I'd be bound by client confidentiality, so if I answer, 'I can't tell you that,' it's as good as a yes."

Sara sighed. "I know. It wasn't fair to ask. I hope you don't think less of me."

He shook his head. "No, I've been backed into that particular corner so many times, I consider it a hazard of the job." He hesitated, then added carefully, "Your grandmother was quite... persuasive about getting information. Especially after your grandfather passed."

Something in his tone made Sara pause. "Oh. OH." She tried to keep a straight face as the implications sank in. Grandma did mention she wasn't celibate after he passed away. Although, notably, she hadn't mentioned it until after she was dead herself. Not wanting to continue with that subject, Sara said, "So, once again, thank you for all your help. And thank you for rushing through this emergency money. I really do need it."

As Sara left the office, she still felt embarrassed that she had tried to take advantage of an old man who had been so nice to her, as well as still feeling a little grossed out that he'd done it with Grandma.

She sat in her car and tried to decide what to do next. She could go somewhere to listen to local gossip, but the only place she could think of was Marge's Diner, which was problematic. She didn't want to eat something that would ruin not only her stomach but also the wonderful memory of lunch at Jen's. But she also couldn't bring herself to sit around and drink a cup of ReliaRoast coffee that had probably been brewed two hours ago. She remembered Marge served Pepsi products. Sara figured she could stomach a Diet Pepsi, and she'd get a slice of pie. If it was bad, she didn't have to eat it.

When Sara and Tom got to Marge's Diner, she was dismayed to find it completely empty. Marge threw a menu down on the table in front of her, like having a paying customer was a horrible imposition. Sara didn't

119

even glance at it. She ordered her drink, asked about the pie, and ordered a slice of French silk.

When the pie came, it was obviously—thankfully—mass-produced and still semi-frozen, so Sara looked through the Downcastle local paper as she sipped her Pepsi and waited for it to thaw. The entire time she sat there, Marge either aggressively wiped the tables around her or stood behind the counter watching Sara like she was going to steal the silverware.

The local paper was less than helpful. The title headline was "Cow removed from road." Despite the non-exciting title, the reporting was decent and included quotes from Adam, Sheriff Robinson, and the local vet.

From there, the paper went downhill, becoming a list of local happenings, thank you notes, and things that elderly people had printed off the Internet and sent in.

Sara forced her fork through the pie, which was still a little hard in the center and turned to the back page. It was a full-page ad for Kelley and Hart Realty with a huge picture of Mark and Dwain Hart under the motto, "If we can't sell your home, we'll buy your home!" Maybe they weren't keeping the land deal as secret as she'd first thought.

After she'd finished the local paper, Tom regaled Sara with stories about what it was like to farm in the nineteenth century. As Sara might have imagined, it was quite difficult. Even though Tom's land grant had been one hundred and sixty acres, he'd only managed to build a house and clear about fifty acres of fields. At this point, Tom went off on a tangent about changes in farming technology and yield sizes that left Sara a little lost, but from the excitement in Tom's voice, she could tell it was a big deal.

She'd finished her frozen pie, and since there was no one to gossip with, she figured she might as well leave. Now that she was ready to pay, Marge was nowhere to be found. Eventually, Sara went up to the counter. There was a little bell, and she rang it.

Marge came out from the back, her eyes were red, making it look like she'd been crying. "I'm sorry. Did you want more diet?"

Sara shook her head. "No, I'll just pay."

"I was in the back, chopping onions."

"Oh, that explains why your eyes are red," Sara said.

"Hey, can you tell me something?" Marge lowered her voice conspiratorially "Someone in here earlier told me you were the one that found the mayor dead, is that true?"

"Yeah. Not how I was planning to spend my evening."

"Do you know if the police found any clues?"

Sara had come in to hear the local gossip, but instead, Marge was trying to get information out of her. "Not that I know of. They asked me a lot of questions, but I didn't really know anything. I mean, he was dead when I got there. It's not like I witnessed anything."

Marge nodded. "I guess that makes sense. Well, thanks for sharing anyway."

"Sure. Have a good day." Sara turned to leave, but as she approached the front door Iris Pilkington walked in.

"Sara, dear." She walked up and clamped onto Sara's hands. "I heard about what happened last night. That must have been so traumatizing."

Sara nodded. "Yeah. It was a bit of a shock."

Shaking her head, Iris said, "You know, whenever we lose such an esteemed leader, it hurts us all. Mayor Hart's murder leaves a hole in our community."

121

Sara bit her lip to keep herself from laughing in the woman's face. Then, she said as evenly as she could. "I couldn't have said that better myself, Iris. With this huge hole in our community, do you think we can continue to hold the Harvest Festival? Or maybe we could postpone it until harvest season."

"I'm afraid not, my dear. Despite our tragic loss, we are going to have to soldier on. Of course, as interim mayor, I could cancel it, but deposits have been made, and we are too late to get refunds. The carnival rides are already on their way, as well as the KISS cover band. The temporary grandstand for the tractor pull is already assembled." She shook her head and patted Sara's arm. "Don't get me wrong, I understand your grief, but we can't let one ill-timed murder get us down. We're going to make this year's Harvest Festival a celebration of life."

Sara was impressed. For most people, that level of pragmatism mixed with insensitivity would have been unreachable. She forced a smile. "I'm sure you're right, Iris. The festival must go on. I'm sure it's what Mayor Hart would have wanted."

Apparently, Sara's attempt to hide the sarcasm in her words had succeeded—Iris's eyes lit up. "Exactly, my dear. And think of it as an opportunity for you as well. The murder will draw more people to Downcastle. They'll meet you at your booth, and when you're ready to open your coffee shop, they'll have a personal recollection of you. If I were you, I'd think about giving out little cups of your best coffee to everyone who drops by the booth."

That thought hadn't crossed Sara's mind, and honestly, Iris had a point. They said there was no such thing as bad publicity. However, she dismissed the idea of making coffee and talking to the dead at the same time, that seemed like too much. "Thank you, Iris. You've given me something to think about."

"I strive to do my best." For a moment, she lost a bit of her usual spunk. "Honestly, there's a lot to do. Mayor Hart wasn't exactly diligent about separating his personal business from his mayoral duties. There were always rumors he was involved in... less-than-honest dealings. If anything shady was happening, I'd bet it's buried somewhere in his office. I barely glanced at his desk today, and there was plenty that didn't look like town business." Her energy returned as quickly as it had faded, and she gave Sara a cheesy wink before sitting down at a table. "Are you sticking around? We could share a table if you want to talk some more."

As badly as Sara needed groceries and didn't want another piece of frozen pie, she couldn't turn down Iris's firehose of information. Sara hadn't even had to talk. In fact, every time she tried to steer the conversation toward the mayor, Iris would recount what he did in a recent city council meeting or bring up some detail about the Harvest Festival. After an hour together, Sara made her goodbyes, unenlightened to anything other than civic politics.

Tom summed up their conversation with the simple statement, "Boy, that lady can talk."

As Sara drove home from the grocery store, she got a call from Joe. She picked it up with the car's Bluetooth, which had always been glitchy, but now worked perfectly. "Hi, Joe."

"Sara. Are you home?"

"I'm about to be, why?"

"Mom wanted me to bring her over, she wants to help some more with cleaning up your house, and I have some initial numbers for you to look over."

Sara didn't want to look at numbers. She had a sinking feeling the price would be much too high, but she had started the process, and she appreciated the work Joe had put in, so she had to see it through, even if it meant disappointing Joe.

She realized she had not answered him. "Of course, I'd love to see you guys. Please stop by."

"Alright. I'll see you in, what, half an hour?"

"Sounds great.

"That is amazing," Tom said.

"What's amazing?"

"How you can talk to someone through the car. In my day, you had to ride a horse or write a letter. If it was really important, you had to go to town and send a telegram. I see a lot of people speaking badly of all the technology in the modern world, but I lived when you could die of infection from scratching your hand with a rusty tool. I think you have it much better."

Sara nodded. "That's a good point, Tom." After spending the day with the old farmer, she'd found she rather liked him. He didn't say much, but when he did have something to say, she found him quite insightful.

When Sara got home, Emily was sitting on the couch texting with someone. No longer in her uniform, she was wearing a pair of sweatpants and a t-shirt that read, "Iowa Law Enforcement Academy." Sara was a bit impressed with how fit Emily looked without her bulky uniform. Chasing down bad guys must be better exercise than watching YouTube videos. When Emily saw her, she smiled and said, "Hey, roomie. I checked in with Adam. He kept an eye on the house, but he said you were gone most of the day. What have you been up to?"

Sara sighed and threw herself down on the couch. "Only all the things I have been putting off since I got here. I got the car started with some help from Adam." She wished she could give Tom the credit, as he had talked down the irate German woman trapped in her engine compartment, but she still wasn't sure Emily would understand the whole ghost thing. "Then I spoke to Grandma's lawyer about settling her estate and got him to represent me for my divorce."

"That's Martin Settler, right?" Emily asked.

Sara nodded. It would make sense Emily would know a lot of the lawyers in the county, especially ones that had been around as long as Martin. "Oh, yeah. I suppose you know him, right?"

"He doesn't take a lot of criminal cases, but I've been cross-examined by him occasionally, and I've testified before him back when he was an associate judge. Don't let the jolly old man act fool you. He knows everybody who's anybody, and he picks his battles carefully. When I'm testifying against his client, I triple-check everything."

"Yeah," Sara said, "he had me fooled too until he told me how he was going after my husband. I almost feel sorry for Brad."

"Screw that guy," Emily said. "He's going to get what he deserves."

"I suppose." Sara realized she'd dropped her story halfway through. "Oh, and I had lunch with my cousin, and opened a bank account. What did you do today, Deputy?"

"I pulled over a couple of speeders. I gave a ride to a couple who got lost biking in the country looking at the tree blossoms. And I took a statement from a Dollar General manager after some teenagers stole a box of candy bars and a case of Miller Lite."

"A full day," Sara said. "Did you find out anything else about Hart's murder?"

"Not me. Walter's following that up."

For a moment, Sara thought about telling Emily what Iris had said, about Hart's City Hall desk being full of personal documents. However, she held back. If there was evidence in that desk, would the Sheriff even bother to follow up on it? And if he found something, he definitely wouldn't share anything with her. Instead, she asked, "Do you think he'll figure it out?"

"Honestly, Sara, there may not be a lot of hope. Hart had a ton of enemies and there were no witnesses. Heck, we don't have the murder weapon. We think he was hit with a rock that the murderer took with them. They could have dropped it in a muddy ditch somewhere, and we'll never find it."

With this extra piece of information, Sara felt even more determined to get a look at that desk herself. But how would she do it? Iris probably wouldn't just let her in. She needed another plan.

"It doesn't help that this is the most remote point in Hawthorne County," Emily added.

"That reminds me. I've been meaning to ask you. You're with the Hawthorne County Sheriff's Office, but when I was in high school, I lived here, and I could have sworn Downcastle and every town around it was either in Linn or Johnson County."

"Technically we're in what they call 'the crooked finger' of Hawthorne County." Emily grinned. "Though, some of the old-timers have a less polite name for it, the crooked penis. Turns out some survey from the 1800s was wrong and we actually stick out a few miles further than anyone thought, so now Downcastle is in Hawthorne. It's inconvenient for everyone, but it will take a legislative act to fix it."

Sara was trying to find the right joke to make about buying pills off the internet when she heard the doorbell ring, got up, and started toward the door. "That will be Joe and Ruby Mae Walker. Ruby Mae was Grandma's bestie, and she's helping me sort Grandma's stuff, and her son, Joe, is a contractor who's going to help me with my coffee shop." She felt a little embarrassed adding that last bit, as she now had some serious doubts about getting it off the ground.

Sara opened the door to find Ruby Mae and Joe outside, as she expected. Ruby Mae held a plate of muffins, while Joe stood beside her, towering like Adonis in a tight t-shirt. He gave her the easy smile that made Sara's heart skip a beat.

Sara smiled, trying to keep her cool. "Hi, guys, come on in."

Ruby Mae handed her the tray. "I made some muffins to go with that good coffee you're always making."

"That's very sweet." She led them in. "Ruby Mae, Joe, this is my um... house guest, Emily. She's staying with me for a few days. She's from the sheriff's department. They were a bit nervous about my safety after I found the mayor's body."

Ruby Mae addressed Emily. "Thank you for watching over our Sara. I appreciate you taking the time to make sure she's safe."

Emily seemed momentarily at a loss for words, but she recovered quickly with, "Thank you, ma'am. I will do my best. It's all part of the job, but it's nice to feel appreciated."

Sara couldn't explain it, but she was sure Joe had noticed Emily's toned figure—perhaps something changed in his demeanor, or he gave off a subtle nonverbal cue. She decided to get his attention. "Joe, you mentioned some initial numbers for the coffee shop"

Joe held up his laptop. "I've got it all in here. We can sit down and go over my estimates now if you like."

Ruby Mae mirrored her son's action, but instead of a computer, she held up the muffins, and a box of clear trash bags. "And you can take these muffins. I am going to get to work upstairs. Call me if you need anything."

"Sure." Sara felt a little guilty letting Ruby Mae do the work by herself. "Oh, and Emily's sleeping in Grandma's room, so maybe stick to the spare room. I'll be up to help as soon as I'm done looking at Joe's plans."

"Don't rush yourself on my account, dear," Ruby said, laughing. "I don't mind doing this kind of work." She started climbing the stairs.

Sara turned to Joe, "Why don't I make coffee and get some plates? We can have some muffins and talk about the shop."

"I can help with that," Emily volunteered.

"I can help too," Joe said, his eyes briefly flicking to Emily before settling back on Sara.

As they all moved into the kitchen, Sara couldn't help but notice how naturally Emily and Joe worked together, their hands brushing as they reached for plates and forks. A small, irrational pang of jealousy twisted in her stomach.

She focused on brewing the coffee, trying to ignore the way Emily laughed at something Joe said—a laugh that was just a little too sweet.

When they finally sat down at the table with coffee and muffins in front of them, Sara forced herself to concentrate on Joe's numbers as he tilted the laptop screen toward her. Good lord, the man was distracting —those broad shoulders and powerful arms from years of football and construction work. She hadn't felt this kind of instant attraction in... well, ever. Even with Brad, it had been a slower burn.

She was tempted to "accidentally" rest her hand on his thigh, a move guaranteed to get any man's attention, but she resisted, uncertain about being so forward, especially when they weren't alone. Also, there was that whole thing about still being married.

"It was a little higher than I expected," he said apologetically. The biggest issue is the plumbing upgrades. But if you do any type of food prep, you have to have them. Plumbing is never cheap."

Sara's eyes went to the bottom of Joe's spreadsheet and looked at the total. Then she looked at it again. She felt like she was going to be sick. "You could build a new house for that amount of money."

Joe sighed. "I was a little worried about this when you told me your plan. Most people think when they have an existing structure that converting it would be cheaper, but usually it's much more expensive. Retrofitting everything to meet code adds up fast. Sure, it makes for a more unique building, but once you factor in all the requirements? It's often easier—and cheaper —to start fresh."

Sara swallowed hard. "Then how does anyone start a new restaurant?"

Joe gave her a sympathetic look. "That's why there's always been one and only one restaurant in Downcastle, and it just changes hands occasionally. The building has all the plumbing for a commercial kitchen and electrical hookups it needs for the appliances. It's basically turnkey."

"Well," Sara said. "It was a nice dream. But I guess I need to start looking for a real job at some point."

Emily spoke up, "But once the coffee shop opened, you'd start making money, right?"

Sara shrugged. "That's a good question. Most restaurants don't even make a profit in the first year, so I'd have to not only fund the upgrades, but I'd have to put a little aside. The only way I could do that would be to mortgage this house on top of putting a fortune into it."

"Don't lose all hope," Joe said. "I'll keep an eye out. Honestly, this old Victorian is beautiful, but it's about the most expensive conversion job imaginable. While there might not be another commercial kitchen space in Downcastle, there may be a building that's easier and cheaper to work with."

"Okay," Sara said. "I won't lose all hope, but I think I'll still start looking for a day job." Considering she hadn't had a job in weeks, she was surprised at how busy she was keeping, with all the divorce and murder issues to deal with.

"Don't you dare give up on your dream," Grandma said from across the table. "I gave you this house so you could do what you want with it. If you have to sell it to Dwain Hart, that's what you do."

Sara thought for a moment before making a statement directed at Grandma that didn't make her sound like a crazy person to the rest of the room. "I'm not giving up on my dream. But I think I should take some time and not make any rash decisions." This placated Grandma a bit, so she finished her coffee and stood up. "Well, I suppose we should go find Ruby Mae and help her clean up."

Joe nodded. "I'll come with you. I didn't figure Mom was going to come with me and not put me to work at some point."

"Do you want me to give you a hand?" Emily asked.

Sara smiled. It was a generous offer, but she felt like Emily was doing enough. "Would you mind clearing the table and putting the dishes in the dishwasher?" It was a nice, simple task that wouldn't leave Emily feeling neglected but also wouldn't tie her up for hours. Yet, even as she made the request, Sara wondered if there was a subconscious motivation to be alone with Joe while keeping him away from Emily.

"Sure thing." She popped up from her chair and started stacking the dishes. "I may nab another of those muffins, though."

"Feel free," Sara said, following Joe toward the steps.

They found Ruby Mae in the bedroom Grandma had always used for storage. Ruby had started three piles based on whether she thought Sara should keep, donate, or discard. From what was there, Sara could tell Ruby Mae was making good decisions. She turned to Joe, "Want to do the garbage first?"

They started bagging up items from the garbage pile. Most of it was outdated paperwork: receipts for appliances long out of warranty, and thick manuals from Grandma's ancient computer—back when they still came with manuals. But there were a few oddities mixed in as well: a record album called Tiny Bubbles by someone named Perry Como, warped beyond recognition; Grandma's trusty Walkman from her long walks, now broken; and an old newspaper clipping about the state's plan to expand the road between Downcastle and the Eastern Iowa Airport to four lanes. A note was paperclipped to the article that said, "Save for Sara."

The note on the article made Sara smile. Grandma had always told her that people only ended up in Downcastle because they got lost trying to find the Cedar Rapids airport after the name change. She no doubt had saved up some kind of joke about people being able to get lost twice as fast now.

Sara and Joe carried the first two bags of garbage down to his big truck and threw them in the back. As he turned to go back in, Sara grabbed Joe's arm. "Can I talk to you about something?" She asked. "I didn't want to say anything in front of Emily or your mom."

Joe raised an eyebrow. "Now you've got me curious." He seemed to think she was asking him out, which was kind of correct, technically, but not the direction she'd intended to go in.

"Look, I know this is going to sound crazy," Sara started, lowering her voice. "But you know how the mayor died right in front of me." This was stretching the truth a little, as she'd spoken to his ghost and then found his body. "I need help with something... not exactly legal."

His expression shifted from flirtatious to concerned, his jaw tightening at the mention of the mayor. "Sara, what's going on?"

"I feel like I have some responsibility to help him find closure. Would you..." she hesitated, then rushed out, "help me break into City Hall?"

Joe jerked back like she'd slapped him. "What? Break into—" He lowered his voice to a harsh whisper. "Are you serious? Why would you even—" He glanced toward the door. "This is why you didn't want Emily or Mama to hear."

"I know it sounds insane, but I have a really good reason."

"It better be life or death, because they have security cameras. I installed them."

"Oh, great!" Sara smiled. "Then you can show me how to avoid them. The um..." She searched for the term. "...blind spots."

"How are you going to even get in? I don't have a set of keys, do you?"

She shook her head. "I don't need keys. I learned how to pick locks watching YouTube."

"Really? What else have you learned from watching YouTube?"

"Well, how to roast coffee, of course. Also, I've been getting into beatboxing lately." She started laying down the bass beat from DMX's 'Party Up,' her lips thumping out a deep rhythm while her tongue snapped out sharp snares. With a grin, she added, "It's surprisingly fun once you get the hang of it."

Joe stared at her for a long moment, then broke into a slow grin. "You're insane, woman. It took you a couple of days to reveal yourself, but you're a crazy person."

She grabbed him by his beefy arms. "Don't be like that, Joe. Trust me, something shady is happening in this town, and Mayor Hart was right in the center of it. I can pick the locks, and you can make sure we don't get caught by the cameras."

Joe gave her a very skeptical look. "To get around the cameras, wear a ski mask and generic clothes. I'd go for something black, less contrast. Now, you shouldn't need me."

"Well," Sara said, "could you also help me sneak out and give me a ride? Emily's staying here at night, and I think she's going to notice if I go out the front door and start my car."

"And when exactly were you thinking of doing this?" Joe asked.

"Tonight?" Sara said hopefully.

He shook his head. "I think this plan is crazy enough that you should sleep on it. Maybe sleep on it a couple of days."

He had a point. Even Sara had to admit she was going a little off the rails. She nodded. "Okay, I'll sleep on it, but if I decide we should do it, are you going to help?"

"Oh, for sure," he said. "A black man breaking into a city building at night? That's a surefire way to stay out of trouble. No chance that I end up full of bullet holes, while the white girl walks away unharmed."

Sara thought she could detect just a hint of sarcasm in that statement, but she decided to ignore it. "I'll call you tomorrow."

Chapter 7

Little Dress, Big Deceptions

The next morning, Sara woke up earlier than usual. As she made her way downstairs, the rich aroma of freshly brewed coffee greeted her. Emily was already up and had left a note on the counter: "Gone for a run."

Tom was again her spectral bodyguard for the day. He greeted her in the kitchen, and after some coffee and toast, they went upstairs to the spare room. The pile of stuff Ruby Mae had said was trash had been removed, but there were still two piles, one to keep, and one for Sara to sort through. However, she also noticed a box off to the side of the "keep" pile. It looked like more signs and tablecloths for the mediumship booth. Atop the box's contents sat a crystal ball. Sara flipped it over and read, "Proudly made in Shenzhen, China for Yoonbao Limited."

In the "sort through" pile, Sara found a curious item: an offer for the house from Kelly and Hart Realty. She remembered Dwain Hart's recent visit, which she had initially assumed was an opportunistic attempt to secure a desperation sale below market value after her grandma's death. However, the document revealed an aggressive offer made during the last harvest festival, indicating their interest in her grandma's house nearly a year prior.

She carried the box down to the garage, and she was setting it next to the canopy tent when Emily came jogging down the street. Seeing Sara in the garage, Emily ran up the driveway, stopping inside the garage door to check her progress on her Fitbit.

"How was your run?" Sara asked.

"Great. You're welcome to come with me if you ever want to."

Sara hesitated, giving it a moment's thought. A few years ago, she might have jumped at the chance for an early morning run. But these days, getting up before the sun just didn't appeal to her. She wasn't really a morning person anymore, and the prospect of jogging through the chilly dawn seemed more daunting than invigorating. The only thing she wanted to do that early in the morning was brew her first pot of coffee.

She realized she'd been spacing out, or wool-gathering as her grandma would have said. She shook her head. "I prefer to sleep in."

"Well, suit yourself. You need help carrying any more stuff down from upstairs?"

"Nah," Sara said, "This is all of it, I think—tent, signs, tablecloth, crystal ball. I still can't believe I'm doing this."

"Well, you never know," Emily said. "You might have fun. Besides, Adam and I will be working there too, rounding up drunks and directing traffic. It's pretty dull work, but the festival budget reimburses the county, and we get overtime. Speaking of overtime, are you doing anything around four this afternoon?"

"No." Sara had been thinking about casing City Hall a bit in anticipation of her break-in, but otherwise, her day was free. "Why?"

"The sheriff wanted me to stop by Mayor Hart's wake this afternoon. Sometimes we do that in a murder case. Usually, all the suspects are in one place, and someone might say something incriminating. I wondered if you want to come along."

Sara nodded. "Yes. That would be interesting."

Well, I'm going to go shower and go to work. See you later."

This left Sara to putter around for another hour to stay out of Emily's way. Yes, it was Sara's house, but Emily had an actual job to go to. Sara's only plan for today was to snoop around and see if she could discover anything about Mayor Hart's murder, and the wake would be the perfect opportunity. The more she learned about the man, the less she cared about him, but she had promised him she'd help.

Waiting for Emily to go to work, Sara went through all the stuff for the Harvest Festival one more time. She even did another pass through the spare room just in case she'd forgotten something. She didn't like to be under-prepared, and once she started doing the medium thing, she doubted she'd be able to get away.

After Emily left, Sara was feeling gross and dusty, so she took a shower. She was getting dressed when her phone rang. She looked at the screen and saw it was Brad calling. She almost sent him straight to voicemail. They both had lawyers to communicate for them —technically, she didn't have to take his calls anymore.

Still, something made her hesitate. What if it was important? Against her better judgment, she swiped to answer. "Hello, Brad."

"Hey, Sara, how's life treating you?" His voice was maddeningly casual, like they were old friends catching up.

"Well, Brad," She said, realizing she wasn't going to remain pleasant at all, "my husband turned out not to be the person I thought he was. He cheated on me and stole my life savings."

"I'm sorry about that, babe. But I had a friend who had just gone through a divorce herself, and she told me that I'd be a fool not to take control of the money. Besides, I figured you had that big house and your grandma's money."

Sara gritted her teeth, knowing the "friend" he was referring to was Kim, his boss with benefits. "Yeah, that's all in probate. I had to borrow money against the estate. I needed a court order to do it."

"But everything worked out in the end, right? That's great. I'm so happy to hear it."

Sara could barely believe what she was hearing. His logic was making her dizzy. "What the hell do you want, Brad?"

"Is the car working okay?"

"It's fine. It was... One of Grandma's old friends came over and fixed it for me, so at least I have transportation now."

"You know, I never wanted to hurt you, babe."

"That's odd. I was just thinking about how much I did want to hurt you."

He ignored her jab and continued, "I just wanted to protect myself. I still care about you, and it hurts that you're mad at me, considering all the good times we shared. Remember the Rockies? We rented that little cabin in Colorado, with the lake behind it. You looked so good in that little bikini."

Sara sighed. She didn't miss the vacations. She missed being able to trust Brad. She missed believing that, although he might seem a little abrasive, deep down he was kind. She could never believe that again. She realized he was still rambling on. "Is there a reason you called?" she asked, fighting her instinct to soften the question with politeness.

"I was just feeling nostalgic and wanted to hear your voice. I know what I did, the affair, was wrong. I know that now. And I understand why you needed this separation, but you know, things haven't been very easy for me, either. I feel like I've lost part of myself. I guess I never really realized how much I depended on you. Every morning, I wake up and make myself instant coffee, and I immediately think of how much I've lost." He sounded like he was practically on the verge of tears. "I'm trying to become a better person. I really am. I now realize that I cheated on you because of some deficiency in my character, and I'm going to have to work on myself to become a better person."

Sara realized he was trying to guilt trip her. However, his sob story about instant coffee had greatly improved her mood. Finally, he paused for a second.

"And your point?" she asked, trying her best to keep the snark dialed down—although honestly, the Academy Awards would not be honoring her for the attempt.

"Well, I hate to bother you right now. I'm sure that with all that's happened over the last week—"

Sara laughed at him. He didn't even know the half of it. She could talk to dead people, she'd found a murdered guy, and she had two guys kind of fighting over her. She even had a cool roommate, even if that turned out to be a temporary situation.

Brad ignored her outburst and continued. "...but I need you to call off the dogs."

"What?" Sara's mind had started to wander a bit, and she wasn't sure where all the dog talk was coming from.

"This lawyer of yours, Martin Settler, has frozen my accounts. I need him to back off a bit. The bank says I can't touch my money because it's under judicial review, and my lawyer won't help me because I can't pay my bill. I can't pay any of my bills."

"Wait," Sara said, shaking her head. "You, the guy who stole my money, is calling to ask for mercy because I am acting in my own interest in a completely legal way?"

"Please, babe. I'm in a real bind."

Sara felt the last of her reflexive niceness evaporate. "No, Brad. Cheating was unforgivable, but then you stole my money on top of that, so if you think I'm going to suffer any more of your shit with a smile now that we're separated, you're in for some serious fucking disappointment."

"But Sara, I—"

"I have to go, Brad. Goodbye." She hung up.

Sara closed her eyes and sat in silence for a moment. She'd learned a lot of lessons in the past week, but the most important one was never to trust Brad again. She thought about how they'd once talked about having children and how happy she was that they hadn't done anything that would tie her to him for decades to come.

She opened up her contacts, selected his name and her thumb hovered over the delete button. Despite the catharsis that might have offered, she was too pragmatic. After all, he would be calling her again, and she wanted to be able to screen those calls. Instead, she hit the edit button and changed his name to Dumbass Mc-Fuckface.

After her conversation with Brad, Sara lost a lot of her motivation. She decided to treat herself to a nice lunch, so she drove to Swisher and tried out their coffee shop. It was top-notch, both the coffee and the menu. It made her a bit worried that if she did open a coffee shop, she would have serious competition less than ten miles away.

After she ate, she struck up a nice conversation with the owner about brewing coffee, and before she knew it, it was time to go back to Downcastle and get ready for the wake.

When she got home, she realized she should have driven into Cedar Rapids and bought some nice clothes. Or possibly she could have negotiated a little with Brad in exchange for her wardrobe. She still only had a handful of outfits and whatever she found in Grandma's closet.

Sara was rummaging deep in Grandma's closet and listening to one of Tom's stories about frontier farming when Emily got home. She hadn't been having much luck—Grandma had owned plenty of black clothes, but none quite right for a wake.

Emily unbuckled her gun belt and hung it on Grandma's headboard. "Hey, Sara, what's up?"

"Looking for a wake-worthy outfit. When I packed up my stuff in Des Moines, I leaned a little more utilitarian than dressy. If I want to go to a wake, I need to find something nice."

Emily waded in behind her. "What about this one?" She pulled out Grandma's little black dress.

Sara sighed. "Yeah, I saw that one. Do you think it's appropriate to wear?"

"Well, it's black." Emily thought for a moment. "Maybe you should try it on, and we'll see how it fits."

Without a second thought, Sara stripped down. Tom, who had been hovering nearby, suddenly stiffened and spun around so fast he nearly lost his spectral balance. "Uh, I—I think Emily's got this covered," he stammered, his voice cracking with old-fashioned propriety. He hesitated for a moment longer, then vanished with a flustered, "I'll just... be over... somewhere else."

Sliding the dress on, Sara said, "I'm not sure I'm comfortable with this." Even in her eighties, Grandma had been a little flamboyant for Sara's taste, and her modesty was screaming this dress was all wrong, the hem was too short, and the neckline was too plunging. The dress fit so snugly she felt like one wrong move might accidentally kick off a burlesque show. "I look like I'm headed to a cocktail party, not a wake."

"I think you look spectacular," Emily said. She bit her lip. "It does ride up just a little on your hips." Emily hesitated for a moment, reached out to Sara's hips, and tugged the dress down about an inch. "You'll have to keep an eye on that." She glanced at Sara's chest. "But don't tug too hard, or you'll pop out the top."

Sara felt her cheeks warm. She was self-conscious enough in the tiny dress, but Emily's close and frank assessment made her feel even more naked.

"Don't worry about wearing it to the wake, though, being overdressed is probably better than showing up in jeans. Plus, everyone knows you fled your unfaithful husband. They'll understand you're working with limited options. Just be careful when you sit down."

Sara nodded. "That's fair enough. Now, for the hard part, help me find a pair of shoes that look good with the dress and fit. Grandma ran half a size smaller than me."

They rushed to get ready, as Emily was supposed to be there for work. Despite their best efforts, they arrived at the wake half an hour behind schedule. Sara couldn't tell which emotion was stronger: confidence that their efforts had paid off and she looked great, self-consciousness about how much skin she was showing, or embarrassment that she was dressed like this at a wake.

The first person to approach them was Iris Pilkington. "Sara! I appreciate you coming. Whenever we lose such an esteemed leader, it hurts us all. Mayor Hart's death leaves a hole in our community."

Sara nodded. "Oh, I know."

"Are you all ready for the big event?"

Sara nodded, not having to ask to know the big event she was talking about would be the Harvest Festival and not the funeral. "Of course. I've sorted through Grandma's things and found everything I need. I even have the cash box so I can make change."

"Oh, dear. You didn't happen to find a credit card reader, did you?"

Sara shook her head. "No, I didn't."

"We've really been pushing the attractions to accept more forms of payment, but your grandmother was a holdout. Most of them are already taking Apple

Pay and Venmo. Well, it's something to remember for next year."

"Of course," Sara said, knowing that she'd never remember anything like that in a year, as she was currently incapable of planning beyond next week. Of course, if she were still living in Downcastle in a year, Iris would no doubt remind her to get a reader, so there was no worry.

Next, she exchanged greetings with a couple of neighbors and other people she'd seen at Grandma's funeral. Downcastle was small enough that if you went to two funerals in a row, you were going to see a few of the same people.

Fitzgerald Bauer walked up to her, his steps slightly unsteady. Since it was four in the afternoon, Fitzy was already pretty drunk, and because of that, Sara already knew he was going to comment on the dress.

"How are you doing Sara?" his breath carried the smell of cheap liquor. "That's a spectacular dress. Looks like something your grandma might have worn. I appreciate a woman willing to show off her assets. Speaking of which, who's your friend?"

Sara had been so preoccupied with her own outfit that she hadn't given Emily's a second thought. Now, as she took a closer look, she couldn't see how Emily was showing off *anything.* Black slacks and a tailored blazer over a crisp white shirt—it practically screamed *certified sexual harassment trainer.* It would've been downright androgynous if not for the undeniably curvy blonde beneath the gender-neutral layers.

"This is Emily," Sara said. "Emily, this is Fitzgerald Bauer, he owns the house next to Adam." She thought about throwing out descriptions like "local character" or "town drunk," but she wasn't sure which term Fitzy might take offense at versus what he might be proud of.

"You two are quite an attractive pair." He lowered the volume of his voice a little. "Are you two, you know, a lesbian couple?"

Sara shook her head. "No, Fitzy. We're just friends."

He nodded. "I was just checking. You can never tell with you young people, all same sex couples and changing your pronouns."

"Emily is just staying with me for a few days. She's a deputy."

Fitzy straightened up and saluted. "Begging your pardon, officer." He lowered his voice again. "Just for the record, I assure you I walked here." This was reasonable enough as the funeral home was only six blocks away. "By the way, do you know if this wake has an open bar?"

"I have no idea." Sara shrugged, and she immediately regretted it when she saw Fitzy's eyes drop to her chest. She reached up to somewhat cover herself, on the pretense of checking on her pendant.

"That's an interesting piece of jewelry," Fitzy said, reaching for it.

Before he could get his hands to her chest, Sara held it out for him to examine. "It's a family heirloom. They say it hexes anyone who tries to see down the dress of the woman who wears it."

Fitzy looked her in the eye for the first time today, "How bad is this curse?"

Before Sara could formulate an answer, Emily put her hand on Sara's arm. "If you'll excuse us, Fitzy, I just spotted Dwain Hart, and I think we should pay our respects."

Dwain was standing at the front of the funeral home, next to the coffin, but far enough away that he wouldn't have to speak to everyone who approached it. Fortunately, today, he had toned down the body spray.

"Dwain," Sara said, "Do you remember me, Sara Jenkins? We met last week. You made an offer on my grandma's house."

Dwain furrowed his brow, a hint of recognition flickering. "I make a lot of offers—it's part of the job —but, yes, I remember now." He paused, his gaze drifting toward the coffin before he met her eyes again. "Weren't you the one who found my dad?" His voice softened slightly. "I'm sorry—I've been a bit out of sorts since...you know."

Sara nodded, trying to look sympathetic. "Yes. I'm sorry for your loss, Dwain."

"Yeah. It's a bit of a shock. I mean, Dad always was there for me. People keep saying that life goes on, but everything seems so fucked up."

"How so?" Sara asked.

He lowered his voice as if wary of eavesdroppers. "Well, like there's nothing in that coffin. The Sheriff says he's holding the body as evidence and there's an ongoing investigation, whatever that means. You were there. Can you tell me if anything was odd?"

"Well," Sara began cautiously, "did they mention anything to you about—"

Emily interrupted gently, "They withhold certain details deliberately. It helps them identify if someone knows more than they should."

Dwain's brow furrowed deeper, and he exhaled slowly. "But this is Downcastle. Everybody here knows something they're not supposed to."

"I think," Sara explained, "Emily means that if anyone knows specific details about the murder, details they shouldn't know, it could indicate their involvement. That's what the sheriff is looking for—a way to find potential suspects."

He pondered this for a moment, then nodded. "I suppose that makes sense."

"Speaking of your father," Sara said more softly, changing the subject with care, "do you have any theories about why he might have been targeted?"

"Maybe," Dwain replied cautiously, "but if I share that, doesn't it mean I'm telling you things you shouldn't know?"

"No," Emily clarified, "that's only true for direct details from the crime scene. It's okay to discuss your thoughts or suspicions about other aspects."

Dwain nodded slowly, as if he was trying to understand and hoped he'd catch up when the nod was over. "Okay. I think I've got that. So, I could tell you about the land deal he was—"

A Chinese woman tapped him one the arm. "Excuse me, ladies," she said with just the trace of an accent. "I need to borrow Dwain for a moment."

The first thing Sara noticed was the woman was also wearing a little black dress, although she was gorgeous and looked much more comfortable in hers than Sara felt. The next thing Sara noticed was a very large, Chinese man standing behind her. He reached past them and placed a meaty hand on Dwain's shoulder, pulling him away.

Dwain was led a small distance away, where Sara watched him engage in a quite heated conversation with the Chinese woman while the big man loomed behind her, personifying the consequences of disappointing her.

He returned a few moments later, looking a little shocked. "It was so nice talking to you, but I think I need to spend more time with my other guests." It sounded very rehearsed considering the short amount of time he'd been away.

Sara leaned in. "Maybe we can talk more about this later? Somewhere private?" she suggested softly.

This is where most men might have tried to steal a look down her dress. Dwain's eyes flickered to the Chinese couple. He shook his head vehemently. "I don't think so. I've been so busy with the arrangements." He walked away without saying anything more.

Sara turned to Emily. "What was that all about?"

"Beats me," Emily said, but there's definitely more going on here than just the murder of a small-town mayor."

Sara looked over to the Chinese couple and saw they were carefully watching Dwain. She wondered how they connected to Mayor Hart. "I think we found some new suspects, at least."

"Yeah. I don't think that couple is from Hawthorne County."

Sara looked over to the coffin, which according to Dwain, was empty. However, it seemed that Dwain was wrong. Mayor Hart's ghost stood behind the coffin.

"I'm going to go up and pay my respects," Sara explained to Emily, hoping to satisfy any curiosity about her moving toward the coffin. Like everyone else at a visitation, she'd have a moment of privacy as others kept their respectful distance.

As she approached the former mayor, Sara focused on him. He made eye contact with her, which seemed good. She got close enough to lean across the coffin and said, "Hello, Mayor Hart."

"Sara, so nice to see you." A hint of sarcasm entered his voice. "A pity about the circumstances, though. However, if anyone had told me I'd have to die to get to see you in that dress, I might have considered it earlier. You should show some skin more often. Very scandalous for a funeral. Your trollop of a grandmother would approve, no doubt."

"Um, it's Grandma's dress." She tried not to look disgusted at his demeanor. "You two didn't... you know?"

"Sadly, no. Not for a lack of trying on my part, however."

Well, at least Grandma had some taste. "Do you have anything to tell me about your murder?"

He shook his astral head. "Nothing more than I told you last time. Someone hit me from behind, and then I was dead."

"According to my grandma," Sara said, "spirits often are unable to come back right away. How can you be here speaking to me?"

"Well," he said, his old snootiness returning, "it's nice to know your grandma doesn't know everything. I was told I could come to the wake on what you might call a 'day pass.' I've already arranged one for the funeral too."

"I don't suppose you'd tell me what the Chinese contingent is doing here?"

"I believe that's none of your business. Let me assure you that they were quite satisfied with my performance."

The way he lingered over that last word made Sara's skin crawl. Despite her earlier desire to question him, she was suddenly desperate to change the subject. "Are you sure there's nothing else you can tell me about your murder?"

Mayor Hart shrugged, a gesture that appeared oddly out of place on a ghostly form. "Afraid not, dear. My departure was rather... abrupt." His eyes traveled down her body in a way that made her wish ghosts could be pepper-sprayed. "You do look stunning in that dress, though. Let me have just a little feel." He jumped across the coffin, his hands extended toward her breasts.

Sara instinctively shoved him away, screaming, "Don't you fucking touch me!" In her panic, she forgot that Hart was non-corporeal and instead pushed over the coffin with a loud crash. As it toppled, her heel caught in the carpet, sending her sprawling backward. It was pure instinct and adrenaline. Only when she found herself lying on her back did she realize that Hart hadn't been able to touch her.

The old man stood above her, laughing his ass off. "Oh, you should have seen your face. Good luck solving my murder." Then he disappeared.

Emily hurried over and helped her sit up. "Are you okay?" She also rearranged the little black dress a bit in a way that suggested Sara had at least shown a few people more than she had intended.

"Um, yeah. I'm fine. I... um... I have no explanation for what just happened. Can we just leave?"

"Yeah." Emily helped her to her feet and started to guide her out the door.

Sara tried to avoid eye contact and keep her head down, but when they reached the door, Iris Pilkington stepped into their path.

Iris shook her head at them. "I appreciate the enthusiasm for promoting your attraction, Sara, but this is not the appropriate time or method for advertising your talents, not when we've lost such an esteemed leader. Something that hurts us all and leaves a hole in our community."

Sara wanted to explain that she wasn't performing a publicity stunt, but she lacked the words to describe her actions, especially in front of Emily, who still thought of her mediumship as a carnival trick. Finally, she said, "You're right, Iris. I'm sorry." With that, she let Emily lead her out of the funeral home.

Chapter 8

Breaking, Burglary, and Municipal Mysteries

When Sara went to bed, she set an alarm for half past midnight and then tucked her phone under her pillow to muffle the speaker. She needn't have bothered; nerves kept her awake. Searching the mayor's office had seemed like a good idea in theory, but now that it was about to happen, she felt like she might throw up.

Still, someone had brought murder to Downcastle —her Downcastle—and that wasn't acceptable. Besides, she was good at puzzles, and this was just a puzzle with higher stakes. And possibly jail time. With that justification, she was finally able to get a couple of hours sleep.

The alarm went off, and Sara started putting on her outfit: black tennis shoes, black jeans, and a black shirt. All the clothes were Grandma's, and for once, Sara was glad Grandma had gone through her My Chemical Romance phase. She probably should have worn some of the emo clothes to the wake, but jeans and a t-shirt hadn't seemed respectful. She even found a black ski mask. After cleaning out the closets with Ruby Mae and rummaging through Grandma's wardrobe multiple times, the winter stuff was easy to find.

As she was dressing, Grandma's ghost materialized beside her, arms crossed. "If you're really going to carry through with this foolishness, then I'm coming along to help," she declared, a mixture of concern and exasperation in her voice.

Sara paused, glancing at her grandmother. "You're not going to try to talk me out of it?"

Grandma sighed, her ghostly form flickering slightly. "You're stubborn, just like me. But someone's got to keep an eye on you. Besides," she added with a wry smile, "breaking into City Hall sounds like fun."

Sara nodded. "I'm sure we can use your help. Like, you can stick your head through the door of a safe, right?"

Grandma nodded. "I can. I can't see anything inside though, no light."

Thinking about that for a moment, Sara said, "But how does that work? You don't even have eyeballs."

"I don't know." Grandma shrugged. "I don't make the rules."

Sara chuckled despite her nerves. "Fine, you can be the lookout.

At twelve-thirty, she walked down the hall. Sara held her breath as she tiptoed past Emily's door. She tried to step lightly, but the old wooden floor groaned like it was feeling its age. She prayed Emily would stay asleep, but luck wasn't on her side.

The bedroom door creaked open. "Everything alright?" Emily asked, her voice too sharp for someone just waking up. She stood in the doorway fully dressed, like she'd been expecting an assassin rather than Sara.

Sara nodded. Her mind searched for an excuse to be fully dressed and sneaking around. "I'm fine. I was just going to go for a late-night walk."

"Wait a minute," Emily said. "I'll throw on some shoes."

"No!" Sara's panicked voice came out too fast, too loud. She cringed. "I mean... it's late. You should go back to sleep. No need to come with me."

Emily crossed her arms, her expression disapproving. "Yes, I do. That is literally why I'm staying here—to protect you. So please explain why you are sneaking out of your own house in all black."

Sara's mind raced, every excuse sounding worse than the last. "Actually, I'm meeting Joe. You know... sort of a... late-night booty call." She forced a smile. "He's picking me up downstairs."

"That still doesn't explain why you're sneaking around dressed in black."

Sara groaned. "You know how this town is. I'd rather not have everyone at church on Sunday talking about me. I'm not even officially divorced yet." She put her fingers on her forehead, burying her face behind her black gloves. "So, Joe suggested ninja roleplay, and I'm already regretting saying yes. But have you seen him wear a t-shirt? My judgment was seriously impaired."

Emily snorted. "Girl, I get it. Those arms, the small-town gossip... Let's be real. I'm here as a precaution, but I'm not Secret Service. I'm just keeping an eye out for you when I'm off duty and patrolling the crooked finger more than it's ever been patrolled before. Just check in occasionally with a text. And maybe don't skulk around like a cat burglar—you're terrible at it."

As Emily's door clicked shut, Sara exhaled, leaning against the wall for a second. That was way too close.

Sara met Joe outside. "So... we're hooking up, by the way."

"We are?" Joe raised an eyebrow, surprised but far from upset.

"Emily caught me sneaking out. I told her it was a booty call."

Joe nodded thoughtfully. "Sounds plausible."

For a long moment, Sara seriously considered giving up on City Hall and just going along with the cover story. It was amazing how good he could look in black jeans and a black t-shirt.

He nodded and motioned for her to follow. They walked two blocks through the alleys to where Joe had parked his truck. Then he drove to a small stand of trees across the street from the back of the city building. "This way the cameras on the outside of the building won't pick up my truck. We wouldn't want to go through all of this just to show my license plate to the camera." Sara thought he had a valid point. He also had his company name written on the door in even larger letters, but she didn't think it was necessary to point that out.

Sara decided to give Joe an out. "Look, I know this wasn't your idea. If you want to bail, or just wait here to be my getaway driver, I'll understand. I can't ask you to do this."

Joe sighed. "I could think of a few better ways to spend an evening. But I was foolish enough to say yes, and if I back out at this point and something happens to you, I feel like your grandma would come back and haunt me."

She nodded. "Yeah. I think you're probably right."

Sitting behind them in the crew cab, Grandma said, "You bet your ass I would."

Sara pulled the ski mask from her pocket. "I guess it's time to pull these on. Thankfully, I found a box of Grandma's winter gear in the spare room. One of these days, I'm going to have to go shopping for some of my own clothes. I packed in a hurry, and I wasn't in the best frame of mind."

"Are you still having car trouble? I could drive you into Iowa City."

The car was actually running better now than when she'd first bought it, so Sara lied. "I took my car out today, but I'm a little nervous about long trips. I'd really appreciate that."

"Cool," he said, as they crossed the street to the City Hall. "Maybe we could go tomorrow. I'm just finishing up a project. I'll get the Fincher brothers started on the trim carpentry and pick you up around nine."

"Hrmm. Can we make it eleven?"

"Yeah, we can do that. And the Finchers could use the extra supervision anyway."

They arrived at the back entrance, a steel security door set into the brick facade with a tiny security light and camera at the top. Sara got down on her knees, set the little wallet with all her lockpicks in it on the ground. She chose a tension wrench and a wave rake and went to work on the lock.

She turned to Joe and found herself at eye level with his crotch. Not a bad place to be, but definitely not the time. She put her hand on his thigh, well outside any sensitive areas, and pushed him back a step. "Just a little more space, please. I think this will take a minute. This lock doesn't want to bulge... I mean budge."

Grandma snickered at their position. "Oh, honey, I bet Joe's got just the tool to open up your lock."

Her face heating to about a thousand degrees, Sara turned back to the lock, put tension on the cylinder, and ran the wave rake back and forth a couple more times. Again, the lock failed to open.

"Um," Sara said. "I think one of the last couple of pins is sticking." Without removing the tension, she set down her wave rake and pulled a hook tool from the wallet. She inserted it as far as she could and pushed up hard. There was a click, and the lock opened. Sara let out a huge breath she hadn't known she was holding. "See, no problem."

Sara's heart thudded in her chest as she eased the door open, the hinges groaning like nails on a chalkboard. Her nerves were so tight she half-expected the sheriff to be waiting with a shotgun aimed at her head. But the corridor beyond was empty, dimly lit by the faint glow of an exit sign. It wasn't surprising, though. After midnight in Downcastle, nothing ever happened —and if it did, there wasn't anyone awake to witness it.

Joe pointed to a door right beside them and whispered, "Here's the mayor's office." Which made sense, as the mayor would have a corner office, and the building wasn't that big.

The door was locked, but it was a much easier lock to open than the one outside. Sara hit it with her wave rake a couple of times and it popped right open. "You go for the cabinets," Sara said. "I'll check out the desk."

"What specifically are we looking for?" Joe asked.

"I don't know." Sara shrugged. "Incriminating stuff."

"I don't know." Joe shook his head. "The woman broke in for 'I don't know.'"

There was a computer on the desk. Sara hit the spacebar, but when the screen came up demanding a password, she knew she was out of luck. Even if she took the entire computer, she'd have to take it to a specialist. Sara decided to keep her mind open about it. If she didn't find anything else, she couldn't exactly take it to Best Buy, but she bet her cousin Jennifer could do something with it.

She opened the center top drawer and found totally ordinary desk items, pens, pencils, notebooks, rubber bands, and other things like that. She looked at the notebooks, but they mostly seemed to be notes from city council meetings. The drawer on the left contained a box of cigars and a handful of USB drives. She pocketed the drives just in case they might have something important on them.

The middle drawer on the left seemed to be stuffed with brochures for retirement communities in South America. Each one was paired with a flyer advertising a nearby brothel catering to rich, older Americans. The girls in those ads looked like human trafficking victims, which made Sara want to vomit. If she did catch the murderer, should she turn them in—or give them a medal?

The bottom drawer was locked, so she used her picks, and it came unlocked in just a second, not being designed for high security. She'd thought the brothel pamphlets had been the weirdest thing she would find, but inside the bottom drawer was a stack of Playboy magazines from the 1970s. On some of the pages, Hart had put Post-It Notes. She put them back without reading the notes. Whatever was written on them, she was sure that 3M would not approve of their product being put to the purpose.

In the top right drawer—also locked—Hart kept a gun and some little baggies of white powder, neither of which Sara touched. Artificial sweeteners, no doubt. Yeah, right.

She popped the lock on the bottom, right drawer and found a large collection of folders, each with a name and address. She found one with her grandma's name, the address of the house, and the number 47. She opened it, and inside, there were detailed plans of the house and where it sat on the city map. One page showed a list of offering prices for the property, there was a low and high, but there were also stages, Stage 2 through Stage 4, each with a high and low that went progressively higher.

"I found something," she said to Joe.

"Good, because I haven't found anything. The file cabinet just has council records and details about city utilities. The bookshelves just have books. And other than the one over here, which is all self-help books about how to be a good manager and how to run a city on a budget, I'm pretty sure he just bought a collection of cheap, leather-bound classics so it looked like the shelves weren't empty."

"Look here,' Sara passed the folder over to him. "It's information about buying my grandma's house. This whole desk drawer is full of them. There must be a file for every residence in town. Downcastle isn't that big."

Joe pointed. "What's that big one in the back?"

Sara pulled the folder. "The label says Yoonbao."

"You mean like that company that's always selling things on Facebook?"

Sara shrugged. "Yeah. I guess." She opened the folder. The first thing inside was a huge map of Downcastle. Every single property had a number. Sara found Grandma's house on the map, and the lot was numbered 47.

She traced the planned development with her finger. Everything in town was marked for replacement except two properties—Jennifer and Nick's place out past the edge of town, and oddly enough, that car wash Hart had been so insistent she buy.

"What the actual fuck?" Sara asked. "Is Yoonbao trying to buy Downcastle?"

Sara looked through the rest of the folder, but all she found were two thick contracts. The first one was in English, but other than the title, "General Power of Attorney for Property in Hawthorne County, Iowa" she couldn't read legalese well enough to figure out what it stated. She flipped to the last page, and there were five signatures, including Michael Hart, Dwain Hart, two that looked like they were signed in Chinese characters, and Martin Settler, who had signed as a witness.

"Well," Sara said. "I guess this is what we came to find out." She took pictures of the first twenty pages and last page of the English version of the document with her phone and started putting things back.

"You're not going to take it with us?" Joe asked.

"Oh, I am, but I'm going to get some pictures uploaded to the cloud just in case."

When her pictures were taken, she stuffed everything into the folder, along with the four stages of estimates for her grandma's house.

"Hey!" Grandma's voice rang through the room like a gunshot. "The Sheriff's outside, and the receptionist's unlocking the front door!"

Sara squeaked, dropping the Yoonbao folder. Contracts spilled across the floor like a bad omen.

Her stomach knotted in fear. "We have to go— now!" She dropped to her knees, frantically stuffing the papers back into the thick folder.

Joe's voice was calm, too calm. "What's going on?"

"Just trust me!" Sara shot to her feet, tucking the folder under her arm. "Time to move!"

They rushed through the office door and Sara stopped at the steel security door. There was no window to see if someone was waiting outside. Normally, Sara would have just had to risk it. Here, she had options, but there was one downside to them. She looked at Joe, sighed, and asked. "Is there anyone waiting to grab us behind this door?"

"How should I know?" Joe asked.

Grandma popped through the door and came back a moment later. "The coast is clear. Go!"

Sara grabbed Joe's hand. "Come on." She pushed the door open and dragged him behind her. Or at least she pulled at his arm for three seconds until he figured out what they were doing, and he started to run, pulling her behind him. As they approached the trees, Sara could see the red and blue lights of the Sheriff's SUV bouncing off the budding branches.

As they got in the truck, Sara held her breath, hoping the rumble of the big engine wouldn't echo too loudly in the quiet night around City Hall. Despite the danger, they couldn't just leave Joe's truck parked near a crime scene, so she stayed quiet as he pushed the start button and the truck growled to life. The moment the engine roared, Joe hit the accelerator, and they sped the half mile to their alleyway parking spot, Sara's heart racing with each passing second.

After parking, they jogged back to the house, the adrenaline still pumping through their veins. Sara had barely caught her breath when Joe grabbed her hand, pulling her up the steps to the front porch. They shared a quick, relieved glance, like two kids who'd just pulled off the ultimate prank.

"I think we're home free," Joe said, a mix of excitement and disbelief in his voice. Sara nodded, a nervous laugh escaping her.

"Yeah, that was... something else."

Without thinking, she leaned in and kissed him—a brief but sweet, conspiratorial kiss that lingered longer than she'd intended. The thrill of their escapade seemed to spark between them. They were still standing there, caught in the moment, when Emily's voice cut through the night air.

"If you're done with your clandestine rendezvous, you can come in and sit down," she said dryly, stepping out onto the porch. "The sheriff is on his way."

Sara groaned, leaning her forehead on Joe's chest. "Let me guess—not a social call, past midnight on a weekday?"

"Funny you should mention that," Emily's tone was desert-dry. "Inside. Both of you."

As Emily disappeared inside, Sara and Joe shared a final glance. Their excitement turned to dread.

Sara turned to Joe. "Are you sure you want to come in?"

He shrugged. "I went along with your insanity, didn't I? I'm not sure if Mom would chew me out more for helping you or for running away. Besides, I think Emily can find me if she wants to."

Sara nodded. "Fair point."

They walked inside and sat down on the couch. Emily sat on the wooden dining room chair that Sara had carried into the room earlier. Probably because Emily was wearing her uniform and equipment belt, and there was no room in Grandma's soft, comfy chairs for the nightstick and holster. Sara was hoping she'd put those on more for purposes of intimidation, and she was not planning to use any of that gear, especially the handcuffs.

Grandma came in and waited in the corner of the room. "It's times like this, I wish I could touch people," she said. When Sara didn't reply, she said, "Don't worry, sweetie. I bet Martin can get you off on an insanity defense." She made her thinking face, screwing up her lips. "Then again, defending you for this might be a conflict of interest, since you stole paperwork from his clients."

At this point, Sara just wanted Grandma to shut up for two seconds, as she was not being helpful. She turned to Emily, and said, "So what now?"

Emily gave her a hard look. "You might as well wait, because Sheriff Robinson is going to be here in about fifteen minutes." It was going to be a long fifteen minutes.

After Emily was done, Grandma said, "Sure, just ignore your poor, dead grandma, who took you in when you were orphaned without any thought of her own wellbeing, who gave up being able to entertain gentleman callers, who made you her sole beneficiary so you could be independent and not rely on your adulterous husband."

"Grandma!" Sara yelled. Then she clamped her hand over her mouth. "Um... Sorry about that." She hovered on the edge of trying to make an excuse or going for the insanity thing. But then she remembered watching *One Flew Over the Cuckoo's Nest* and thought the better of it. "I was just nervous, and I was imagining what Grandma might say if she was here. I guess my imagination got the better of me."

Emily raised an eyebrow. "Is this some sort of insanity plea thing?"

"No." Sara shook her head for emphasis, as her voice didn't sound so sure.

"If you want to go for insanity, beatbox for her," Joe whispered.

As she had guessed, the next fifteen minutes seemed to stretch to eternity. She felt like she should say something, maybe apologize to Emily. But she wasn't sure what to say, so she just remained silent, which she supposed was her right.

The doorbell rang.

Emily stood. "I'll go and get that, if you two will sit still." She used a normal voice, but the way in which she stressed "sit still" made it clear that any shenanigans would be met with harsh consequences. Sara realized that her friendly roommate Emily was gone. This was the hard-edged Emily who had questioned her after she found the body.

Sara was beginning to feel a little nervous. Maybe she could get Nick and Jen to provide her with a lawyer if Martin couldn't take the case. She just had to get through the next moments without incriminating herself, which meant she shouldn't say anything.

Sheriff Robinson, who had seemed so nice the other day, looked extremely displeased. He unbuckled his gun belt and set it on the floor next to him before settling into one of the comfy chairs. "You know," he said with gravitas, "I don't like getting out of my bed to drive the entire length of the county in the middle of the night."

Despite Sara thinking very hard about not saying anything incriminating, or in fact, anything at all, her mouth seemed to have different plans. "Yeah, how did you get here so fast?"

"You've got to remember," Robinson said, "this is a small town, and from what I can tell, about thirty years behind when it comes to racial tolerance."

163

Joe snorted. "Probably more like seventy."

"So, when my dispatcher woke me up and said that she was getting reports from Downcastle, that there was a black man walking around behind their house, that there was a black man abducting a white woman, and that there were two black men stealing a truck out of the alley in the middle of the night, I decided to drive over here and check things out before someone decided to put together a lynch mob."

For the life of her, Sara didn't know how she was mistaken for a black man, but she was equally amazed that there were three people awake after midnight in the two blocks between her house and where Joe had parked his truck.

The sheriff looked back and forth between them. "Before I say anything else, do either one of you wish to make a statement?"

"That depends," Joe said. "Are we under arrest or are we being detained?"

Sighing, the sheriff said, "You know, I never heard those questions before everyone got the Internet. Now everyone's a legal expert. For the record, you are currently being detained. I'll decide about arresting you based on how forthcoming you want to be. But look on the bright side, if I do end up arresting you, I have better food in my cells than what Marge has over at that diner."

Of course, a Salisbury steak frozen dinner was better than anything at the diner. For the moment, Sara nodded. She saw Joe do the same.

Sara asked, "Am I going to need a lawyer?"

"You have the right to one, obviously. We've all heard it on the TV cop shows. However, if you want Martin Settler, you're going to have to wait until tomorrow. He takes his hearing aids out at night, and anything short of the trumpet that fell Jericho will not wake that man until his border collie gets him up for walkies."

Sara contemplated this for a moment. She was trying to think of something to say when the sheriff began speaking again.

"All right then, let me also say this, I can't just let everybody break into an office anytime they think something suspicious is going on. If people went breaking into other people's properties every time they thought something was going on in this town, I'd never get any sleep at all. You both got that?"

They nodded.

He leaned back in the comfy chair like he was preparing to listen to a story. "So, tell me what you found."

"What?" Sara said in total surprise.

"Well," he said, "you obviously broke into Downcastle City Hall. I looked at the video, two people wearing ski masks—some call them balaclavas—went through the mayor's office and took a folder. You two are currently wearing all black, there's a ski mask sticking out of your pocket, Sara, and there's a big, fat file folder sitting between you on the couch. Now, I'm no big city detective, and I only won my last election by a few dozen votes, but I think I have cracked the case of the City Hall Bandits."

Joe shrugged. "We might as well show him what we have."

Sara glanced at Grandma, who nodded her approval. Then she put the folder on the coffee table. "So, this is what I think the mayor was up to." She opened the folder and spread out the map. "He was trying to buy up the whole town on behalf of Yoonbao, the Chinese retailer. They plan to turn it into some kind of giant warehouse or factory or something."

The sheriff thought about this for a minute. "And are they using illegal means to obtain this property?"

Joe shook his head. "Nah, it looks like they're planning to pay above the market rate."

"But," the sheriff said, "what if they still don't want to sell?"

Joe took out the four-stage plan for Grandma's house. "If you don't sell right away, they keep upping the offer. If you hold out to the very end, they're planning to offer almost three times what the properties are worth. Honestly, I wouldn't hold out that long myself, I mean, you'd just have to sit in a town with fewer and fewer people as Yoonbao started to build around you."

"But why?" Sheriff Robinson asked. "Why would they want to dismantle a small town and put an industrial facility?"

"Funny you ask," Joe said, "because I've been thinking about this a little bit as Sara was planning to turn this house into a coffee shop. Renovations like that aren't very practical for several reasons, like OSHA regulations and grease traps, but say you wanted to tear down the house and rebuild, you'd still have electrical service, municipal sewer and water lines, even a street made to carry the weight of a loaded delivery truck. All these costs add up, and if you're Yoonbao, you don't want to build that infrastructure yourself, or deal with a city that's going to hassle you about every little thing."

Nodding, the sheriff said, "But if you controlled the whole town, because you bought it, you could do whatever you wanted."

"You got it," Joe said. "And Mayor Hart just tapped into the city's reserves to do some major upgrades. He built up the main streets, he did some much-needed repair to the sewage lines and the treatment plant, and he convinced the co-op to upgrade the electrical service."

Sara remembered the newspaper clipping. "The county is upgrading the road all the way to the airport, four lanes."

Joe nodded. "All he did was make the town nicer so Yoonbao could move in quicker."

Sheriff Robinson shrugged. "Well, it's a shame to see a small town fall apart, but as you said, there's nothing illegal here."

Sara pointed at the sheriff. "Still, I thought maybe someone might have found out about it and wanted to murder Hart."

Sheriff Robinson let out a huge yawn. "I'm sorry, I'm just not seeing it. We can look into it more deeply, but I think this is a dead end. I mean, how many people love Downcastle more than they love selling their house for double the market rate?" He turned to Sara. "So, was that all you stole from City Hall?"

Sara hesitated, thinking about keeping the rest hidden, but they could have been having this conversation behind bars. She reached into her pocket and held out half a dozen thumb drives.

Sheriff Robinson scowled as he glanced at the drives, clearly not at ease with anything more complex than his revolver.

Emily took them, turning one over in her hand. "These need to be logged into evidence." She paused, then added carefully, "Of course, given our department's limited resources, it might take me a day or so to process them properly. Especially since I'm off duty tomorrow."

Sara nodded, catching her meaning. They'd have a day to go over the information on those drives, and if they were password-protected or something, her cousin Jennifer and her husband could help.

He nodded. "You keep those drives for me, and make sure they get logged in the moment you start your next shift." He gave her a serious look. "Be it on your head, Deputy."

Emily swallowed and nodded as if she wasn't used to hearing this dire a warning from her supervisor.

Sheriff Robinson's serious gaze lingered for a heartbeat longer. Then he slapped his thighs and stood up. "Welp, I don't know about all of you, but I, for one, am going back to bed." He bent over, retrieving his gun belt from the floor and buckling it on.

Joe asked, "So you're not going to charge us with anything?"

The sheriff sighed. "Have you ever heard of a statute of limitations?"

"What?" Sara asked, her mind stumbling over the words. She knew what the term meant, but the context left her confused.

The sheriff yawned. "Just this once, I'm looking the other way. You didn't hurt anyone or break any locks. It's late, and if I arrest you now, I'd have to process you, then get up early to feed you breakfast. And for what? So Martin Settler can plea felony breaking and entering down to criminal mischief or some other slap-on-the-wrist misdemeanor? I've got a dead man on my hands and better things to do."

He folded up the maps and tucked them into the folder, leaving behind the plan for buying Grandma's house. "Let's have this particular piece of paper get lost. I wouldn't want anyone getting ideas about who broke in." Tucking the folder under his arm, he headed for the door.

"Once you're done with the thumb drives, I'll take them and this folder back to City Hall. Good night, and if you ever think about doing something this stupid again, do it in another county. Remember, you confessed in front of me and my deputy, and I've got a three-year statute of limitations to change my mind about charges."

Chapter 9

Salacious Secrets from Slyly Sequestered Supercomputers

Sara had easily pulled all-nighters in college without any ill effects. Once, she had taken mushrooms at a party, walked halfway across Iowa City to eat fries at McDonald's, and then turned around and walked all the way back. She still made it to Environmental Chemistry at nine the next morning. But now, just staying up half the night to rob City Hall and plan a cabal with the local sheriff was taking its toll.

She went downstairs to find Emily had made herself some of Sara's Ethiopian Yirgacheffe, a good choice, it was her favorite bean other than Kona, which was prohibitively expensive. Of course, Sara didn't have any bad coffee. Even her Arabica was higher-quality beans, picked on a single estate in Nicaragua.

Touching the pot, she determined the coffee was still hot and poured herself a mug. As she was doing so, she found a note on the counter. "Went for a run. Don't start the hunt for clues without me."

Her bodyguard ghost for the day was Maggie, the schoolteacher. Maggie was in a talkative mood, launching into a long story about the menswear shop her husband had run. Sara let her mind drift, thinking of Emily's body and whether looking that good would be worth all the running. Weren't you supposed to get hot and fit after your divorce to really stick it to your ex? Still, she'd barely started the legal work. And last night, she'd had to run away from the police—that surely counted as a workout.

First, she called Joe and told him the clothes shopping trip was off. "I know we didn't really think about it last night, but the sheriff only gave us today to look at this stuff."

Joe's voice had that familiar, easygoing tone. "Yeah, I figured as much when the sheriff caught us. So, what's the game plan now?"

Sara leaned against the counter, her tone turning playful. "Oh, I still expect you to take me clothes shopping. We're not skipping that."

Joe laughed, catching her tone. "You sure about that? It seems dangerously close to one of those movie montages where the guy has to sit through a dozen outfit changes. I'm not sure I'm cut out for it."

Sara grinned, enjoying the banter. "Oh, come on. It'll be fun. I promise I won't make you hold my purse —unless you really want to."

Joe's voice dropped to a teasing whisper. "Well, as long as I get to pick out at least one outfit, I might survive."

Sara felt a little thrill at his words. "Deal. But just so you know, I've got high standards."

Joe chuckled softly. "That makes two of us."

After talking to Joe, she sat drinking her coffee and wondered if Emily was interested in Joe. If she was, Sara didn't want to get in her way. She liked Joe, and he was cute and fun to flirt with, but she wasn't ready for anything serious. She sighed, not knowing the right answer.

She decided to spend some time on things she could control and looked up information for green coffee bean wholesalers. Until now, she'd been buying off Amazon, sticking to five pounds at a time. She found a couple of companies that seemed to have a good buzz on the coffee roasters forums, and she bought a ten-pound bag from each of them, an Ethiopian Yirgacheffe from one, and a Tanzanian Peaberry from the other. She was pleased to find out they both had free shipping on orders over sixty dollars, which brought the price down to seven dollars a pound.

Coffee in hand, she checked social media to see which of her college friends were having babies and which ones were getting a divorce—or worse, both. They had all pretty much reached that stage in life. She hadn't announced her own intentions yet, not because she wasn't committed, but because she had other things going on and didn't want to spend the entire day answering the same direct message: What happened?

She was deep into doom-scrolling when Emily walked back in, glistening with sweat but still somehow looking irresistibly attractive—like a fitness model in one of those commercials about yogurt that makes you poop better.

"I'm going to take a quick shower," Emily said. "Then we can go through those thumb drives."

"Cool," Sara said. That left her with very little to do for the moment.

After Emily headed upstairs, Grandma wandered in. She fixed Sara with a mischievous grin. "So, how's Downcastle's very own cat burglar doing this morning?"

Sara groaned. "Grandma, please."

"Oh, don't 'Grandma, please' me," she chuckled. "I'm just saying, when I was your age, the most exciting thing I ever did was sneak into the drive-in movie theater or go on a date without wearing underwear. For that matter, I usually did both at the same time."

Maggie let out a nostalgic sigh. "Oh, that reminds me of my own courting days. You think sneaking into drive-ins was a lot of work. If we wanted to get away from our parents, a horse had to get involved, and that did not always go well." She stared off into the distance, seemingly lost in a memory.

Sara looked between the two ghosts, wondering if she should ask for details. The way Maggie was staring into space suggested some stories were better left in the early part of the twentieth century. "So," she said, trying to get Grandma back on topic, "you were saying?"

Grandma grinned. "Just that you're out here playing Nancy Drew meets James Bond."

"Is this supposed to be helpful advice?" Sara asked.

Grandma grinned. "Who said anything about helpful? I'm just enjoying the show. But if you want advice, here it is: maybe stick to sleuthing in broad daylight. You're not exactly master-spy material, honey."

Sara couldn't help but smile. "I'll keep that in mind."

"That's my girl," Grandma beamed. "Now, about that kiss on the porch... I may be dead, but I'm not blind. Spill the details, honey. Was it as steamy as it looked from my vantage point?"

Sara felt her cheeks warm. "It wasn't... I mean, we were just caught up in the moment."

"Honey, the best kisses always are," Grandma said, her eyes twinkling. "So, on a scale of wet fish to fireworks, where did it land?"

"Grandma!" Sara exclaimed, but she couldn't help smiling. "It was... nice. Really nice, actually."

Grandma raised an eyebrow. "Nice, huh? Well, 'nice' is how it starts. Next thing you know, you're sitting in the back seat of a Chevelle watching *Smokey and the Bandit* and waiting for your date to realize you're not wearing underwear."

Sara laughed despite herself. "I think I'll stick to breaking into municipal buildings for now, thanks."

"Your loss," Grandma shrugged. "But I notice you didn't deny the fireworks."

Half an hour later, Emily was downstairs looking fresh and glowing with health, which made Sara feel greasy and gross by comparison.

Sara was afraid things would be awkward, considering her criminal activities, but Emily just held up a laptop bag and asked, "Ready?"

"Sure." Sara grabbed the flash drives off the coffee table, where they'd sat since two in the morning, and brought them over to the table. "I'm glad you have a laptop, I was afraid we'd have to do this on Grandma's computer, which is ancient. I'm not even sure it would work with flash drives."

"Hey!" Grandma said. "That's a perfectly good computer. It always did what I needed it to do."

Sara was pretty sure new computers were a must every decade or so, but she couldn't argue with Grandma with Emily sitting right beside her.

Emily made a face. "None of these file names make any sense. It looks like the drive is either corrupted or he had some kind of encryption. I know how to keep chain of custody on electronic files, but that is where my knowledge ends."

They looked through two or three more drives, but they seemed to all be the same.

Sara held up her phone. "I'm going to call my cousin. I'm not sure she can do anything, but she's got to know more about this stuff than us."

By the time Sara had showered and dressed, and they had driven out to Jen's estate, it was after ten. Jen and Nick both met them at the door, and Nick buzzed with excitement. Without a greeting or any small talk, he waved and said, "Come with me."

Jen rolled her eyes and motioned for them to follow him. "He's been waiting for a challenge like this for quite a while."

Nick led them to a bookcase at the end of the living room and pushed. The bookcase swung open to reveal a staircase, and Nick descended as lights turned on automatically ahead of him.

Sara would have thought they were descending into a dungeon, but the air was too sterile—no musty smell at all. When they reached the bottom, rows of lights flickered on, revealing a room with a couple of large desks in the center, each holding monitors and keyboards, and one wall completely covered in computer equipment.

"Technically," Nick said, "I'm not supposed to have this. It's on indefinite loan from the Department of Defense."

"How did you swing that?" Sara asked. She was sure that the military took that kind of thing seriously.

Jen sighed. "Baker Dental is now the sole supplier to the Army Dental Corps. And we're not making anything on the deal."

"We might actually be losing a little on it," Nick added.

Jen shot him an annoyed look.

"Hey," he shrugged. "I own the company. I'm allowed a toy once in a while. I wanted a toy."

"And he couldn't just buy a Ferrari like a normal man-child," Jen summed up.

Sara held up a handful of flash drives. "Before you two start arguing, do you mind taking a look at these?"

Nick nodded and plugged the first drive into the machine. "First, we're going to isolate all these files on this laptop and scan for viruses. It's not a perfect solution, but by air-gapping the devices and using write-once media..."

At this point, Sara began to lose interest. To her, the process seemed very boring. Nick would load files onto the laptop, type something, and wait, then carry a fresh drive to the wall of computers, type something, and wait again, before returning with another drive for them to read. Each drive took about an hour to decrypt, even on the huge computer Nick wasn't supposed to have.

When the first drive was complete, Nick walked it over to them. "You're lucky. The encryption is 1024-bit RSA, pretty common stuff and a little outdated. Still, it would have taken a long time on a regular home computer."

"Like how long?" Sara asked.

Nick hesitated, scratching his head. "Well... I'm not up to speed on the latest video card performance, but if they're pushing around ninety teraflops..." He paused a moment as if running the calculations in his head.

Jen cut him off. "At least a decade or two."

Emily started scanning through the first drive. It contained a series of Word documents. She opened one and started to read. "This looks like some kind of science fiction story." She skipped ahead. "Okay, now the main character's masturbating." She skipped ahead more. "I think this is science fiction, dinosaur erotica."

"Do you think he wrote it?"

"Not unless his pen name is t'Sade. I think he just collects it. There's actually quite a lot of files on here." She opened another one. "More erotica. I think he got this one because he subscribed to the author's Patreon."

When the file names appeared on the second drive, Sara immediately recognized them. They were the same as the files she'd found in the desk last night. "These are copies of all the paper files in his desk. Did he scan the paper files, or did he print out the electronic ones?"

"The guy was a Boomer," Emily pointed out. "I'm betting he printed them out. Although he seems quite handy with a flash drive."

Sara pointed to one of the files. "Open this one." When the document popped up on Emily's screen, Sara said, "This was their plan for buying my Grandma's house."

The fourth drive was surprising to say the least. Most of the files were images, and they popped up as large thumbnails. They were mostly naked women, but also a few couples.

"And a selection of amateur porn," Emily said, "What a horny old goat."

When Sara looked a little closer at the thumbnails, she felt the blood drain from her face. "Um, it's not pornography. Well, it is, but I think these are all Down-castle locals."

Sara was glad that Maggie had decided to explore the house a little. This might be a little much even if she had been progressive for the horse-and-buggy days. For that matter, she was glad Tom wasn't around.

Going back to the thumbnails, Sara saw a few pictures of a blonde woman she knew. "That's Marge, the lady that runs the diner." She pointed to another. "That's Steve Hollister, the postmaster. I don't know the other two with him. That one's probably a farmer, with those tan lines and the John Deere tattoo." A few of the pictures were posed, as if the subjects knew they were being photographed—like the one of the post-master—but most looked more like stills from home security cameras.

"Speaking of tattoos," Emily said, as she brought up the next picture. "Who gets a tattoo of Rick Astley on their butt. Is that some kind of sick joke, like they are Rick Rolling the guy who's doing them from behind."

"I never understood that," Sara said. "Rick Rolling, I mean. It's not the worst song ever."

Tapping her lip, Emily said, "I've heard about these small-town swinger's clubs, but I didn't think we had one in our county. Now, this is a possible motive for murder. A guy gets too close to a woman, somebody gets jealous, and pretty soon, someone gets a landscaping paver to the back of the head. Something similar happened in Anamosa a few years ago."

Sara quickly scanned through the other pictures, wanting to know and not wanting to know. Thankfully, she didn't see any of her Grandma or her cousin Jen. She did see her high-school Spanish teacher though, and she wondered if that had something to do with the school board sending her on continuing education trips to the many Spanish-speaking countries of the world. Then she started thinking about Mariachi music. "Enough. Bring up the next drive before I get sick."

Emily pulled the drive out and put another one in. "More fan fiction, but this is all Harry Potter smut, and something called Supernatural Sam slash Dean."

"Not as exciting as finding out about a swinging group in Downcastle," Sara pointed out.

Emily shrugged. "At least he enjoyed reading. It's a shame more people don't pick up a book these days."

Sara asked, "So, um, what do we do from here?"

"You go about your life, relax, move on. I will take these over to the sheriff. I mean, yes, everyone in these pictures might be a suspect, but having twenty suspects is only slightly more useful than having none. Now, if we'd gotten two or three to pressure, that would be something, but a four-person department can't effectively put pressure on twenty people."

Sara wanted to argue, but it was hard to focus on strategy when her mind kept replaying the sight of the postmaster wearing nothing but tan lines from his little uniform shorts.

Emily pulled into Sara's driveway and put the cruiser in park. "I'm going to grab a drink of water before I go check these drives into evidence." She kept her tone casual like she was just thirsty, and she totally wasn't going in because someone had recently broken into the house and she was doing a security sweep.

Sara had always thought the saying, "The guilty always return to the scene of the crime," was just a trope for mystery novels, not something that actually happened in real life. Yet, the day after breaking into

City Hall, she found herself driving back there to have a chat with Iris Pilkington.

Her need to talk to Iris stemmed from something Sheriff Robinson had asked her last night. Who loved Downcastle more than getting double the value of their house? When she really thought about that question, Iris was the first person to pop into her head. The woman was working herself to death and blackmailing Sara merely so Downcastle would have more attractions than Swisher Fun Days.

Speaking of the Harvest Festival and Iris's blackmail, Sara was tempted to tell her, "I can't afford to renovate Grandma's house, so I won't need any permits. And I won't be attending the festival as the village psychic." But a few things held her back. The booth was already set up, she kind of wanted to give it a shot, and in a town this small, she couldn't afford to burn bridges with someone as connected as Iris.

She even felt a strange sense of appreciation for Iris. A middle-aged woman skipping an orgy wasn't exactly headline news, but after seeing so many people she knew naked that morning, Sara was immensely relieved Iris wasn't one of them. Sometimes, small mercies really did bring the most joy.

When she arrived at City Hall, things were all kinds of chaotic. People were putting up signs about the Harvest Festival. Some people were carrying chairs out, and some people were carrying chairs in. A troop of Girl Scouts seemed determined to make sure everyone stayed hydrated, pushing cups of water and tea into people's hands, whether they wanted it or not, with relentless focus and surprising authority.

Maggie looked the building over. "I'd heard they'd changed City Hall about fifty years ago or so. I'm not sure I like it. It looks a little too fake, like they were trying to be quaint."

Sara walked up to Deb, the receptionist. "Hi. We met the other day. I'm Sara. How are you doing?"

"Things are crazy around here. There was a break-in last night. And then Iris wanted the chairs put out with the tables, but then they said there would be rain overnight, so she's bringing the newer chairs back in and taking out the cheap folding chairs to re-place them."

"Oh, that sounds fun," Sara said with sympathetic levels of sarcasm. Then she said, "Thank you," to the Girl Scout who had just pressed a cup of iced tea into her hand.

"Iris tried to do the same thing last year, but May-or Hart said moving all the chairs a day early would be too disruptive. I hate to say it, but I don't think he was wrong."

"Speaking of Iris, is she here?" Sara asked. "I was hoping to have a word with her."

Deb laughed. "I can tell you don't know Iris. There's no way you'd catch her in the office on the day before the Harvest Festival. If you want to catch her, just head downtown. Since she can't shut down main street to start the real setup until six, you might be able to get her to sit still. After six though, she'll be running around until everything is done and ready for tomorrow morning."

"Okay, thanks for the advice."

Sara walked over to the center of the main street, which was named Ruebens Road after Mayor Hart's an-cestor who'd founded the town. She looked up and down the street, quickly spotting the towering red updo under which she would find Iris. Sara moved in that direction only to quickly lose sight, as Iris popped into one of the downtown shops, possibly the post of-fice, but it was a little hard to tell from the distance.

For a petite, yet plump woman, Iris could move when she wanted to.

Sara picked up her pace, dodging around a woman with a stroller, a wooden barricade ready to be moved into the road, and a couple of early vendors who were already setting up.

Pushing open the post office door, Sara was greeted by the familiar musty scent of old paper. The lobby was quiet, except for a conversation between Iris and Steve Hollister, the postmaster, known for his love of town gossip, stamp collecting, and—according to Sara's recent discovery—his bisexuality. Good for him, honestly, but still not something she'd needed to see. She shuddered slightly at the not-soon-to-be-forgotten photos.

Maggie also had things to say about the post office. She thought selling off the original land and putting the post office in a modern storefront was somehow criminal. Thankfully, Downcastle no longer had an old-time menswear shop, as that had been Maggie's husband's business, as she would, no doubt, have some opinions on what they were doing wrong.

Sara approached slowly, hoping to catch some of their conversation. However, Iris must have seen her reflection in the well-polished fronts of the post office boxes. She spun around. "Sara! How is our resident medium? Everything ready to go for tomorrow?"

Sara nodded. "Yes, Adam Mitchell and Joe Walker are going to come over first thing and help me set everything up."

Iris raised an eyebrow. "Two big strong men at the same time? They'll have you finished in no time."

Sara winced at the woman's phrasing. She probably wouldn't have even noticed it if not for the photos she'd seen earlier. "I really appreciate their help." She desperately needed to erase those images from her mind, but even as the thought came to her, she knew they were there to stay. The image of kindly old Mr. Hollister spread naked on a red velvet chaise in a pose no senior citizen should assume was seared into her memory for good.

Wanting to step away from Mr. Hollister, Sara took Iris by the arm and guided her away from the postmaster. "Iris, I wanted to ask you about Mayor Hart."

"What did you want to know, dear?"

"Well, I don't know if anyone's told you this, but after I discovered the body, the murderer came after me."

"Oh, my goodness." Iris seemed genuinely concerned, although whether it was for Sara's well-being or the possible cancellation of the mediumship booth, she was unsure.

"Yes, the sheriff has been having his deputy, Emily, sleep at my place just as a precaution, and I have Adam next door, so I feel pretty safe." Actually, she hadn't at first, but now she was feeling better. Eventually, though, Emily's perpetual sleepover would have to end, and Sara wasn't sure how she felt about that.

"You poor thing, and here I am bothering you about a booth just so we can get one up on Swisher."

"I'm fine," she said, which was just about true. "But you knew the mayor pretty well, right?"

"Well, Mike and I argued about things occasionally, but I do believe he understood that, deep down, I always had the town's best interests at heart."

"Since you knew the mayor so well," Sara said carefully, choosing her words, "I was wondering about something you mentioned the other day—those rumors about shady dealings?" She paused, then added casually, "Or maybe... any relationships he might have had around town?"

184

Sara watched Iris's reaction carefully. Sure, she already knew about the mayor's extracurricular activities, but maybe Iris would let slip something that would connect the photos to the murder.

Irish shook her head. "I don't know that he was doing anything illegal, and you don't want to speak ill of the dead."

Sara thought about telling Iris about Hart's plan to sell the town to Yoonbao. After all, if anyone would care about Downcastle being turned into a giant warehouse, it would be Iris. But revealing that would mean explaining how she knew about it, and Sara wasn't ready to confess to breaking and entering. Instead, Sara went for the other approach. "If you tell me what you know, it might lead somewhere that helps me find his killer."

"But, sweetie, what if I tell you something and then the murderer comes after you again?"

After all this back-and-forth, Sara hoped Iris had something juicy. "Don't worry," Sara said as if she didn't have a care in the world. "Emily is still staying over at my place, and if someone can catch the killer, I won't have anything to worry about."

"Well, okay, if you think it's safe."

Sara kind of wanted to throttle the woman, but she made herself remain calm. "I'll be fine."

"I think the mayor might have been dating Marge from the diner. She sure seemed to hang around with him a lot."

Sara wanted to scream "Because they belong to the same swinger's club!" but she didn't. She kept her calm, she nodded, and then she said, "Thank you so much, Iris. You've been a great help. I'll be there tomorrow."

"Tomorrow!" Iris jumped like she'd received an electric shock. "The Harvest Festival is tomorrow. I need to get back to work."

As long as she was on the main street, Sara decided to stop by Marge's Diner. There were a few more people in the diner than usual. Sara wondered if it was because it was a Friday afternoon or because people had come downtown to see the setup for the Harvest Festival.

Sara went in and, when she smelled food cooking, her stomach complained that she had not eaten today and was subsisting on a cup of Yirgacheffe and some of the awful iced tea the girls scouts had been passing out. However, she heeded her grandmother's warnings as she looked through the menu. She figured it was difficult to get food poisoning from fries, especially as she was reasonably sure they were taken out of a freezer bag and dropped directly into the boiling grease.

She got lucky. Marge was waiting the tables. Sara had several questions about the sex club, but they could wait until after she'd ordered and eaten. She exchanged greetings with Marge and ordered her fries and a Diet Pepsi.

Sara took out her phone and pretended to look at something. She whispered to Maggie, "You're invisible. Go around and see what people are gossiping about."

Maggie gave her a curt nod, walked over to the next table, and started to listen.

The fries came out about fifteen minutes later. Sara reached for a ketchup bottle, thinking ketchup from a bottle was another thing Marge couldn't screw up. Although, she had to admit the bottle was kind of gross and sticky. She looked through her purse and found a wet wipe.

Marge came over as she was cleaning her hands. "Is everything all right," she said nodding to the wet wipe.

"Not a problem. My ketchup bottle was just a bit sticky. Someone probably spilled some ketchup earlier."

"I'm so sorry about that." Marge extracted a rag from her apron, one that appeared even grungier than any potential residue on the bottle, and meticulously wiped the glass surface.

Sara smiled as authentically as she could manage. "Great. Thanks!" She'd already gotten ketchup anyway, so it wouldn't kill *her*.

When Sara was almost done with her fries, Marge swung by again and pointed to her Diet Pepsi. "Need a refill, honey?"

"That'd be great, thanks."

Marge returned with the fresh drink, and Sara seized the moment. "Hey, Marge, I'm really glad to see you doing better than the other day. You seemed pretty shaken up about the mayor's murder."

Marge stiffened but kept her smile. "Well, yeah, he is... or was, our mayor. Of course, I was upset." She shifted as if to walk away.

Sara leaned forward, trying to sound casual. "It's just that... no one else seemed quite as upset. Not the receptionist at City Hall, not Iris—she's worked with him on the city council forever."

Marge gave a small shrug. "I guess I'm just an emotional person."

Sara lowered her voice. "I heard you might've had a more personal relationship with him. Some folks were talking about it.

Marge's eyes darkened, her smile vanishing. "That's none of your business. Who told you that?"

Sara's pulse quickened as she felt the weight of the other patrons' eyes shifting toward their table. She tried to stay calm. "Just something I overheard. You know how people gossip."

Marge's voice rose, clearly for everyone to hear. "Maybe people should mind their own goddamn business." She snatched up the last of Sara's fries with a sharp motion that startled her, and stormed back into the kitchen. A few heads in the restaurant turned away, pretending not to notice.

Eating most of her fries before starting the conversation had been the right move. Now, she was stuck in a restaurant where she clearly wasn't welcome, staring at a full Diet Pepsi. She took a couple of sips, set it down, and slipped outside.

Sara walked back toward her car, along the area which tomorrow would presumably be vendor booths. Currently, there were only a handful of "booths" set up, basically canopies like her grandma's but with various features and levels of quality.

All the rest of the vendors or attractions, as Iris called them, currently consisted of tables and folding chairs with masking tape that indicated their area. Each folding table had a piece of paper with the name of the attraction on it. She found hers, "SARA JEN-NINGS, MEDIUM," sighed at her misspelled name, and sat down at the table for a second.

Maggie sat down across from her, firmly in the chair, but partly in the table, which played tricks with Sara's eyes. "I stuck around and listened to people's conversations. They all think you're a horse's ass for harassing Marge."

Sara nodded. "Yeah. They're probably right too."

"I don't know about that. You sometimes have to rattle people a little to get a response out of them. Look at your grandma. What if she'd just taken antidepressants and become a subservient housewife, as so many of her generation did? Do you think you'd see her in the same light?"

"I'm not sure," Sara said. She had always been proud of Grandma's fierce independence.

"In my day, you had to work extra hard to be a free spirit. If you wanted to go parking with a boy, there was a horse and buggy involved. I would have lost my virginity a full year earlier, but a flatulent horse is a mood killer."

"Maggie!" Sara said, "You were a little wild. No wonder you and Grandma are friends."

"The biggest thing that's changed between then and now is the quality and availability of the birth control. Also, the men take baths more than once a week, which was a more effective birth control than what we actually used. That's the reason I married a man who owned a store, farmers might eat a little better, but working with animals means you get a little ripe before the weekly bath."

Sara smiled. "I admire your pragmatism."

"And I've always liked you, Sara, even if you are a bit of an ass. From what I could gather, the folks in the diner weren't necessarily on Marge's side; they just thought you were being a little insensitive. Still, the way she reacted... she might have known the mayor would try to nail anything that moved, but I don't think she was happy about it."

"Well, that's not surprising," Sara said. "I think he was hooking up with half the eligible women in this town, and quite a few of the married ones, according to the pictures I saw this morning." She thought for a second. "I supposed that happened in your time too?"

"More than you would think. They didn't have paternity tests back then."

Iris strolled up, robbing Sara of all the juicy details. "Hello again! Getting a feel for your booth?"

Sara yawned, still tired from the night before. "That and giving my feet a much-needed break." She gestured toward the flurry of activity downtown. "You sure know how to keep everyone busy."

"Anything worth doing is worth doing right," Iris said with a proud little nod. "Speaking of which, how's the mediumship going? Have you unearthed your grandmother's secrets yet?"

Sara nodded, biting back a grin. Since Grandma's ghost had taught her those secrets, she felt pretty confident. "I think I'm on the right track. Want to help me practice? I left my crystal ball at home, but I could improvise."

For a split second, Iris's eyes lit up like a kid sneaking candy before dinner. "I really shouldn't, though... There's so much to do." Her hesitation sounded only half-convincing.

"Oh, come on! You deserve a break."

Iris hesitated for the briefest moment, then slapped the table with a grin. "Alright, you talked me into it. I can't resist."

Sara reached for Iris's hands, still faintly scented with lavender hand cream. She closed her eyes and took a deep breath. Time to work her magic.

Chapter 10

The Medium and the Mustache

Sara closed her eyes. "I'm just putting myself in a trance."

"Your grandma always said a mantra out loud," Iris said helpfully.

Sara nodded. "I'm still trying to memorize the words. For now, I will do it silently."

"I'm sorry. I'll be quiet now. It's always been one of my weaknesses to be able to chatter away." Iris paused, then added, "Mom always said I could talk the ear off a corn stalk. Not that corn has ears. Well, it does, but not the listening kind. Oh dear, I'm doing it again, aren't I?"

Sara waited patiently for Iris to wind down. This was probably good practice for tomorrow, when she would be dealing with paying customers that she couldn't just tell to shut up.

Iris continued, her words tumbling out faster, "Okay, zipping it now. Silent as a... well, not a ghost, I suppose. Maybe a mime? When mimes come back as ghosts, do they talk? Well, I suppose—" She clapped a hand over her mouth, eyes wide with apology.

As Iris finally fell silent, Maggie turned to Sara with a knowing smile. "Did you know, dear? She's a descendant of mine. That nonstop chatter runs in the family. My sister was just like her—could talk for hours without taking a breath. You could walk out of the room and come back, and she'd still be going."

Sara took a deep breath and let it out. "Speak the name of the spirit you wish to speak to."

"I would like to speak to my father Karl Pilkington. The one from Downcastle not the British guy on TV, Ricky Gervais's friend."

Just for effect, she spoke softly in a breathless voice. "Karl Pilkington, the one from Downcastle, not the British one. Come to me. Your daughter wishes to speak to you."

Sara waited for a few minutes, then she heard a man with a slightly nasal voice say, "If you opened your eyes, you'd see that I'm standing here waiting for you." Then he added, "Oh, hello, Maggie."

She opened her eyes. A man stood before her in an old-fashioned suit, one with the big lapels like they had in the sixties. He had a daisy in the buttonhole, and dark red hair with a pointy mustache. "Your father was a tall man with red hair and a mustache."

"My father didn't have a mustache," Iris complained.

"I did once, for a week," he said. "June, Mrs. Pilkington, didn't let me keep it. But she can't stop me now. Until death do us part."

192

"He says that he always wanted a mustache in life, but he never grew one. So, he chooses to appear that way to me."

"Father!" Iris said. "Is it really you?"

"Of course it's me," he said. "Who else would it be?"

Sara decided that she needed to act as a bit of an intermediary. "He says he's here, and he loves you."

"Ask him if he's well."

Karl Pilkington rolled his eyes. "I'm dead. It's not like I'm going to get more dead. It's not like I'm going to catch a cold."

"Where he is," Sara said, "he is beyond such considerations. He says he loves you and wishes you the best life."

"I did not say that," he grumbled. "I do, of course, but you shouldn't put words in my mouth."

Sara nodded. "Yes, I agree." She turned to Iris. "He didn't say that much when he was alive, but he does mean it."

Iris clasped her hands to her chest, and she started crying. "I know, Daddy. I know." She briefly dug in her purse for a tissue, and finding none, pulled out a long receipt, to Sara it looked like a CVS, and started blotting at her eyes. The blotting only made the damage to her makeup worse.

Sara made a note to herself to bring a box of tissues, or two, tomorrow. "It's obvious you love him very much, and..." She looked directly at him. "...not everyone is easy to love."

"That's enough of you," he said. "In my day, young women knew to respect—"

A dark-haired woman with cat's-eye glasses appeared. "Yes, Karl, everyone respects you just fine." She gave him a dismissive wave.

Karl harumphed and disappeared.

193

The ghost shook her head. "Uh, I can't believe I was married to him. A ginger mustache is a horrible look. It was true then, and it's true now." She turned to Iris. "Hello, my little darling." She gave her daughter a wave.

Sara blinked, momentarily thrown by the domestic drama unfolding in the afterlife. She made a mental note: Ghost couples therapy could be a lucrative side gig. They didn't carry money, though, so maybe not.

Regaining her composure, she continued. "Your mother is here now. She's waving at you." On one level, it felt kind of odd just telling someone what the invisible person next to them was saying and doing, but it wasn't like it was hard, and she planned to charge fifty dollars for a twenty-five-minute session so she could live with a little awkwardness.

"Oh, ask her how she's doing."

June Pilkington said, "Oh, tell my darling girl that mommy loves her so much, and I am happy and fine."

"She says she loves you, and she is happy and fine."

Iris's eyes narrowed. "That's what you said about my father."

Sara shrugged. "They've passed on. If they were under a lot of stress, what hope would the rest of us have?"

Iris nodded. "You make a point. Can you ask her where she left her recipe for fudge cake?"

This one Sara repeated nearly verbatim. "The recipe card is in her polka-dot apron, but if you can't find that, there's a very similar recipe on page 83 of the *Iowa Grange Cookbook*. Just add eight ounces of cream cheese."

"Thank you, Mom."

"Goodbye, darling," June said as she faded away.

"Oh," Iris said, "one more question."

Sara shrugged. "Sorry, she's gone. Do you want to try to call her back?"

Iris shook her head. "No, you're right. I really do need to get back to work."

"Wait," Maggie said. "Tell her that Great-Grandma Maggie is here and says hello."

"Is that all?" Sara asked. When Maggie nodded, she said, "Your Great-Grandma Maggie is here also. She says hello."

Iris looked surprised. "Well, hello to you too, Great-Grandma. Thanks for stopping by."

"There," Sara said, "Now I'm done."

"Aren't you going to do that cleansing thing and ground me?" Iris asked.

Having no idea what the "cleansing thing" was, Sara made a circular motion with her hand and said, "Okay, you're good to go."

"Thank you for the reading." Iris's usual measured tone wavered slightly. "That was... remarkable. Your grandmother never achieved quite that level of clarity. I hadn't expected to be so moved."

"Um, Iris, you might want to fix your face."

Iris's eyes went wide. "Oh, yes. Thanks again." She took off down the street, no doubt looking for a business with a brightly lit restroom, her long receipt streaming behind her.

That night, Emily and Sara packed all the canopy parts into her car. She had to put the back seat down and bungee the trunk closed, but she got it all in. Then she got out the big cardboard boxes with signs, tablecloths, bunting, a crystal ball, and a battery-powered white noise generator. She supposed that last one made sense, it was probably difficult to give someone a heartfelt missive from a lost loved one when the cotton candy vendor in the next booth kept asking people if they wanted pink or blue.

Later that evening, she had Grandma walk her through the beginning mantra. Grandma used a spooky voice and said, "Beyond the veil thin, where spirits begin, I beckon to the boundless skies, where nothing but enigma lies, the candles glow, in the mystical flow, let the spirits astound, in these ancient echoes profound."

Sara made a face. "You really said that?"

"I did."

"But it's so cheesy."

Grandma nodded. "Yes, Sara. Believe it or not, people who come to a small-town festival and pay a psychic usually don't want to talk to Mom and Dad. They want the cheese, and the cheese we must bring!" She said the last bit in her spooky voice.

Sara sighed. "Okay, let's go over it again." They rehearsed it a couple more times, and Sara wrote it all down.

"For tomorrow," Grandma said, "just hold it in your lap or pin it to the back of the tablecloth. Then you can look down like you're praying and read it."

"Great idea." Sara nodded.

"Now, are you ready for the closing statement?" She paused.

Sara took up pen and paper and gave her a nod.

"We draw this circle closed and thank the spirits for the wisdom they have shared today. With good intent, we release the energy that binds us to the beyond. May the mysteries unveiled today guide us on our sacred journey."

"That's not as bad as the opener," Sara observed.

Grandma shrugged. "Well, it's meant to be a grounding statement, no need to use lofty words."

The next morning, Sara's alarm went off at five. She startled awake, scaring the ghost cat who had been sleeping on the pillow beside her. She fumbled with her phone, trying to turn off the horrible noise. She knocked it to the floor. It bounced on the rug and went under the bed.

As Sara was trying to extricate herself from the sheets, the alarm turned off and her phone floated up from the ground. For a moment, she was confused, but then she reached over and touched the amulet, which she'd left on the bedside table. The German factory worker, Greta, appeared.

At first, Sara was a little nervous, after all, the woman had been her own personal automotive poltergeist. "Greta?"

Greta said something in German that Sara did not understand. *"Ich fühle mich für all das Leid, das ich dir zugefügt habe, leid. Ich möchte Wiedergutmachung leisten, wenn das möglich ist."*

"Wait," Sara said, "you can move things? No one else can move things."

Greta answered, *"Ja, ich habe diese Fähigkeit. Tom sagt mir, dass sie sehr selten ist."*

While Sara had no idea whatsoever what Greta was saying, Greta seemed to understand her, and she wasn't swearing at her, as far as she could tell, German could be a bit difficult that way.

"You up?" Emily asked through the door. "Today's the Harvest Festival."

"Yeah. Thanks for checking on me. I have a lot to do today."

"Speaking of today, I'll probably be working the festival all night. Why don't you drive over to the airport tonight and get a hotel room, just as a precaution. That way I won't have to worry about you."

Sara thought about it for a minute. She wasn't thrilled with the idea, but it did sound like a reasonable idea. "Sure, I guess that makes sense."

"You take a cold shower to wake you up, and I'll put on some coffee."

That reminded Sara that she had ordered those two ten-pound bags. She hoped she would have time to do some roasting soon.

She still didn't feel awake when she got out of the shower, but she'd laid out clothes already, so getting dressed was just going through the motions. She basically wore what she'd worn to break into City Hall, all black clothes, but with the addition of a cape with moons and wands on it and a witch's hat—thank you to Grandma and her love of cheese.

She staggered downstairs to find a mostly full pot of coffee and Emily, already looking awake and alert, bordering on perky. Sara resisted the urge to growl her, especially since she was handing over a cup of coffee.

Without a word, Sara sat at the counter and drank. The coffee was a little too hot, but she didn't care. After about ten minutes, she began to detect signs of life within her body. She took a deep breath and said, "Good morning. Thanks for the coffee."

"No problem, roomie."

"That reminds me. How long are you thinking of staying here?"

"Why?" Emily asked. "Have I already outstayed my welcome? I refill the coffee pot. I even did the dishes yesterday."

"Oh, wow. I actually hadn't even noticed. No, you can stay as long as you want." Once the words came out of her mouth, they seemed a little open-ended, but on the other hand, Sara did feel a lot safer with her around.

"Well, I don't know about as long as I want, but I was planning to at least spend a week here. Especially since we still don't know who tried to stab you."

Although she agreed, Sara was guessing that whoever killed the mayor was not a professional killer. Chances were, now that they knew Sara didn't have any evidence to give the sheriff, they weren't coming back to finish the job.

Sara sipped her coffee, lost in thought about the strange turn her life had taken. From reluctant medium to almost-murder-victim to... what next?

As if in answer to her unspoken question, Emily cleared her throat. "However, beyond this protection duty, I've been considering the unique challenges of law enforcement in this area," Emily began, her tone casual but her eyes intent. And I wondered if you'd like to make the situation a little more permanent?"

"How so?" Sara asked.

"Because our county has its unusual shape, and the county seat happens to be located about as far away from Downcastle as you can get. That's why having Adam here to assist is a relief, but honestly, it might be a good idea to establish a field office in this area. I was wondering if I could rent a room for that purpose, unless, of course, Yoonbao decides to come in and tear everything down, in which case, they would probably bring in their own private security."

Sara nodded. She kind of liked having Emily around. "I might consider that if you are serious." She wondered what Grandma would think of the deal. As long as she didn't start talking about roommates with benefits.

When Sara had made plans for the guys to meet her to set up the booth, she'd overlooked one small detail. The street had been blocked off at six the previous evening, and they weren't opening up the barricades to let attractions in. It looked like most of the larger attractions and merch tables had set up last night.

She ended up having to drive through the alley and pull around to the front parking area of the Kelley and Hart Real Estate office. Grabbing a box, she headed toward her table. Adam and Joe were already standing there making small talk, so she hurried, thankful she had worn tennis shoes and not been tempted by Grandma's more exotic offerings. She didn't need to be three inches taller to sit at a table anyway.

As she approached the men, she felt a little embarrassed that she hadn't thought to bring coffee for them. Emily had made it, after all, Sara would have only needed to fill two travel mugs. Three really, she thought as she realized she'd be trapped in her tent all day without any way to get coffee without asking for help.

Joe was wearing a flannel shirt and jeans, in deference to the morning chill. Adam was wearing a police uniform with enough flair to border on bling.

"Hi," she said, approaching the guys. It was early for her, but politeness seemed like the least she could muster. They were here to help, after all, even if part of her suspected their motives weren't entirely selfless. She guessed they were both hoping this might lead somewhere, and someday, she may even be ready to entertain the idea. But today wasn't that day. She wasn't ready for serious romance. She had to focus on divorcing Brad and surviving the mess she was in. "Thanks for coming. The car's parked over by the real estate office."

As they were walking to the car, she asked Adam, "So, why the uniform?"

"I'm working the event. The sheriff asked me, and it's easy overtime. I'm not above directing traffic once in a while."

This surprised her a bit. "I didn't know Downcastle was big enough to need traffic direction."

"Normally, it's not, but a lot of people come to town for the Harvest Festival, and shutting down the main road and adding a parade doesn't help. It's not like there's a lot of places to set up detours."

Sara nodded. "Good point."

Between the three of them, they managed to get everything, or it might be more accurate to say that the guys managed to get everything, and Sara got the last cardboard box. She wasn't sure if they were carrying so much to show off or compete, but it seemed to be a bit of both.

While the two men might consider themselves in competition, they showed themselves capable of playing nicely with others. Her tent was done in under ten minutes, which had seemed impossible when she'd first strewn the plastic pipes out on the garage floor.

When the tent was finished, Grandma appeared in the corner. She gave Sara a thumbs up. "You're going to do great, and if you have trouble, I'll be here to give you advice."

Then, without direction, the men set up the table and chairs, complete with tablecloth and bunting, which left Sara with nothing to do for twenty minutes but put up some signs, pin her mantras to the bunting behind the table, and set out her crystal ball and box of tissues.

At first, Sara had thought she would have to print her own signs, but she found out that Grandma had used the stage name "Madame Celestina Delphine," so she just used the old signs.

"Wow, guys. That was absolutely amazing, and so fast. I couldn't have even done it without you two." As she talked, she touched-up her makeup. She'd gone a bit goth, with a pale foundation, smoky eyes, and black lipstick. "Joe, I hope I'm not keeping you from a job site."

"Not at all," Joe said. "I don't have any pressing deadlines, so I figured I'd take the day off. I always have a light day during Harvest Festival anyway because the Fincher brothers won't work. Apparently, they love the mobile carnival rides."

"They just ride carnival rides all day?" Sara asked.

Joe shook his head. "No, they watch the people riding them, waiting for an accident. They claim they've run the numbers, and with the age of the rides and the probability of shoddy maintenance, it's only a matter of time."

"And you employ these men?" Adam asked.

"Well," Joe said, "I've had guys that weren't as weird, but they did worse work even when you watched them. And I've had guys that worked for less money, but they drank or they stole from the site. One guy took a water heater home. I was like 'Dude, we were going to notice the house didn't have a water heater.'"

"Well," Adam said, "I'm going to go check in with Emily, she's basically running security today."

Joe nodded. "And I should go around and look at all the attractions. I hear we have more than Swisher this year. That's impressive."

Sara nodded. "All right, I guess I'll see you guys this evening when it's time to tear everything down."

"Yep," said Adam.

"I wouldn't miss it," Joe said.

Sara took a last look around and then sat down. From the open flap of the canopy, she could see other people wandering in to set up their tents or tables.

A middle-aged guy poked his head in the door. Sara didn't need psychic powers to tell the guy was a farmer. He had the permanent tan of someone who worked outside, he wore work boots and battered jeans, and parked on his head was a hat with the words "Pioneer Seed Corn, a DuPont Company." He looked sheepishly around her tent, and winced a little bit when he saw the crystal ball, but he still took another step in. "Hey, are you open yet?"

Sara nodded. "Sure. I am. Do you want to speak with a loved one?"

"I sure do, but um, how do I know you're not putting on a show?"

Sara passed over one of the pamphlets her Grandma had printed up. "It is just a show. I make no guarantee that any information will be accurate. I do however offer your money back if you're not satisfied."

"And how much money is that?" he asked.

"Fifty dollars for twenty-five minutes."

The farmer whistled. "You do think highly of your skills."

Sara shrugged. "It's the Harvest Festival. Everything's expensive. You want a reading or not?"

He nodded and sat down. "Let's do 'er." He reached over to shake her hand. "I'm Ted Miller, by the way." He got out his wallet and counted out fifty dollars, which Sara put in her cash box.

Sara looked down in her lap, where she'd pinned her opening mantra and read it in Grandma's spooky voice. When she looked up, the farmer seemed ready to bolt for the door. She asked him, "Who do you wish to contact?"

"I want to talk to my grandfather, Joe Miller."

"Joe Miller," she said, "come to me. We would hear your words."

A man appeared behind the farmer that could have been his twin. He was wearing a suit from maybe the 1950s. His head did a slight nod, and Sara realized he was acknowledging her grandma.

"Your grandfather is here. A very handsome man. I can see you take after him."

"Ah, shucks," he said, looking down. "So, I need you to ask him where the well is on the old Johanson place. I know when he bought it, he knocked down the pump house, but I'd like to start watering the cattle over there, and it would be better to start with a well that's already dug. The well-digging company has quoted me fifteen hundred, and that's just to dig the hole, that don't guarantee we'll find water."

A furrow appeared on the forehead of the ghost. "The Johanson place... If I remember, the road was north of the homestead. So, if you came off the road heading South, the house was... fifty, no seventy yards..."

Sara tried to repeat his words. "The road was north of the homestead... but on the road heading south... The house was fifty... The house was seventy..." She gave up. "He's thinking about it."

"Well, can you tell me or what?" the farmer said.

Finally, Joe shrugged. "I don't know. It's there somewhere."

Sara shook her head. "He cannot recall. Do you want to know anything else?"

He shrugged. "No, not really. I'll take my fifty dollars back now."

Sara wondered if she should do the grounding statement, but she decided to skip it. She got out her cash box and gave Ted Miller his money back.

As he was walking out the door, Ted Miller and his grandfather said in unison. "Well, that was a complete waste of my time."

Sara sighed and slumped in her chair.

"Don't worry," Grandma said from her corner. "It will get better. There's always some rough ones."

"Should I get you a chair or something?" Sara asked.

"No need to worry about me. I don't have a body. I'm just appearing to you this way so you're more comfortable."

"I'd be more comfortable if I didn't feel like you were standing over my shoulder."

A chair appeared behind Grandma, and she sat down. "Better?"

Sara paused for just a second, wondering if she should mention the times she'd rearranged the living room furniture for the comfort of Grandma and her friends. She decided against it. "Much better."

Chapter 11

Divorces and Dummkopfs

Despite Sara's misgivings, the rest of the day went much better. The next two appointments were much like her practice session with Iris. These were followed by a few, "They love you, and they're proud of you," moments and a couple of, "Where did that recipe/heirloom/stock certificate go?" question and answer sessions. Unlike old Farmer Miller, however, most of these spirits had a general idea of how to find the thing in question.

Once a teenager popped in and offered to pay her double for winning lottery numbers. Sara told him, "I talk to the dead. I can't see the future," to which the kid left her tent and loudly told his friends, "She's a total fake."

She did get one more odd one in the morning when a middle-aged woman came in asking to speak to her father. When the ghost appeared, he wore what could only be described as a shit-eating grin.

"Your father is here," Sara said. "He's smiling at you."

The woman nodded. "Can you ask him to share a memory with me?"

The man answered. "Outlook not so good."

"Um..." Sara said, "he says the outlook isn't good."

"Is that exactly what he said?" she asked.

The man repeated. "Outlook not so good."

"He says, 'Outlook not so good.'" Wasn't that the name of Microsoft's email program? "Do you have another question?"

"Ask him if he sent my dog, Scruffy, away to live on a farm?"

Sara repeated the man's answer. "Better not to tell you."

The woman thought for a moment, then she pulled a piece of paper out of her purse and unfolded it. After glancing at it a second, she nodded.

"Okay," she said. "One more question. Am I going to win the lottery this year?"

Sara was about to tell the woman that she couldn't answer questions like that, when the father said, "Don't count on it."

Since this was as good an answer as any, Sara repeated, "Don't count on it."

The woman's eyes went wide. "Daddy! You're really here."

The ghost said, "Holy shit, Becky. We did it. Fuck Harry Houdini."

Sara said, "Holy shit, Becky. We did it. And then he said, 'Fuck Harry Houdini?'"

She gave Sara an inquisitive look. "You're the real deal, aren't you? You see, my father had a weird sense of humor, and he always told me that if I tried to contact him through a seance, he would answer me with things written on the Magic Eight Ball. We never thought it would work. Harry Houdini did something similar, leaving code words with his wife."

"Also," Sara said after listening to the father for another minute, "he says he's fine, he's proud of you, and he loves you very much."

"That's not just something you all say?" the woman asked.

Sara shrugged. "No, that's just something *they* all say. Generally, they don't have a lot to say. They've moved on from their lives, but they want you to feel loved and happy in yours."

She nodded. "That makes sense. Thank you, Madame Delphine."

The next visitor to her tent was Dwain Hart. The young man looked like he was hesitating to come in, but then he steeled his resolve and strode in like he owned the place. "Hello, Sara... I mean, Madame Delphine. I'd like to contact my father and ask him a few questions."

Sara looked back at Grandma, who shook her head. "Generally, after the initial shock spirits disappear for a while. There are a lot of theories why that is, but nobody knows for sure. I think you should tell him to keep his money, but give it a try if you want to."

Sara nodded. "Come in and sit down. Before we begin, we should go over a few things. Because your father just died, I probably won't be able to contact his spirit. There is a period of time when the spirit is unable to talk to the living. However, I will try if that's what you want."

He sat down and nodded. "Sure. Just try your best."

Sara went through the mantra, just because she'd gotten used to saying it, and it kind of helped put her in the mental frame for contact. When she finished, she said, "Mayor Hart. Mayor Mike Hart of Downcastle. Come to me." She waited. He did not appear.

She shook her head. "Sorry, Dwain. It looks like he's not coming."

Dwain shrugged. "Makes sense. He never had time for me when he was alive, just 'Dwain, do this' and 'Dwain, do that.'"

"I know it's difficult to lose a parent. I lost both my parents in a car accident when I was in high school."

"Can't you just, you know, talk to them? Isn't that why you're here."

"It's not always that easy," Sara said. "Just because I can talk to them doesn't mean they have much to say. I've been doing this all morning, and do you know what the most common message is? 'I love you. I'm proud of you. I still care about you.' That's usually the only message they have."

"I'm not sure if we'd get that from my dad," Dwain said, "but I was hoping he could tell me where he left the Yoonbao contracts."

"Oh, I can help with that," Sara said before she could think to close her mouth.

"How so?"

Sara searched for words. "Well, um." She remembered seeing Martin Settler's signature on the document. You could ask the other party in the agreement —Yoonbao, you said? Or you could contact their attorney..."

He shook his head as if to clear it. "Of course! I bet Martin Settler has a copy. I guess I wasn't thinking. What with the funeral and all the details, I just couldn't deal with digging through Dad's filing system again. Thanks, Sara. I hope the rest of the..." He waved his hands around to indicate the tent. "...the whatnot goes well."

Sara stopped him before he could run off. "Say, Dwain, who do you think killed your dad?"

"That's kind of an odd question." He stopped and thought about it. Then he shook his head. "The sheriff asked me the same thing, and I'll tell you what I told him. I have absolutely no idea, but he must have pissed someone off royally. He was kind of good at that." Then he did turn his back on her and hurried away.

Sara sighed, and said to his back, "You're not going to get your contracts today. Martin Settler is five booths down, selling cotton candy for the Lutheran Church."

After that, things went back to the type of readings that Grandma called "regular," mostly people wanting love and assurance from their deceased loved ones.

However, one customer did really stand out. A young woman came in around two in the afternoon, and Sara could see that she had been crying. She looked vaguely familiar, and Sara wondered if they'd been in high school at the same time.

"Hi," Sara said, trying to sound like she hadn't noticed the woman's distress. "What can I do for you?"

In a shaking voice, the woman said, "I'd like to speak to my mother."

Sara nodded. "Let's see if we can make that happen. Have a seat." She didn't bother to ask for money, she didn't want to make it awkward if the woman couldn't afford her fee, because she was going to get a reading whether or not she could afford it.

She looked down at her mantra, even though she could have made it through by memory, as she had now done over a dozen readings. Still, it was a nice safety net. When she was done, she asked the woman her name and her mother's name. During the day, Sara had learned to ask the name of the customer as well as who they wanted to contact, otherwise it got confusing when the ghost began referring to them by name.

She nodded. "My name is Nichole Davis, and my mother was Susan Turner."

"I'm calling to Susan Turner. Will Susan Turner come to speak to me? Your daughter Nichole wants to hear from you."

A very stern-faced woman appeared beside Nichole. At first, they didn't seem to have much in common, but as Sara looked more closely, she noticed some small similarities, their matching eye color, the high cheekbones.

"Your mother is here," Sara said. "What do you want to ask?"

"I want to know if it was a mistake getting married to my husband."

Sara looked to the mother who was shaking her head. Sara almost answered when she saw that, but she was lucky she waited just a minute. "I told that girl it was a mistake hanging around him at all. My biggest regret was not stopping her from marrying him just because she was pregnant. I should have stood up in the church and called him a no-good son of a bitch."

Sara translated. "She believes there were mistakes all around, but in hindsight, she does not believe he was the best match."

Nichole burst into tears, and Sara pushed the box of tissues an inch closer, to give Nichole the hint. This was another trick she had learned during the course of the day.

Taking a tissue, Nichole continued. "I mean, I knew Eddy was a few cards short of a deck. But I wanted to be a good wife, and when he said he wanted to spice up our marriage... I tried to make him happy. He kept saying it was normal, that lots of couples in Downcastle did these things. But when we joined this club..." She twisted the tissue in her hands. "I never thought I'd be forced to do things like that, with married people..."

And suddenly, Sara realized where she knew the woman from. She was the woman with the Rick Astley tattoo.

"That's when she should have divorced him," the mother said matter-of-factly.

"Your mother says that if you feel you should get divorced, she supports you."

"Hey!" Susan yelled. "Don't tell her 'I'm being supportive.' Tell her I want her to dump that pervert right now."

"Your mother informs me that she wants me to use stronger language. She wants you to get that divorce."

Nichole nodded. "Yes. I will go do it right now."

"You may have to wait until tomorrow, Martin Settler is working in the cotton candy stand."

"I didn't even know he was Lutheran."

"As long as you're here," Sara asked, "do you mind if I ask you a question?"

Nichole nodded. "Sure."

"This... adult social club you belonged to, was Mayor Hart a member?"

Susan made a face. "If you're going to talk about... those people, I'm leaving. I don't hold with that kind of thing, and I'm not going to listen to my daughter talk about fornication." She disappeared in a huff.

Nichole hesitated, her fingers twisting the tissue. "I'm not supposed to say. I mean, we're supposed to keep that kind of thing a secret." She gave a brittle laugh. "Besides, can't you just ask him? I mean, he's dead. That's kind of your thing."

"I'm just trying to understand what happened to the mayor," Sara said, her voice soft and a little uncertain. "These things can be complicated."

"He probably pissed someone off," Nichole said. "He was good at that." Her laugh this time was sharper, tinged with something between bitterness and relief.

"Besides," Sara added, "what are they going to do, kick you out? He's dead, and you didn't want to be there."

Nichole nodded, some of the tension leaving her shoulders. "Fair enough. Yes. He was a member."

"Was there any particular person that he had a thing for?"

She nodded. "I think he and Marge had a thing. I mean, it would be him and Marge and someone else, or a couple of someone elses, but they usually seemed to end up together somehow."

Sara nodded. "Thank you, Nichole. You've been most helpful."

She shook her head. "No, thank you, Madame Delphine. I feel better already."

"I am merely a conduit to those who have passed beyond. Now we shall do the ritual of grounding." As Sara went through the lines of the grounding, her mind raced. She'd suspected Marge was more than just a member of Hart's club. She couldn't wait to tell Emily tonight when she got home.

But what could she do with the information? Nothing right now. Peering outside, she saw a line of people each awaiting their turn. Some were there to communicate with their departed loved ones, and then there were the more unusual requests—like the man this morning who brought in his corgi, hoping to connect the lively pup with his deceased wife, just to reassure the dog he was still a good boy. The most bizarre part? It seemed the corgi was aware of her presence.

As Nichole left, Sara took a moment to breathe. The tent suddenly felt too small, too crowded with the emotions and secrets of the living and the dead. She glanced at her grandmother's ghost, still quietly observing from the corner.

"Grandma," Sara said softly, "did you ever feel... overwhelmed by all this? The weight of people's hopes, their grief, their unfinished business?"

Grandma's ghostly form shimmered slightly. "Oh, honey. Every day. But you learn to carry it. And sometimes, like with Nichole, you realize you're not just talking to the dead—you're helping the living."

Sara nodded, a small smile tugging at her lips. She'd started this against her will to placate Iris. But now... now she was beginning to understand why her grandmother had continued doing it all those years. There was something profoundly moving about being the bridge between two worlds.

She was about to say more when the tent flap rustled, announcing her next visitor. A waft of Old Spice cologne accompanied a man dressed in what Sara thought of as "farmer chic." He was wearing new blue jeans, fancy cowboy boots, a button-up shirt, and a clean cap with just a tasteful Pioneer logo and no words.

"Hi," Sara said. "Who are you trying to contact?"

"Well," he said, sitting down across from her and gazing at her with warm, hazel eyes flecked with gold. "You."

"Um..." It had been a long day, and Sara had kind of been getting into a groove, but she wasn't sure how to answer that.

"I'm Kevin Pfeiffer. I sat by you in biology class. We dissected a fetal pig together."

"I think I might have blanked out that entire memory," Sara admitted. "Dissection is not really my thing."

"I did most of the actual dissecting, actually. You made the labels and put them on the pins."

Sara nodded. "Yeah, that makes sense."

"Anyway..." He blushed, which was actually kind of cute. "I had a bit of a crush on you back then, but then you went away to college and got married. Anyway, I heard you were getting a divorce, and I wondered if you might want to go out next Saturday night."

Sara realized she was nodding. "Sure, I would love to."

He smiled, which showed cute little dimples under his otherwise rugged features. He took out his wallet and removed a business card. "Give me a call. I look forward to it." He held her eye contact for a moment and then strode away confidently.

Sara picked up the card, The center of the card was dominated by a large cow with "ORGANIC" written over it and "Beef to Order" under it. At the bottom of the card was written, "Pfeiffer Farms Inc, Kevin Pfeiffer, Proprietor" with his address and cell number.

"So, you're up to three suiters now?" Grandma said from her spot in the corner.

Sara shrugged. "I don't know. The other two haven't asked me out. Maybe this will motivate them."

At the end of the day, Sara was waiting for Joe and Adam when a wild-eyed man came into her tent. He was wearing bib overalls and dirty boots, and by his smell, he'd been working with animals before he decided to invade her tent.

"I'm sorry," she said, "but I'm not taking any more clients today."

"Oh, I'm not a client," he said. "I'm Eddy Davis. You told my wife to divorce me." He was slurring his words enough that she could tell he'd been drinking.

Sara held up a finger to stop him. She was honestly scared beyond imagination, but she figured if she could keep him talking, Joe or Adam would eventually show up. "I'm afraid you misunderstand. I spoke to Nichole's mother, Susan. She's the one that thinks Nichole should get a divorce."

"That's just a bunch of bullshit. You're just one of those man-hating women. You're probably bisexual and have a liberal arts degree."

Sara hated that stereotype. "I have a Bachelor of Science in Chemistry from Iowa."

"What's wrong, you can't keep a man of your own, so you got to ruin everybody else's marriage?"

Now Sara was wavering between the point of being scared and being seriously angry. However, she did not doubt that Eddy could inflict severe damage on her person, and she really didn't want to wrestle with someone smelling of manure.

Gretta appeared in the tent. She walked over and picked up the crystal ball, an impressive feat of strength, considering other ghosts Sara had met could pick up nothing at all and that crystal ball was heavy. Greta walked over to Eddy.

To Eddy, it must have looked like the crystal ball levitated off the table and hovered over to him. He stopped to watch it move, a look of stupefaction on his face. His mouth hung open for a moment, and then he said, "What the heck?"

Gretta hit him over the head, and he dropped to the ground unconscious. She replaced the crystal ball to its previous location and said, "*Dummkopf!*"

Sara let out a huge sigh of relief. "Thank you, Gretta."

She gave Sara a dismissive wave. "*Nichts zu danken.*"

Just then, Adam came in and looked at the farmer crumpled on the floor of her tent. "What in the hell happened here?"

Sara shrugged "He came in here drunk and yelling. Then he got dizzy and went down hard on the concrete."

Adam rolled his eyes. "They're not supposed to get that drunk until later." He got down on his hands and knees. "And he stinks. At least he has a pulse and he's breathing."

Sara thought about that for just a moment and shuddered at the idea of being haunted by Eddy. "Yes, thank god."

"Well, I don't feel like carrying him to my car and driving him to the drunk tank. But he has a head injury, so I guess he gets to ride in an ambulance, not that he's going to remember it. He picked up the radio off his shoulder and said, "CRPD492 to Hawthorn dispatch."

His radio beeped, and a voice replied, "Hawthorn Base. Go ahead. Adam."

"We have a drunk who's hit his head on Reuben's Road, outside the real estate office. Request ambulance."

"They're getting started early, huh?"

Adam replied, "Affirmative. CRPD492 out." He sighed. "Now we're going to have to wait for an ambulance before we can tear the tent down."

Sara was quite tired after dealing with people all day. "Can't we just roll him out the door?"

Adam bit his lip. "When I said I could carry him to the drunk tank, it was mostly in jest. Once someone's knocked out, you have to be pretty careful with them. You don't want to move him only to find out his injury is worse than it looks. Head injuries are tricky."

"Great." Sara sat down heavily. The perfect ending to the perfect day. On the bright side, though, she had made close to a thousand dollars in cash that she had no intention of reporting to the IRS.

Joe showed up about five minutes later. "Sorry I'm late, I was talking to the Fincher brothers. They were feeling depressed because another year is almost gone and there have been no major accidents." He looked at the guy laid out on the floor. "What's Eddy Davis doing here?"

"You know this guy?" Sara asked.

"I built a hog-farrowing building for him."

Sara nodded seriously as if she knew what that was. "An ambulance is coming for Eddy. Do you think that might cheer up the Finchers some?"

Joe shrugged. "It wouldn't hurt to ask. I'll be right back." He returned five minutes later without them. "They are going to take their chances with the carnival. Personally, I think that's a sunk cost fallacy, but they're nothing if not stubborn."

While they waited, Sara told them about her day starting with how most people wanted to know their loved ones were happy and safe, and ending with the farmer who wanted to find a capped well. She didn't, however, mention the revelation that Marge was Mayor Hart's... she tried to think of a word for the odd situation... primary sex buddy? She knew Emily and Sheriff Robinson might want to keep that information for themselves.

219

Before the ambulance got there, Eddy sat up and pointed at Sara. "She used her Voodoo magic on me!"

Adam walked over and leaned down to speak to him. "You fell and hit your head. Sit still, an ambulance is on the way."

Eddy stood up abruptly. "I can't afford no ambulance." He clumsily rolled to his feet and hurried out of the tent.

Joe shook his head. "Another sad commentary on the state of the American healthcare system." He sighed. "Okay, let's tear this thing down and get your car loaded up."

Adam put his hand on his radio. "CRPD492 to Hawthorn Dispatch. Better cancel that ambulance." He took his finger off the button. "Technically, we're not supposed to let them move with a suspected head injury. But we can't do much if they make a run for it. What am I supposed to do, chase him down, tackle him, and make it worse?"

As they started to tear down the tent, Sara couldn't help but marvel at how quickly she'd gone from reluctant medium to someone who could calmly explain away a ghostly crystal ball assault.

Right as they backed the last box into the car, Emily's voice came over Adam's radio, she said a couple of codes, and then "half an hour."

"It looks like your house guest is taking a break to go home and have some supper," Adam said. "You might run into her if you hurry."

Sara stifled a yawn. "Yeah. Though, I'm so tired I doubt I'll be good company. Today was fun, but dealing with the public is exhausting."

Chapter 12

Criminals and Cranial Complications

Exhausted from the day's events, Sara drove the few blocks home. When she turned off the car, the sound of a KISS cover band performing "Detroit Rock City" immediately invaded her space. She was glad she'd made a reservation at the Radisson. No matter how tired she was from running her booth, it seemed unlikely she'd get much sleep if she stayed here. She just needed to pack an overnight bag.

When she stepped out of her car, her whole body felt heavy. However, she wanted to get the car unpacked before she did anything else. She didn't put anything away; she just stacked it all in the garage to deal with later, left the car in the driveway, and shut the door on the whole mess.

"I'll put everything away tomorrow," she told herself. "Or the day after."

As she left the garage, her mind wandered over the day's events. Despite the physical drain, there was a satisfying weight of a thousand dollars in her pocket. More importantly, she felt like she'd helped a few people get closure with the untimely deaths of their loved ones, which she found very rewarding. And Iris seemed to be warming up to her. Despite her attempt to blackmail Sara, she seemed to mean well.

Stepping into the house, the thump of the band followed her. She just needed a change of clothes and her travel bag, and then she could escape the noise. She usually didn't sleep well in hotel rooms, but she was betting that wouldn't be an issue tonight.

Before she could collapse on the couch, Grandma ran in waving her arms. "Sara, get out of the house!" There was a loud noise in the kitchen that seemed to punctuate this.

Sara was frozen for a moment, not knowing what to do. She felt ripped in half, part of her wanting to investigate the noise, and part of her terrified of what had frightened her grandma. She felt so drained. She shook her head to clear her thoughts, and she realized she needed to just listen to Grandma and go.

Before she could find the will to move, Marge appeared in the doorway to the dining room. In one hand, she held the remains of what had been Sara's favorite coffee roaster, now a mangled piece of metal. In the other hand, she had a gun.

Even as Sara felt the heat leave her body to be replaced by the icy certainty that she was about to die, she was still a little pissed off that Marge had broken her coffee roaster. It had cost eight hundred dollars, and it was the only thing nice she bought when she got her job at Verdegrowth. "You bitch, you know how much that thing costs?"

Marge didn't look impressed. "No, and also I don't care. I think it's more than a small bit of payback for ruining my life." She practically spat the words in anger.

Sara tried to think about what she might have done. "I did what now?" She really had to keep her mouth shut. She bit her lip.

Marge glared at her with burning hatred. "You roll into town with your fancy coffee and start talking about building a restaurant. Do you know what everyone going to my cafe was talking about? They couldn't help but yack away about how much more they were going to enjoy going to your coffee shop than coming into my place and eating every day. Do you know how fucking low the profit margin is in a place like mine? Do you even realize how hard I work to keep the place afloat?"

Sara bit her tongue and kept silent even as a voice in the back of her head told her to say, "So low you can't afford new grease for the deep fryer." It may have been a good quip, but not one worth dying for.

Internally, she screamed for Emily to come home and get her sandwich. Sweet Emily with her gun belt.

"I knew you were on to me," Marge said, "and I could tell what you were up to. Palling around with the local cops. Asking stupid questions. Cornering me in public. You knew it was me from the start."

Sara opened her mouth to argue that she didn't, that she was only slightly beginning to suspect something was up, but she slammed her mouth shut. There was no reason to antagonize the crazy lady with the gun.

"But I see what you're thinking," Marge said, smirking.

The voice in Sara's head said, "That you're a crazy bitch?" She bit her lip harder.

"It was the Davis couple. After Nichole tipped you off that I was close to the mayor, she felt so guilty that she ran right over and confessed to me. Then later, I heard you assaulted Eddy. He said you hypnotized him and hit him with your crystal ball. I had him all worked up to kill you in a fit of passion for breaking up his marriage. Some men are so easy to control once you've slept with them a couple of times."

Sara's lip-biting strategy had failed, she just had to ask, "So is that your game, use the men of the swinging group to do your bidding?"

"Do my bidding?" She laughed. "That's a bit dramatic, isn't it? I mean, I started the group because there's not much to do in Downcastle. I didn't want to join a bowling league, and I like sex. Being able to manipulate the more weak-willed members was just a bonus."

Sara imagined Emily walking through the kitchen door for her sandwich. She had to keep Marge talking. "But Mayor Hart found out about your manipulation, and he was going to put a stop to it." Sara guessed.

Marge shook her head. "Hart was a pompous idiot, which made him very easy to control. Unfortunately, that meant that he was weak-willed with other people too. I'm not sure what kind of hold you had over him, but when he told me that he'd have to approve your coffee shop..." Marge took a deep breath and continued in a more reasoned voice. "All I ever wanted to do was own a cheerful little café. Instead, I ended up working sixty hours a week over a frier. There's only one burner on the stove that works, and the walk-in freezer is dying. Then Mike Hart, the one person I thought I could trust, just gives up a permit for a coffee shop? He wouldn't even discuss the subject with me."

She mimicked Hart's voice. "There's nothing I can do, Marge. I have a plan. I'll get her to buy the carwash, Marge." Then she growled. "That's when I decided he had to go."

Sara could have sworn she heard the kitchen door just barely through the thump of the KISS cover band. Was it just her imagination? She needed to stall. "But that was all Iris. She said she'd clear the way for all the permits and zoning and things. He was just embarrassed because she'd outmaneuvered him. She just wanted me to run a booth in the Harvest Festival."

Marge paused, looking a bit deflated. "Hmm. How sad. Mike died for nothing, and now you're going to have to as well." She raised her gun.

Suddenly, Patches the ghost cat ran across the room, hissing and spitting. She jumped at Marge with her claws out... and passed through her.

Somehow, however, Patches's attack must have had some effect, because Marge paused for a moment, looking confused.

That's when Emily came out of the kitchen door, hooked her nightstick around Marge's ankle, and pulled her foot out from under her. There was a deafening crack as the gun went off. Marge landed with an "Oof," and the gun slid across the living room floor, ending up under the couch.

Emily put her knee in Marge's back and cuffed her. "Good thing I decided to take a break. You okay?" she asked.

"Oh, I'm fine," Sara said. "I'm just a bit dizzy." She tried to sit down in one of Grandma's chairs, but she missed it. On her way down, her head caught the corner of the coffee table before she hit the hardwood floor.

225

Sara walked into the light, a radiant, enveloping glow that was unlike what she'd seen when other people crossed over. This was the big–budget movie, tailored just for her. No Liberace, though. Maybe the difference was that she was the one who was dying. The light was comforting and warm, inviting her to move into the unknown.

But as she walked, a sense of disappointment washed over her. After a start as a meager lab assistant with a cheating husband, she'd begun living a life of adventure solving mysteries, breaking into buildings, and finally having a gun drawn on her. Despite all this, she'd been done in by an ordinary coffee table. Then again, there were much more embarrassing ways to die: slipping in the shower while you were home alone, having a heart attack on the toilet, and other undignified things like that.

As she moved into the light, her thoughts moved to her life. Maybe the manner of death wasn't as important as the life that preceded it. Her mind wandered through all the things she had done, good and bad, and she re–lived all of those moments, both through her eyes, and through the eyes of those around her, learning more about herself, the people who felt better to have known her, and the people who she had made enemies of without even noticing it, like Marge.

After all this review, she knew that she'd had a small, yet positive impact in the people and the world around her. These were the things that truly mattered, and her disappointment was replaced by a sense of peace. The worries of everyday life floated away from her.

As Sara moved deeper into the light, she found herself surrounded by familiar faces. Grandma was there, giving her a comforting smile, just as she had in life, except that she was still appearing twenty years old and scantily dressed.

Gretta was there too, dressed in her BMW factory uniform. She nodded at Sara and said, "*Willkommen im Jenseits,*" and Sara understood her. She was welcoming Sara to the other side.

Then there was Ethan, the love-sick harbinger of horrible poetry. He stood slightly apart from the rest, clutching a bouquet of roses. Sara found the roses simultaneously endearing and quite awkward, as if he was there to symbolize the innocence and purity of first love, along with the stupidity and horniness.

Her parents stood to the side, their faces seemingly a mix of emotions. Seeing them there, Sara wished she would have gotten more time with them, but at the same time, she felt their love had never left her even though their bodies had left the Earth.

Sara walked up to her mother, a knot of emotions tightening her throat. "I meant to call," she said, her voice tinged with regret. "But one minute I got the amulet, and after that, I just got busy."

"Nothing to worry about," her mother said dryly. "I only gave birth to you. It's not like I'm anyone important or anything." Despite the sarcasm, Sara could tell that she understood.

Her dad, always the peacemaker between them, came up and put his arms around her mother. "Carol, let's give the girl a break. She's been mostly dead all day." Sara's heart warmed as he referenced *The Princess Bride*, their go-to movie for father-daughter bonding when she was little. "I think what your mother meant to say was that we both love you very much, and we're proud of you."

Sara smiled. "I know. I guess we're going to get to spend a lot of time together, now that I'm dead."

Her dad pointed at her and said in a very bad Billy Crystal voice. "Not necessarily. You're only *mostly* dead."

"What do you mean?" Sara asked.

Grandma interjected with her usual straightforwardness. "You took a nasty bump to the head, but it's only going to be a near-death experience—if they can get you to the hospital. The traffic from the festival is holding up the ambulance."

Dad turned to Grandma and said in a soft voice, "Did she have a thing with that weird kid with the roses?"

Grandma shook her head, and Sara could see her mouth twist as she tried to speak in a deadpan voice. "No, they only got to second base. Her boobs caused him to cross over, though. They're magic, you know."

"Mom, I do not want to hear about the supernatural quality of my daughter's anatomy. My interest in those things begins and ends with the feeding of any possible grandchildren, and even then, I'd rather not have a lot of details."

"So," her mother said, redirecting the conversation. "What else have you been up to?"

"Well," Sara said, "I kind of caught the mayor's murderer. Well, actually it would be a little more accurate to say I flushed her out. As she got nervous and came after me."

Her mother nodded, and she took on her dry, sarcastic voice again. "Oh, that's nice, dear."

As Sara began to recount the tale, the edges of her vision started to blur, the figures of her loved ones becoming hazy. The light began to fade, and reality started to reassert itself. Sara couldn't help but think how typical it was. She'd finally gotten a chance to catch up with her parents, and the universe couldn't even let her finish one story. She'd just have to summon them later and fill them in on the details. She should probably tell them about Brad too.

Sara woke with a dull headache. She tried to turn over and go back to sleep, but there was something attached to her arm, and there was a railing in the way, so she just kept her eyes closed tight. This went on for quite some time, but she heard someone humming. She could have sworn they were humming that old song "Rhinestone Cowboy."

She opened her eyes and slowly turned her head toward the sound. Ruby Mae and Grandma were sitting next to her bed. No, it wasn't her bed. The sheets were rough, and there was an antiseptic smell in the air. She was in a hospital bed. She tried to say something, but her throat was so dry, she just croaked. She wanted to swallow, but her throat felt like it was glued shut.

"Oh, good." Ruby Mae stood up and crossed the room to her. "You're awake. I'll call the nurse." She sorted through the tubes and cables attached to Sara, found a call button, and pressed it. "There we go. You had us all worried." Her voice held a tinge of relief.

Sara listened, her throat too dry to produce sound, and Ruby Mae filled the silence. "Your friend Emily stayed with you overnight, and when I came to visit this morning, I sent her home and said I'd stay with you a while. Iris Pilkington came by too. She brought you a banana bread and said something about a business proposition. However, I doubt you're going to be up to eating banana bread or ready to talk business anytime soon."

Sara tried to croak out a yes.

"Joe's downstairs getting me a cup of coffee. I made him drive me into town. I get around Downcastle alright, but I'm not as good in Cedar Rapids."

Sara managed to nod slightly. She was probably in St. Luke's Hospital. They'd probably brought her here because it was the closest to the interstate.

A nurse came in. "I see you're awake, Ms. Jenkins." She turned to Ruby Mae. "If you want to give us a moment of privacy, I'll get her cleaned up and give her some water."

Sara nodded emphatically when she heard water. The nurse saw her reaction, and even as Ruby Mae was making her way out, the nurse poured a cup of water and put the tip of a straw in Sara's mouth. Sara took a deep drink from the straw and nearly choked.

"Go easy," the nurse said. She set the water aside. "Let's see how that sits while I take some readings." She took an electronic tool off her lanyard and scanned codes in from several pieces of monitoring equipment.

Sara was finally able to swallow. "How long have I been here?" she asked.

"They brought you in last night," the nurse said. "You suffered a severe concussion, and you were unconscious for several hours. You also needed a few stitches for the cut on your scalp. The doctor wants to do a CT scan before giving the all-clear, and as long as everything checks out, you might be able to go home later today. Just make sure to rest and take it easy for a few days. You should also check in with your primary doctor in about a week. They may want to do some follow-up tests."

This seemed like a lot of information to give someone who'd just suffered a head injury. Sara just nodded.

When the Nurse was finished with her, Ruby Mae and Joe came in, both holding small cups of coffee.

Sara reflected on how nice it was to see a man she was attracted to while lying down without a bra on and a bag of urine hanging by her feet.

As they made small talk for the next hour, Sara felt gratitude for their presence, despite the throbbing in her head and her less-than-flattering hospital garb. However, after a while, she could tell Joe was beginning to feel antsy.

The nurse came in again and said, "The doctor reviewed your vitals and has given the green light for your CT scan. The imaging team will send someone in soon to inject the dye." She gestured to the tubes and wires attached to Sara. "But we can start getting these out of the way." Then, turning to Joe and Ruby Mae, she added, "This might take a little time, so if you'd like to grab some lunch, now would be a good time."

"Actually," Joe said, "I need to swing by the job site. I left the Fincher brothers alone, and I need to know what they've done while I've been gone."

Ruby Mae wasn't accepting that. "No, we're going to stay here until Sara needs a ride home."

Sara decided to settle things before the two began to fight over her. "I'll be fine. You go home, and if I need a ride, I'll call you."

"And you make sure you do call us," Ruby Mae said. "No going behind our backs and calling that Youber."

"That's Uber, Mom," Joe corrected gently as they stepped into the hall.

As they were leaving, Sara heard Ruby Mae outside her door saying, "Don't sass me, young man. Who cares if it's Youber or Uber, or whatever? She knew what I was talking about."

Chapter 13

Pastries and Propositions

Despite being unconscious for half a day, Sara still felt exhausted. Aside from the CT scan, she slept through most of the four hours it took for the hospital to clear her for discharge. When she wasn't asleep, she drifted in and out of consciousness while Emily and Adam watched over her, swapping cop stories. At one point, she even recalled Grandma commenting that she was tired of their stories and would see Sara at home.

During her trip for the CT scan, the presence of ghosts in the hospital halls had unsettled her. At first, she thought the place was simply overcrowded with injured people. Then she saw some of them were walking through closed doors and other objects. They reminded her of Mayor Hart, when he didn't know he was dead. She found it both sad and disturbing knowing there were so many there, and at the moment, she didn't think she had the energy to help them. She grew anxious to be released.

Before she could leave, a nurse handed her a thick packet of information on head injuries. The key takeaway was simple: she needed to watch for symptoms like dizziness, memory loss, or difficulty concentrating, and follow up with her primary care doctor.

As she got dressed, Sara noticed something strange. Her amulet—the one that allowed her to see spirits—had been in a bag with her belongings the entire time. And yet, she had seen Grandma and other ghosts throughout her stay. Was her ability to see spirits growing stronger because of all the practice, or had the near-death experience brought her even closer to the dead?

Once she was home, Emily sat her on the couch, tucked her under Grandma's blanket, and gave her the TV remote. However, her headache was bad enough that she just wanted to nap anyway. Every once in a while, she'd wake up, and Emily would ask if she needed anything. This was the way the next day went, with Emily fetching her things when she wasn't working.

Finally, on the third day, Sara got bored of being waited on. She felt fine and needed to get out. She got up, showered, dressed, and went for a long walk. She didn't feel dizzy, and she knew where she was, so she figured she was okay. She probably did need to find a local doctor, though.

When she got home, Grandma was waiting for her. "Are you finally feeling better?" she asked.

Sara nodded. "Very well, thank you."

"Are you hungry?"

She shrugged. "I could eat."

"Great. I'm going to teach you how to make muffins from scratch. My cookbook is in the cabinet above the refrigerator. It's in a shoe box."

Sara took down the shoe box from the tiny cabinet over the fridge. It was covered in dust. "Did you even use this, Grandma?"

"Of course, the first time I did a recipe, I wrote it down for reference, and I usually needed to look at it a time or two more before I got it down. However, I haven't really needed to look at anything in there for quite a long time."

"Okay," Sara said. "What kind of muffins are we going to make?"

"That depends, dear. What kind of fruit do you have in the fridge?"

Sara took a look. "We have apples."

"Apple cinnamon, then." Grandma smiled. "Let's get started. Find the recipe card that says, 'Fruit Muffins.' First, look at all the ingredients on the recipe card, find them, and line them up on the counter. There's nothing worse than getting halfway through a recipe and having to run to the store, especially back when the store didn't even open on Sunday. And don't forget to add cinnamon, it's not in the basic recipe."

When the ingredients were assembled, Grandma said, "Now, measure out all the amounts. Usually, it's not a big deal, but you're just starting out, so we'll take baby steps."

Sara did as she was told, letting Grandma guide her through the steps, cutting the apples into tiny chunks, sifting the dry ingredients, learning which ingredients to measure exactly and which she could be less exact with.

"Now, we're going to preheat the oven. Every oven is different, but the one in this kitchen takes about seven minutes to warm up. They usually tell you to turn on the stove immediately, but we're taking it slow today."

Beyond just the cooking instructions though, Sara was having fun. As they worked, Grandma told her about the time Ruby Mae hid a bottle of vodka in her oven and they almost burned the house down, and Grandma explained that the old mixing bowl was so horribly discolored due to a cheap hair dye Grandma bought at the drug store when she decided she wanted to be a redhead.

Finally, the batter was spooned into the muffin tins, and Sara sat down at the kitchen table while Grandma told her stories about learning to bake from her own mother. The house slowly filled with the sweet smells of baking, first just a hint, then growing stronger and richer until it made Sara's mouth water. After about twenty minutes, she noticed the scent had changed subtly.

"Thank you for the baking lesson, Grandma." Sara sighed. "It's just a shame that I won't be able to have a coffee shop. I bet I could sell the hell out of your muffins."

Grandma grinned. "I think there's an innuendo in there somewhere, dear. But take a big sniff of the air. What does it smell like?"

Sara shrugged. "Muffins."

"Cooking muffins or cooked muffins?"

"Cooked muffins," Sara answered.

"Then go get a toothpick and poke it into a couple of the muffins. If it comes out without batter on it, they're close to done. Timers are handy, but your nose will double-check when things are truly baked."

Sara did as she was told, and she was surprised when the toothpick came out clean, despite the timer having another two minutes. "I think they're done."

"You can take them out, then. You could wait another two minutes, but people like a moist muffin better than a dry muffin."

Sara knew what Grandma was doing with her "moist" comments, and she refused to take the bait. She pursed her lips and shook her head. "Don't say it."

When they were all out of the oven and had cooled just enough, Sara brewed a fresh pot of Tanzanian Peaberry. With her coffee properly prepared, she selected a muffin and broke it open, releasing the steam that carried the rich smell of apples and cinnamon to her nose. The texture was perfect, baked through without being dry, and it melted in her mouth.

"I think, Grandma, we make one hell of a team."

The only thing that made Sara sad was that Grandma couldn't taste the muffins when she was done. However, Emily would be home soon, and Sara would have an objective taster.

When Emily got home, she took her into the kitchen and served her a muffin and coffee. When she took her first bite, she just said, "Wow." As Emily was eating her second muffin, she said, "These are really good. You have a talent."

"Thanks," Sara said. "My grandma taught me."

"I was talking to Sheriff Robinson today. Since you're feeling better, he's told me I can move back to my apartment, but he's still open to setting up a satellite office in Downcastle. Are you still interested in a roommate? I mean, my lease isn't up for a couple of months, so we can iron out the details later. What do you think?"

Sara nodded, weighing the comfort of Emily's company against the uncertainty of having a new roommate. A renter was a much bigger commitment than a houseguest. If she thought there would be a chance of converting the house into her dream coffee shop, she'd say no, but that vision seemed impossible now. The house could stay a house, at least for now.

"Yeah, that sounds fun," she replied, trying to project more confidence than she actually felt. Someone had already tried to murder her in the house—not once, but twice. Having a well-armed, trained roommate would definitely make her feel more secure. But it wasn't just about safety. With a small grin, she added, "As long as you let me help solve a case every now and then."

Emily smirked. "Right, because a civilian partner is just what I need," she said dryly. "Remember how we just got you out of the hospital?" Without missing a beat, she shifted the conversation. "So, you said this is your grandma's recipe. What was she like?"

"Grandma?" Sara laughed. "She was wild. Let me tell you about the time she and Ruby Mae blew up the stove—"

Sara's phone rang, and for once, it wasn't her ex. Iris Pilkington was calling. She answered, wondering what Iris wanted. "Hi, Iris. What's up?"

"Sara, I was wondering if you could meet me downtown tomorrow, at Mel's Diner around noon?"

Sara noticed she'd used the old name, "Mel's Diner" instead of its newer moniker of "Marge's Diner." Apparently, now that Marge was a known murderer, Iris didn't even want to speak her name. "Sure, I can do that, but is it open with Marge in jail?"

"Oh, it's open for me. Don't worry about that." And with that enigmatic statement, Iris hung up.

Sara drove the car to "Mel's Diner" the next day to meet with Iris. She brought a little basket with the leftover muffins wrapped in plastic as a thank you to

Iris for the banana bread—it had been tasty, but not up to Grandma's standards. Still, it was the thought that counted.

When she arrived at the diner, she was surprised to find Joe's contractor truck parked outside. She parked behind it and walked to the front door. She pulled on the door and found it locked, but she squinted against her reflection in the glass, and she saw Iris walking toward the door to let her in.

"Come and sit down." Iris led her over to a table where Joe was already sitting. "I'm so glad you could both come. I was thinking about you-know-who's arrest. And it occurred to me that the loss of a shared eatery and meeting place could hurt us all. It could leave a real hole in our community."

Sara nodded. She put her little basket on the table. "I brought some muffins," she said.

"Oh, wonderful. It's too bad we don't have anything to drink with these... Well, I suppose you-know-who won't mind if we borrow some drinks. She has other things to worry about." Apparently, Marge was now like Voldemort, and they weren't supposed to speak her name.

Iris walked over to the counter, where a cooler displayed canned beverages and pulled out an iced tea. "Sara, what would you like?"

"I'll take an iced tea too," she said.

"Joe?" Iris asked.

"Yoohoo," Joe said.

Iris walked back and sat down the three cans. They took a second to open their beverages, take a sip, and unwrap the muffins. When Iris took the first bite, she lifted her hand to her chest as if in shock. "Oh, my goodness, Sara. This is so good, just like your grandmother used to make. This is the best food that's been served in this diner... ever as far as I know."

"Thank you." Sara smiled.

Joe, his mouth full, nodded his appreciation. "Mmm," he said.

"That kind of brings up why I brought you two here," Iris said. "As interim mayor, I started looking through Mike Hart's things. He was not very good about separating his personal business and town business. His desk was full of folders and documents that pertained to a land deal he was involved in."

Sara feigned surprise and Joe did the same.

"Are either of you familiar with Yoonbao?" Iris asked. "They're kind of like Wish or Temu?"

They both nodded.

"Well, I found all these contracts in Chinese, so I took them over to Yingyi Wilson, Bob Wilson's wife, and asked her to read them. Well, she said they were a bit complicated, being legal documents, but it looks like Yoonbao had hired Mike and Dwain Hart to purchase every property in town."

"That's weird. What would they do that?" Sara had been burning to know if Joe's conclusion about making the town into a Yoonbao distribution center was correct.

"It turns out that Yoonbao was looking to do a major US expansion, and part of that was building a large US distribution center in the Midwest. Downcastle has existing infrastructure, a ready workforce in the corridor, and a highway directly to the airport. They were going to level our beautiful town and turn it into a warehouse." Iris, usually jovial, seemed quite angry about this. "Knowing that Mike Hart was doing this while he was supposed to be a pillar of the community makes me think that maybe he got..."

Iris bit her lip and took a breath. "Mayor Hart and Yoonbao thought this was a worthless town that anyone would want to leave if they got a halfway decent

offer. Well, my family has lived here for five genera-
tions, and I am going to fight them."

"I admire your determination," Joe said. "I was
born and raised here myself, but how are you going to
fight such a big corporation?"

She smiled. "With this town's greatest resource,
its people. They don't own this town yet. We're going
to make them regret going after our town. And that
starts with you two."

"Us?" Sara asked. She had absolutely no idea
where Iris was going with this, and she was beginning
to think the Yoonbao news had driven her over the
edge.

"Yes. Sara, you want to own a coffee shop. Joe,
you have the expertise to rehab a fixer-upper. And I
have two things I can offer you. The town's economic
development fund, which has gone unused through the
tenure of Mayor Hart, and this building which I happen
to own."

Sara had to think about this for a moment. "So,
you're Marge's landlord?"

"Yes, my great-grandfather owned a menswear
shop, and this was his place of business. The storefront
has stayed in the family all these years." She paused.
"And I don't think you-know-who is going to be able
to keep making her rent payments. So, as soon as I can
evict Marge, I'm willing to offer Joe some money to fix
the place up, and I'll give you very favorable terms on a
new lease."

Sara couldn't believe what she was hearing. She
needed a moment for it all to sink in. Of course, Iris using the economic development money to remodel her
own building was a huge conflict of interest, but she'd
let Iris and the city council worry about that.

Iris was at the edge of her seat, waiting for an answer. "So, do you want to start a coffee shop?"

"Yes! Yes!" Sara said as fast as she could.

Iris was so happy, she got up from her seat and did a little dance. Sara found herself joining in. Joe shook his head and laughed at the two of them.

Sara saw someone else out of the corner of her eye and looked over to see Grandma and her parents looking at her with approval. As she wondered how long was appropriate to continue a group happy dance, she reflected on how much her life had changed in just a couple of weeks, and how a broken-down car and the discovery of her husband's infidelity might have been the best things to ever happen to her—although she'd never admit that out loud.

About the Author

Shannon Ryan lives in Marion, Iowa. He writes weird, funny stories in the urban fantasy genre, featuring satanic telemarketers and awkward vampires.

In addition to writing, he enjoys making furniture and other items out of wood, writing computer programs, designing models for 3d printing, editing books for others, and playing with kitties.

Minion of Evil

Have you ever wondered if your boss is evil?

David Graves is having a bad life. A bill collector is threatening him with grievous bodily harm. His girlfriend thinks he's an incompetent loser. His human resources manager, a creature of nightmare, is sexually harassing him. And when he finally meets a girl he likes, she seems more interested in rebuilding engines and committing random acts of violence.

Still, David thinks he is doing all right—until he discovers his bosses are Satanists and his employment contract dooms him to an eternity of telemarketing and damnation....

Minion of Evil is frightfully accurate portrayal of identity theft, computer hacking, wrench wenches, monomaniacal supervisors, and what really goes on behind closed doors in customer service.

https://weirdauthor.com/evil

MINION OF EVIL

SHANNON RYAN

Merger of Evil

Tired of working McJobs and the gig economy, Amy Love thinks she'll never amount to anything. Then an angel visits her and tells her to take a job with Tommy Norman, a famous psychopath.

Tommy has come to Iowa to assist in a merger between a satanic telemarketing company and an evil cable company. Amy takes the job to find out her former boss, David Graves, a man she fears and despises, is one of the chief negotiators.

Amy must face lawyers, guns, and demons to assist some unfathomable heavenly plan.

https://weirdauthor.com/merger

Fangs for Nothing

Not everyone who gets turned into a vampire becomes a sexy rock star.

At twenty-seven, Vincent Lester still looks seventeen, acne and all. He lives in his parents' basement, playing PlayStation and barely surviving by licking the blood off raw hamburger trays. His parents nag him to find a day job, but he's afraid the sun will make him burst into flame.

One night at the bar, Vinny picks up a drunk girl, literally, and gets his first taste of fresh, human blood. Then things get really weird.

http://weirdauthor.com/fangs

Panic No More

Even the best families can have dark secrets.

Some people would say Nick Baker has it all: the trust fund, the family connections, and the country club membership. However, the Baker dynasty is in decline, and being a Baker comes with obligations as well as a family history of insanity.

Already prone to panic attacks, when Nick sees a supernatural creature dancing outside his office window, he wonders if he's just hallucinating or suffering a complete mental collapse. However, the creature is all too real, and it has come to collect on a promise made by one of Nick's ancestors, the secret of the Baker's success. Nick must choose between thwarting the ambitions of his family or facing the wrath of an ancient god.

https://weirdauthor.com/panic

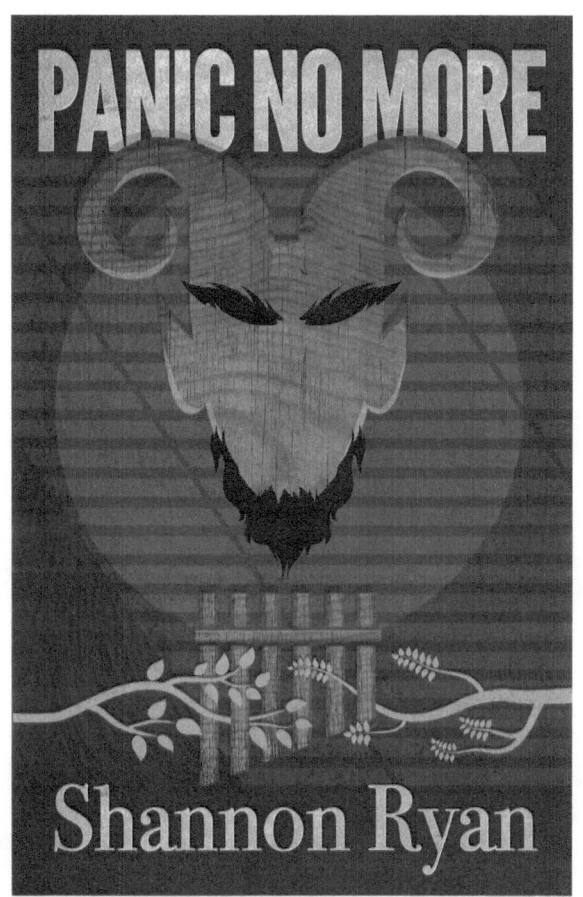

www.ingramcontent.com/pod-product-compliance
Lightning Source LLC
Chambersburg PA
CBHW060540190726
48283CB00003B/798